A Shade of Winter

Book One of The Perth Paranormal Series

A.B. Hooser

Printed in the United States of America
First Printing, 2023
ISBN-979-8-9866027-5-2

The Henlo Press
P.O. Box 1694
Ashland, KY 41105

www.thehenlopress.com

This book is dedicated to Amber, my most ardent cheerleader and Jane to my Daria.

"It's nice to meet you, Pansy, why don't you have a seat over there and we'll get started, yes?" Dr. Noonan closed the heavy wooden door to his office before my sister replied, but I could hear the low murmur of her response. Knowing Pansy, she was probably being as agreeable as possible. That was her default with strange adults, pleasant and eager to please. Mine was to be suspicious and mouthy, but then again, we were identical in looks, not personalities. Since I'd only be a distraction if I followed her in, I decided to occupy myself in the waiting room.

I'd only tagged along to this farce of a therapy session in case Pansy needed me afterwards, but the very idea of being in a Psychiatrist's office made me itchy and ready to bolt. Our father, who'd been the one to decide that Pansy needed therapy in the first place, had parked his butt in a chair by the windows and was already engrossed in a car magazine. To a stranger, he probably looked like he didn't have a care in the world. Everyone in our family could tell you that that was a lie.

I began a tour around the room, my combat boots making no sound on the thick, baby blue carpeting. Blue is a soothing color—I'd read that in a magazine once. I ran my hand over a mercury glass mirror; its spotted finish giving it the appearance of something old and expensive. In fact, everything in the waiting room looked old and expensive, from the art on the walls to the bookshelves filled with leather-bound volumes towering behind the receptionist. The waiting room serviced two other doctor's offices and from the looks of it, all of them were doing very well for themselves.

Pansy had actually asked Dad how much he was paying for all of this, hoping to use the cost as an excuse for why she shouldn't have to do this, but he'd told her not to worry because the insurance was covering it. Since that plan was shot down, that left us with Plan B—pretend to be normal and that everything was fine. If she could trick the doctor into thinking that there was nothing wrong with her, we figured she may only have to do this two or three times. Besides, if anyone needed therapy, it certainly wasn't Pansy. In the last few weeks, Dad had spent more and more time at work, and Mom, well—she spent her few waking hours lying in bed, staring at the wall. When Mom and Dad had closed the door to their bedroom to brainstorm this great idea, one of the few times since the funeral that they'd even spoken to one another, we'd assumed that their conversation would be about Mom's need for therapy, not Pansy's. Clearly, Pansy was not the one that needed her head shrunk, but no one asked for our opinion.

The parents thought that Pans wasn't showing enough depth of despair, or grief, or whatever, over the accident. Which was true, but not for the reasons that they thought. Pansy hadn't just caved and accepted this emotional poking and prodding into the most private aspects of her life. No, it had been a conditional surrender and I was proud of her for standing her ground. Dad had accepted her terms, strange as they were, and now we were scheduled for Saturday morning therapy for the foreseeable future. Hopefully she'd appear so normal that the doctor would say, "You don't need to be here, you don't need to come back." She certainly couldn't tell the truth or I'd be visiting her in the looney bin.

The door opened and I paused in my perusal of the bookshelf to make sure that whoever was coming in wasn't someone we knew. We were a full hour's drive from our small town, so the odds were slim, but there was still a risk. If word got out that Pansy was seeing a Psychiatrist, she'd be all but shunned by the rest of the school. Being a very small high school, it would take less than forty-eight hours for that kind of juicy gossip to make the rounds and we had enough drama without adding that kind of pressure, thank you.

To my relief, the woman who entered was a complete stranger.

Disaster averted, I continued pacing the room. Dad was oblivious to my boredom and didn't look up from his magazine as I made another loop around the room. I hadn't wasted nearly enough time, but since I'd circled back to the door where my sister was being 'treated,' I eased into Dr. Noonan's office, anyway. With daffodil yellow walls and oversized windows that let in as much of the weak winter light as possible, it was almost cheerful.

Dr. Noonan wasn't at his desk, but sitting in an overstuffed armchair across from Pansy's. He didn't look up from his notes as I entered, but Pans gave me a warning glance. It was her way of telling me to behave without having to speak to me directly. Her eyes were red and I could see that she'd already been crying. Was she laying it on too thick? After all, we wanted the doctor to believe she was well-adjusted and capable of grieving, not that she was a big blubbery mess.

"But you were driving the vehicle, at the time, correct?"

"Yes, sir." Her eyes dropped to the tissue she was twisting back and forth in her hands. *Avoid eye contact—good thinking, Sis.*

"Your parents feel like you're not processing your grief—that you're suppressing the incident—and that's not a good approach to healing. Can you explain to me exactly what it is that you're feeling?"

Oh, good grief.

Dr. Noonan leaned back in his chair, crossing an ankle over his other knee. He smoothed his longish, dark hair from his face before settling back with a yellow legal pad balanced on his leg. I assumed this was his 'observation' mode—getting comfortable so he could watch Pansy's reactions while she recited her prepared list of 'feelings' we'd brainstormed the night before.

"Good, good, tell me more," he said, scribbling on the legal pad in his lap.

Pansy wasn't deviating from the script, so I wandered off to explore the office. I looked over the framed degrees and certificates on the wall behind Dr. Noonan's desk, and noticed that they were mixed in with photos of a woman and two kids. *Must be the family.* One frame held individual Glamour Shots, and I turned with the intention of telling Pansy that she needed to check out the hilariously cheesy pictures.

Before I could open my mouth, my eye was caught by a different photo. There, lying on Dr. Noonan's desk was a printed copy of a Polaroid. It was our car, the red Cavalier crumpled and torn. It had been a present for our sixteenth birthday the year before and we'd loved that car. It looked like the whole file was there, or at least a copy of it. The police report, the diagrams, the crime scene photos, all spread out across his desktop. I could see pages of what looked like the statements the police had gathered: the first responders, one from my sister, and one from the Justin Woodbridge guy. *The drunk.* There was a hand-drawn diagram of the accident scene showing the placement of vehicles in relation to the bridge. It looked so nice and neat on paper. Almost orderly.

It hadn't been orderly. It had been pure chaos. There'd been screams followed by the screech of metal deforming and being pushed into places it wasn't meant to be. Then a brief moment of silence interrupted only by the *whump whump* of the windshield wipers and a soft ticking from the ruined engine. And then there was more screaming.

Wailing.

Pansy sobbing and crying my name.

That's what I remembered the most, her screaming for me. My chest suddenly tightened like I couldn't get enough air—which was ridiculous, really. I glanced at the photo again before moving over to the windows, away from it. The roses in the flower bed outside the window had been cut back for the winter, their woody stems whacked off at strange pointy angles, and I stared at the ugliness until I got myself under control. Dr. Noonan had resumed talking, but I hadn't been listening until Pansy's voice brought me back to the present.

"I know it's not my fault. I know that. But I'm afraid I'm never going to forgive myself. Maybe I could have reacted faster. If we hadn't been out so late it wouldn't have happened, but I was the one who wanted to stay at the party. Why Gerri? Why not me?" Her words held a hint of panic, pulling my attention away from my own feelings. I didn't know if she was acting for the doctor or if she meant it, but my intuition told me she was being sincere. I frowned.

"It's not your fault." She shook her head and I couldn't tell if that meant she was agreeing with me or not.

"Survivor's guilt is common in these kinds of cases," the doctor was using his soothing voice. I began to wonder if part of the therapy was to hypnotize the patient with his voice. *Hypnotherapy was a real thing, right?* Mostly recomposed, I moved to stand behind her.

I laid a hand on Pansy's shoulder. "It's not your fault," I said again, more firmly this time. I couldn't get the image of the photo out of my head. The front end of the car had been smashed and crumpled, but it wasn't the force of the oncoming car that had killed me. No, the broken end of the guardrail forced through the passenger side door and through my body is what ended my life. I shivered with the memory and Pansy laid her hand over mine, or tried to, anyway. To Dr. Noonan, it probably looked like she was touching her own shoulder for no reason. Dr. Noonan could suck it.

My twin was the only person who could see and hear me since I died four weeks ago. Until this moment, I'd thought we were adjusting as well as we could to this unexpected turn of events, but obviously, we had more work to do.

2

"I swear I want to marry Chris and have his babies."

"Well, that would be awkward. Ya know, being dead and all."

"Rub it in."

Pansy was curled up on one end of our living room couch and I was pretending to be curled up on the other end. I had to concentrate to keep myself from sinking into the couch. Like, literally, into and through it. We'd found reruns of Northern Exposure on cable and I was busy lusting after John Corbett's character, smooth-talking, philosophizing, radio host, Chris Stevens. *Just because I'm dead doesn't mean I can't appreciate his beauty.*

"He is cute, but I like Dr. Fleischman."

"Too neurotic," I said, waving my hand in dismissal. "Who wants that much drama in their life?"

"Aww, I think his neurosis is cute. What I really like is Maggie's hair. Do you think I should cut mine off?" Although 1995 was almost over, the pixie cut was still popular with our classmates. Cutting her hair that short would be a drastic change since Pansy's dark hair currently brushed the top of her waistband.

"I think if you do, you'll look even more like Wynona Ryder and then you'll get, 'Why do you look so familiar?' crap everywhere you go." I mean, it happened enough now, but with short hair, it would be even worse. I knew because mine was already shorter, not Wynona in *Reality Bites* short, but it was shoulder length and had been down when I died. I was never going to have to worry about how to cut my hair ever again. And, since there was no such thing as after-life hair bands or ghost scrunchies, I was stuck with it down and in my face forever. Ugh.

"These stupid big eyes," she grumbled. That was it, really, as best we could figure. We didn't think we looked like the famous starlet, but we had the big eyes with dark lashes and eyebrows that were the same shape as Wynona's. We also had the same short, thin shape, and strangers regularly stopped us so they could try to figure out why we looked familiar. It was super annoying.

"You know what?" Pansy asked, looking over the top of the magazine she was reading. "We're never going to walk into a room and have people ask us if we're twins again."

"I guess not." I mean, it was obvious we were, but people always felt compelled to ask stupid questions.

"Isn't that sad? I think that's really sad."

"Who are you talking to, sweetie?" Mom had walked by and heard Pansy talking. *Great.* From my vantage point, I could see our mother in the hall at the bottom of the stairs. *On her way back up to spend more quality time alone with her pillow, no doubt.* She was wearing a bathrobe, even though it was four in the afternoon, and judging by the look of her hair she hadn't showered in a week.

"Just myself, Mom."

"Tell her the psycho told you it would be beneficial."

"Dr. Noonan told me that pretending Gerri was still here and that I could talk to her again would be beneficial to my grieving process." *Ooh, that sounded like real quack talk. Good job, Pans.*

Mom looked at her with a blank expression and nodded her head like that made perfect sense. Turning, she walked up the stairs without saying another word. Pansy and I shared identical facial expressions of frustration with one another.

"She isn't getting any better."

"At all," Pansy agreed.

With a sigh, I nodded toward the magazine spread out next to her I'd been reading during the commercials.

"Turn, please."

"I swear to God, I'm going to invent a robot to turn the pages for you."

"Quit whining. There are people out there who would love to turn pages for a ghost."

"Do you know how I know you aren't a figment of my imagination? Because I would imagine you much more self-sufficient and not nearly as irritating," she grumbled before turning my page.

There were definitely some downsides to being dead. The floating and spying on people was fun, but I'd never recommend dying before you've ever really lived. Now that I was a ghost, the only trick I'd mastered was floating. Doors and walls were no impediment to me, I went right through them. 'Walking' was really just me floating above the ground and trying to remain somewhat level to avoid sinking down into it. I had tried to sink all the way down into the earth my first week back, but it was dark and the idea of dirt and worms millimeters from my invisible eyeballs was too freaky. No, thank you.

Topping my list of *Things About Dying That I Find Irritating* was that I couldn't touch or move anything. Talk about inconvenient. Okay, well that actually might be second, right behind how sad my friends and family were about it, because, clearly that was top of the list. Third, I was also stuck forever in the clothes I'd died in, which, in retrospect, wasn't so bad and could have been worse. I raised a foot, admiring my favorite pair of Doc Martin boots in oxblood red. My ripped jeans, Green Day t-shirt, and fluffy gray wool socks were my permanent togs for the rest of my life. Or my non-life. Existence. Whatever. At least I hadn't died in my bathrobe, or naked, or had a big pizza sauce stain on the front of my shirt or something. Oddly enough, the damage caused to my wardrobe by the actual act of dying wasn't represented in my ghostly form. Thank goodness for small favors.

It had been a warm day in October and I'd tossed my coat into the back seat before we'd left the party. Again, I was grateful, because I would look crazy ridiculous come summer if I was still wearing my ski jacket with a scarf and gloves. Not that anyone could see me but Pansy, and it wasn't like I was going to sweat, I couldn't feel hot or cold, it was the principle of the matter. The ghosts you see in movies are always wearing fabulous flowing gowns and I'd hate to be bundled up against a Colorado winter for all eternity.

"Earth to Geraldine. Why are you staring at your boots?"

"Nothing. Just thinking. What time is our meeting tonight?"

"My meeting is at six. I don't know where you think you're going." She continued flipping through the channels like I was going to accept that answer and move on.

"Umm, hello? It's a PPS meeting, how do you plan on stopping me from attending?" She couldn't touch me any more than I could touch her. It wasn't like she could restrain me.

"I think it's too dangerous. What if they have some way to see you? What if they try to exorcize you or something?"

We had never, ever in our lives, believed in ghosts or things of a paranormal nature so we weren't exactly up to date on how the Perth Paranormal Society detected its ghosts. In fact, we weren't clear on how many 'ghosts' they'd actually found. Pansy had read about the group in the paper after they had discovered electrical problems in an older woman's home that could have caused a fire. She'd chalked her flickering lights up to ghosts, as one does, and had called the PPS instead of an electrician. Luckily one of the members actually *was* an electrician and had quickly fixed the problem. No ghosts were found.

Being allowed to join the group was how Dad had bribed Pansy into going to therapy. My twin, six minutes my senior, thought she would be able to protect me if she learned the ins and outs of ghost detection, lest some bright doorway open up and suck me into the great beyond.

In the six weeks since I'd been dead, I hadn't encountered any other ghosts in town, not that we'd left the house more than a handful of times. Still, you'd think there would be someone haunting the school or the girl's locker room or something. Nothing, nada. Apparently when the average person died their souls did not get up and wander around, but I never saw a bright light, a door, or a portal to heaven. We had a lot of questions and no one to ask.

"I'm going. There's nothing you can do to stop me. In fact, I could have gone to the last meeting and you wouldn't even know about it." I had been standing right next to her when Dad told her that the group met every other Friday night at a place called The Buffalo Chip. I didn't need an invitation to attend if I wanted to go.

"Well, I guess you could have. But if you had, you would have already told me everything you'd learned." She was smug, but correct. Between the two of us, I was the one who could never keep a secret. I liked to talk and be social. Pansy was the one who could hole up in her bedroom for a week with no contact from the outside world and be perfectly okay with that. Having her as the only person I could talk to was probably going to get old after a few months, but what else was I going to do?

"Of course I haven't. I'm waiting to share the experience with you." I saw her lips tighten as she tried not to smile.

"Fine. I can't stop you from going but I want it noted, for the record, I think it's a bad idea."

"Duly noted."

"You know, come to think about it, you really don't need permission to go anywhere. It's not like you need a permission slip or have to worry about breaking curfew. You can go do whatever you want whenever you want to. You could go to New York and see every Broadway show. You could see every movie in the theaters as many times as you wanted. You could even go to every concert at Red Rock." Pansy was sounding wistful and maybe even a trifle jealous, which I thought was weird.

"Yeah, I mean, I guess I could do all of that. But how would I even know where to go? It's not like I can pull out the Rand McNally and flip through the pages state by state. If you opened the map and I studied it before I left I might make it to Red Rock and back. Maybe. But New York? What if I got lost? I can't ask for directions and it's a really big world out there." I mean, I was fast, I could keep speed with a car traveling at like, sixty, but how long would it take me to float to NY? What if I got lost in Kansas along the way? I didn't have a ghost compass and it's not like I ever learned to navigate by the stars.

"Well, it wouldn't kill you to at least go explore the neighborhood."

"A waiting room is one thing, but I don't want to see any naked people if I can avoid it."

"Maybe you'll find another ghost."

"Sure, but what if ghosts can hurt other ghosts and I find a big scary one that's like, the ghost of a psycho killer or something? Huh? What then?"

"God, you're such a baby."

I stuck my tongue out at her and she closed the magazine I was still trying to read, tossing it on the coffee table before standing to stretch. I was never going to finish that article on how to create the perfect beach wave hairstyle.

"Since you're not feeling adventurous, let's get back to me. Should I eat before I go? Do you think they eat while they're there?"

"Why else would they meet in a restaurant if they aren't going to eat while they're there?"

"I don't know. Maybe they eat before the meeting and I'm not invited to that part. I should eat something in case there's no food."

"Whatever, loser. I'm going to float over here on my corner of the couch and work on turning my own pages."

"Concentrate."

"This isn't freaking *Beetlejuice*, Pansy. Unless you have a copy of the *Handbook for the Recently Deceased* lying around somewhere and haven't told me, I could be wasting my time."

"Well, you've got plenty of that." She said as she walked out into the entryway and started toward the kitchen. I heard her murmur to herself, "I hope."

Yeah. You and me both, sister. You and me both.

3

I like to think of our little town of Perth as being firmly wedged in the butt crack of Colorado. I picture the mountains as one cheek, the high plains as the other, and Perth Canyon as the plunging cleft between the two. The town clings to the eastern rim of the canyon and the shallow waters of San Isidro Creek meander through an arroyo delineating the eastern and southern borders of the town. The San Isidro cascades through a series of inconsequential rapids until it meets up with the dry riverbed of Perth Canyon, where it is absorbed and disappears.

Perth, being a small town, boasts a handful of restaurants, two banks, two gas stations, and not a single red light, unless you count the flashing caution lights in front of the schools. We are not a destination town, we have no tourist attractions, and no one ever stops here on their way to anywhere else. We're ten miles north of the New Mexico border and centrally located in the middle of nowhere. Almost everyone who lives here has at least one family member working for the gravel quarry southeast of the arroyo. As far as I can tell, it's the only reason anyone ever moved out here in the first place. As a result, everyone knows everyone else in town and their noses were all up in everyone else's business.

The Buffalo Chip was just over the East Bridge and since it was snowing, Pansy had taken the city bus. It was the only bus and its route ran in a loop around town, so we arrived fifteen minutes early. As one might gather from the name, The Buffalo Chip wasn't a high-class place. Decor consisted of wood plank flooring, wood planks on the walls, lots of neon beer signs, and a full-grown, taxidermied bison to greet you at the door. I'd always found Bill, as he was affectionately called, really creepy with his beady, glass eyes. I examined the layers of dust-crusted oil attached to its coat while Pansy loosened her scarf and futzed with her notebook. She assured herself for what had to be the hundredth time in the last hour that her signed permission slip was pressed neatly between the pages.

"How do you think, exactly, one cleans a stuffed buffalo?" I asked, attempting to irritate her into forgetting her nervousness.

"What? Leave it alone and quit talking to me," she hissed, pushing a stray strand of hair behind her ear. After twenty minutes of agonizing over how to wear her hair tonight, she'd gone with straightened and parted in the middle. "I'm trying to make a good impression. I don't want them to think I'm crazy."

"Well, good luck with that," I muttered as I floated up to straddle the buffalo. Waving one arm over my head, I pretended to ride it, much to her displeasure. When she continued to glare at me, I mimicked the motions for zipping my translucent trap and throwing away the key.

So. Much. Eye. Roll.

After shooting me a final look of disgust, my dear sister took off through the busy dining room, stopping and starting as she avoided bustling waitresses carrying large trays of food and drinks. The staff wore jeans with cowboy boots and black tee shirts with *The Buffalo Chip* printed across the back. They reminded me of an army of black ants scurrying all over the room. Floating through everyone and everything, I made much faster progress crossing the length of the dining room. We met at the back of the restaurant leading to a separate room, the space reserved for parties and special group meetings. A printed piece of copy paper hung on a cork-board by the entryway:

Reserved
PPS Meeting
6:00pm-8:00pm.

The windowless room was empty except for one woman sitting at a table with a steaming tea cup and, judging by the cover, a romance novel.

"You must be Pansy," she said, placing a cross-stitched bookmark between the pages before walking over to greet my sister. "Randy said you'd be joining us this week."

I'd seen her before in town, but we'd never been formally introduced. She stood about five-four, two inches taller than Pansy, and wore her light brown hair in dreadlocks decorated with various beads, pieces of string, and shiny things pulled back with a tie-dyed kerchief. Think 'bird's nest' if the bird had taken some design courses. She gripped Pansy's hand in both of her own like she was consoling a grieving acquaintance. I'd seen a lot of those handshakes since my funeral.

"Yes, I'm me. That's me. Pansy. I'm Pansy, yes." Apparently, my sister, who had been told for years not to speak to strangers was now incapable of doing so. When the woman chuckled and patted her on the shoulder, Pansy closed her eyes and turned a cute shade of pink. "I'm kind of nervous. I've never done anything like this before."

"Aww, don't be nervous, Sweetie. We don't bite. You can hang your coat up over there," she pointed toward a coat rack in the corner which already held a bright red wool peacoat. Pansy took off her puffy silver ski jacket, hanging it on a peg. "Come on and you can have a seat right here, next to me. I'm Summer Hopkins and I own Wild Harmony—it's the yoga studio downtown?" Pansy nodded dutifully, indicating she knew where it was. "I've been a part of this group for the past four years. Randy is our Fearless Leader; he's the one who started the group about ten years ago. He and Greg were two of the original members."

Pansy took a seat next to Summer at a dining table that seated six. There were two rows of tables, five to a row facing a folding table at the front of the room. "There's Greg now." She waved as a dark-haired man with a full beard and mustache came in pulling a handcart loaded with equipment behind him. He was dressed like a grunge lumberjack in a heavy red-checked flannel jacket, jeans, and work boots. A full beard hung a good six inches off the end of his chin. I guess he thought all of the extra hair would keep his face warm. *The Grizzly Adams look is never going to come back into style, buddy.* Stopping next to Pansy, he held out his hand.

"Greg Abernathy, nice to meet you. Are you thinking about joining the team?"

"Yes," Pansy said, giving his hand a perfunctory shake before opening her notebook and pulling out the signed form. "My Dad signed the permission slip."

He laughed and held his hand out to take the slip. "I'll make sure Randy gets this for his records. I'll warn you, our meetings are kind of boring, but we cover a lot and try to familiarize ourselves with upcoming projects. Are you going to go with us tomorrow night?"

"Oh, I hope so."

"Good. We'll try to get you up to speed tonight then." He had a nice baritone voice with a hint of an accent, possibly Texan. I watched him loading equipment onto the folding table. I was looking at the projector, something I'd only seen at school, and was pondering where someone would buy a projector for their own use when a six-foot-something guy pushed a television cart through me. His arm went through my head, although he didn't react at all. *Some ghost catcher he is.*

"Randy," Summer called, "I want you to meet the newest member of our crew, Pansy Bellafini."

"Nice to meet you, Pansy." He walked to their table to shake her hand briefly before turning back to the television cart to untangle the wires and power cords needed to plug it into the VCR on the shelf under it. Also bearded, Randy looked to be about 40 years old, soft around the middle with a bald spot that formed a perfect circle at the crown of his head. If Kevin Costner needed a back-up Friar Tuck, Randy was ready to fulfill the role.

A short woman with pale skin and straight bobbed hair dyed a fantastic shade of cranberry walked in with a man, at least a foot taller than her, and with skin as dark as hers was pale. They were laughing as they came through the doorway, but both of their smiles widened when they spotted Pansy.

"Chandra, Shawn, this is Pansy. She's our newest member." Summer announced.

"Oh, I know Pansy. They're at the Firefly all the time." The Firefly Café was a popular spot for the teenagers in town and Chandra was the manager. Located across the street from the high school, we stopped for snacks, dinner, or caffeine and late night study sessions on the regular. "How are you doing, kiddo?"

The sincere concern in Chandra's voice made tears spring to Pansy's eyes but she managed to blink them back. Shooting a wavering smile in Chandra's direction, Pansy received a pat on the back in response. "As well as can be expected, I see. It's good to get you out and about, honey." Turning to her companion, she introduced him as Shawn, her husband, and explained he was the electrician of the group.

"See, what a lot of people think are supernatural phenomena are really just normal, everyday problems with their house," Chandra explained. "Noises in the walls or in the attic? It's probably some kind of vermin. That's where Randy comes in," she pointed toward Friar Tuck, who was still getting the cord situation under control. "He's an exterminator. Shawn is an electrician. Greg is a plumber. Nine times out of ten, whatever the problem is, it's one of those things that've gone wrong."

"I read the article in the paper about the bad electrical wiring. Does that happen a lot?"

"Not a lot, but sometimes. Flickering lights or high EMF readings which can make the hairs on your arms stand up, it usually ends up being faulty wiring." Shawn replied, his voice surprisingly soft for someone who had to duck to get through the doorway.

"Do you ever actually find ghosts?" *Good question, Pansy*, I thought, practically rubbing my hands together. *Here we are, getting to the meat of the issue.*

"Well, we don't like to use the term 'ghosts', it always makes me think of Ghostbusters. I like to think of them as spirits. We sometimes find spirits or unexplained occurrences which can be attributed to paranormal activity in a home," Chandra said.

"Unexplained but regular occurrences," Summer said. I saw her mouth the word, 'ghosts' to Pansy as soon as Chandra and Shawn had turned to take their seats.

"Okay, so, since Blake is probably stuck behind a snowplow or something," Friar Randy said as he focused the projector, transforming the blurred spot on the front wall into a hand-drawn image of a house plan. "We'll go ahead and get started without him, he can catch up later. Anyway, Greg and I went to do some recon earlier this week. The client we'll be visiting tomorrow says her children keep having nightmares and swear they're seeing someone walking past their room in the dark. She said they always see this figure around three in the morning."

"Oooh, the witching hour," I heard Summer mutter under her breath. Fascinated by being in a room full of people who were dedicated to finding ghosts, and yet, who also seemed to be completely unaware of my presence, I decided to do some testing of my own. Since no one had looked in my direction at all, I assumed no one could see me. Deciding to go for sound, I stood in the middle of the room and yelled, "Tin roof! Rusted." Pansy turned immediately and shot me a dirty look. Trying to disguise her sudden motion, she started fluffing the long drape of her poet sleeves. No one else turned, flinched, or gave any other indication they'd heard me.

I opted for a more physical approach. I started with Friar Randy, and when he showed no response to my hand resting slightly *in* his shoulder, I moved on to Shawn. Ditto for no response. Chandra, on the other hand, flinched and brushed absently at my hand, which could have been a coincidence. I decided to come back to her again later. Scientific method and all that. After testing everyone else in the room, including my sister who I had to sneak up on so she wouldn't see me coming, no one else showed any particular response to my touch.

Going back to Chandra, I laid my hand on her other shoulder and was rewarded with instant feedback. She immediately raised a hand to brush at her shoulder, squirming in her seat. Interesting.

The Good Friar caught my attention again when he started talking about the woman in front of me. "Okay, Chandra has listened to our EVP's over the last few days and we've picked out a few good ones that we want to go over with you from our last session." He was turning toward a large boom box on the front table when another man came in and started unwinding a scarf that had been wrapped around his head. The tardy Blake, I assumed as he removed his coat and gave his light brown hair a good shake. The weather must be getting worse. *Fantastic.*

Friar Randy hit the 'play' button, listened for a few seconds to make sure the tape was where he wanted it, and then hit 'pause' again. Summer leaned over to Pansy and jerked her thumb back to Blake who'd taken a seat at the back table in their row.

"Blake is a history professor at the community college," she whispered. "He likes to do all of the research on a house before we start a job."

Lumberjack Greg started passing out pieces of notebook paper and ink pens. "Okay, this was from the weekend before last. The job over on Birchwood," Randy continued. "Shawn was downstairs checking the electrical and was recording, you can hear him here on the recording mumbling to himself," there were a few chuckles, "and then I want you to listen to what happens next. I want everyone to write down what they think they hear."

"This is the way we normally do it," Summer told Pansy. "People hear what they want to hear, it's called pareidolia. It's like when you hear some random noise, but your brain interprets it as being a voice speaking in your own language. It's the normal human condition, you can't help it, but writing it down helps eliminate the power of suggestion."

Accepting the piece of paper and holding the pen like she was about to start the hundred-yard dash in ink, my sister leaned forward, eyes intent on the stereo as Friar Randy hit the 'play' button.

There was a lot of static, and Shawn's voice was muffled like the recorder had been in his pocket at the time. I could hear him mumbling that he was surprised the entire place hadn't caught on fire and then there was a banging sound, metal on metal. Real-time Shawn offered up a bit of commentary, "That was me closing the electrical panel."

After another few seconds of unintelligible mumbling on the tape, there was another voice, much deeper, but also muffled. "Burn it down," is what I heard. Everyone in the room started writing on their papers after a brief second of surprise at being able to hear a voice so clearly.

Pansy had written, "Come around" and Summer had written "Burn the ground" So, obviously, the human condition also included hearing whatever you wanted.

"Okay," Friar Randy said, rewinding the tape. "Listen again and then we'll compare."

He replayed the 'voice' five times before all of the members of the Perth Paranormal Society felt confident in what they'd heard. They went around the room telling everyone else their variation of what they thought they heard and the results were widely varied.

"Well, so we mostly agree the first word was 'burn' but the rest is up for debate," Randy said, leaning up against the table at the front of the room.

"The voice was obviously a man but when I researched the house I didn't find any men, or women for that matter, who died in or near it." This from Blake at the back table. "The house was built at the turn of the century and the electrical was updated in the forties and needs a complete overhaul, but there's no record of anyone ever dying in the house. The original owners had sold it to their children, they died in New Mexico, the children then sold it shortly afterward to a young couple who only lived there for a few years and then sold it to the current owners. There's nothing to suggest anything terrible ever happened in the house that would make a spirit claim it."

"Was there anything else on the tapes?"

"Yeah, was there anything else on the tapes?" I asked, forgetting for the moment no one could hear me.

"Yes," Friar Randy answered, "a few more spots where it seems like the same voice, although if the spirit is actually trying to say something it's completely unintelligible." He put in another tape which had already been queued up to the correct spot. After two or three listens no one could agree if it was actually a voice, let alone the same voice.

"Anything else? Cameras, videos, meters?" Summer asked.

"I have some video for us to look at, but I think it's just dust." He pushed the TV cart into position and pressed play on the VCR where I could see Summer and Chandra sitting in what looked like an attic asking questions like, "What's your name?" and "Did you die here?" There was something that floated by and Randy rewound it, playing it frame by frame. After some discussion, it was decided we were seeing dust floating across the screen. The general consensus in the room was that anything perfectly round was light being reflected from dust in the air, creating bokeh on the lens, and could not be a supernatural spirit. Good to know.

"We have to experiment when we get home," I whispered in Pansy's ear. For once, she looked like she was having a good time and eagerly nodded her head.

A waitress came in with drinks and appetizers which she set up on one of the empty tables in the back of the room and we took a break to eat and drink. Or, at least all of the living people in the room took a break to eat and drink. I stared at the food with no small amount of jealousy. Getting bored and wanting a cheese fry so bad I could almost taste it, I decided to carry out my experimentation in the greater dining room of The Buffalo Chip. I ran my hand along each and every diner. There were only two who responded and one of those only brushed their shoulder the first time, my second and third attempts didn't provoke a response at all.

After my second pass of the dining room I figured most of the noshing had to be over, so I returned to the meeting room where Lumberjack Greg was now standing at the front. He'd removed his flannel shirt, revealing a plain white tee, and was flipping through a handful of papers. Drifting over to hover directly in front of my sister, I saw everyone now had the same printouts—land deeds for a house and improvement permits. When Summer, still sitting next to my sister, turned her page to what looked like statements from the members of the family, I could see that there was the mom, Maryanne, and two kids, Kaitlyn, age 14 and Josh, 9. No mention of the father. Complaints were of noises, scraping sounds at the windows, pictures and objects being moved, and rustling on the roof and in the attic two to three nights a week.

"Did the kids seem credible?" Shawn asked, looking at the statements skeptically.

"The kids are freaked out and the boy, Josh, is actually staying with his dad on most weekends because he's too afraid to stay in the house."

"So, the mom thinks it's not an animal?"

"I took a look when I was there," Friar Randy, who I recalled was the exterminator, replied. "There's easy access to the attic from the inside and I didn't see anything torn up, no insulation pulled out of the walls or boxes chewed up. No scat anywhere. If it's an animal, they're really clean and considerate."

"Could they be imagining it?"

"Anything is possible. Pansy, do you go to school with Kaitlyn?"

I could see panic flash in Pansy's eyes because she had been called to speak in front of strangers, and adult strangers at that. Her shoulders straightened and even though her eyes were wide her voice didn't waiver. Much. "Kaitlyn? Umm, yes, I think so. I think she's a freshman." We didn't know any freshmen personally but had heard a few of their names. Not that we had a particularly large high school, less than four hundred students in all.

"Well, maybe you can talk to her. She may open up to you since you're closer to her own age. We may be able to work with that."

"So what's the protocol if they find out someone is lying their butt off?" I asked, and much to my surprise, Pansy opened her mouth and repeated my question. You could have knocked me over with a feather, if I had, you know, a body or something.

"Well, it does happen," Lumberjack Greg said. "Usually, we take the person behind it and play them whatever evidence we have of them perpetrating the supposed 'haunting' and most of the time they'll admit to it."

"We did have one kid over in Crandall who swore up and down he didn't do it even though we had him on tape banging on the walls and then running back to his bedroom when his parents came out to see what was going on," Shawn offered.

"Hidden cameras, man, they'll get you every time," Summer whispered to Pansy.

"Maybe he was possessed by a demon," I said. Pansy started to open her mouth to repeat my statement but caught herself, choosing to ignore me instead.

"So, the house is three stories if you include the attic," Blake said, pushing wire-rimmed glasses up his nose as he looked over the papers.

"Attic is really only half a story, the highest point is down the mid-beam," Lumberjack Greg said. "I still had to stoop to make it through. Bedrooms are on the second floor and the first floor is the main living space. There's a full basement which isn't completed, dirt floor, concrete block walls, lots of plumbing, and exposed electrical." He scratched his beard while looking over the room.

"So, any other questions before we wrap up here?" There was some mumbling and the chairs scraped against the hardwood as they were pushed out from the tables.

"I think that's it. Pansy, you're sure your mom knows you're going to be out until the wee hours of the morning?"

"Yes, sir. She knows."

"And you're good with driving home so late? In the dark?"

What he meant was alone in the dark and cold with the ice on the roads and the fresh memory of her last wreck and the consequential death of her twin. Not that he actually said any of that. He didn't need to. Pansy just nodded.

4

The following evening, we were upstairs in our bedroom getting ready for our first night of ghost hunting. We'd shared a room and giant closet for our entire lives. Her side was done in purples, my side in greens, with twin-size beds that were separated by a single nightstand that we shared. While the walls on my side were covered in concert posters and the torn-out pages of *Teen Beat* magazine, hers was covered in framed posters of Monet artworks. Our closet was also divided. My set of folding doors displayed mostly blacks and grays, while Pansy hoarded every color of the rainbow behind hers.

Not owning a single pair of shoes suitable for creeping around an attic or basement without risk of scuffing suede or breaking an ankle in three-inch platforms, she borrowed a pair of my old combat boots in plain, unadorned black. I almost died, again, when she actually laced them all the way to the top before double knotting them.

When she realizes that she can't bend her ankles, she'll rethink that plan, I thought. After pulling a gray hooded sweatshirt over a tee, she tugged her hair back into a French braid.

"Okay, Gerri, do I look like a professional paranormal investigator?"

"You look like a high school kid heading out to a bonfire. What does a professional paranormal whatever look like, anyway? Did you get Dad's Maglite out of the cabinet?"

She patted one of the side pockets of the black cargo pants she was wearing, also mine. "I don't know, and yeah, I've got it. Should I pack a first aid kit, do you think?"

"I'm pretty sure they already have one. They're adults, surely they're prepared for these kinds of things."

She stood in front of the full-length mirror that hung on the wall between our closets and I watched her as she patted at her hair again. We'd shared clothing when we were younger, not so much as we'd grown and developed our own tastes, but I supposed that everything in both closets was all Pansy's now. Although, I would have to tell her to keep her paws off any concert tees that she hadn't actually attended, like the Poison tee or the Stone Temple Pilots. You can't wear the tee for a concert that you didn't actually attend. That was the rule, according to Robbie, our older brother. Three years our senior, he had taken us to most of the concerts we'd attended.

I watched Pansy nod at her own image in the mirror, sure that she was giving herself a silent pep talk. With a sigh, and a final nod in my direction, we were ready to go. I hated to say it, since between the two of us Pansy was definitely more of a clothes horse, but I missed the process of standing in front of a mirror and trying to decide if I looked like the best possible version of myself. The makeup, messing up my eyeliner at least twice, sometimes three times, as I tried to make both sides even. Sure it was easier knowing that no one could see you, but I wouldn't pretend that I didn't miss it.

Heaving my own sigh, which was entirely for theatrical effect since I didn't actually need to breathe, I followed her down the stairs.

"Gerri?" The horror in our mother's voice made my non-existent heart break.

"No, Mom. It's me. I'm wearing Gerri's clothes."

"Why would you do that?" Mom clutched the corner of the wall leading to the living room, a glass of wine in her other hand. She leaned slightly forward as if to get a better look, needing to make sure it was really Pansy.

"We've always worn each other's clothes, Mom. And I can't go ghost hunting tonight in Mary Janes and a sweater vest."

"I…" She stopped and I noticed that her eyes were glazed; this obviously wasn't her first glass of wine for the evening. It took a moment before she seemed to realize that Pansy was still standing there waiting for her to finish her sentence.

"Okay. Be careful." She didn't look back up at us, but leaned against the wall staring into the glass of red like she was waiting on a fortune to appear in a Magic 8 Ball. Maybe some answers would float to the surface for her soon. I hated to see her like this, so lost and disconnected from everything. I wished that I could wrap my arms around her and tell her that I was okay. Tell her that I was still with Pansy.

I caught Pansy looking at me and shrugged. I wasn't equipped to handle our mother's grief. Neither was our father, apparently, since he'd been working later and later each night since the funeral. "Should you hug her or something?" I asked. It was Pansy's turn to shrug as she continued to the front door. We'd talk about it later.

"You ready?" Pansy asked as she climbed in behind the wheel of Mom's Explorer. Determined that I wasn't going to be a downer, I nodded.

Since I couldn't adjust my floating speed fast enough to keep up every time Pansy braked for a stop sign, I floated alongside the SUV. Seeing me half in the dashboard or flying through the back of the seat made her uncomfortable. Understandably.

The members of the PPS were supposed to meet in the parking lot of Sycamore Plaza before heading to the McAllister house. Since our neighborhood was also on the northern end of town it only took about five minutes before Pansy, stressing the Explorer's speakers with our *Nevermind* CD, was pulling into the freshly paved lot of the strip mall. Being early November, it was already full dark at seven o'clock, but the white van we'd been told the group used to haul equipment shone like a beacon under a street lamp.

We parked next to the van and Pansy waved at Friar Randy and Lumberjack Greg through their open passenger window before walking over to Summer.

The beads woven into Summer's dreads twinkled under the street lights as she leaned against an old VW Bug. I couldn't tell if the car was really blue or if the paint only looked blue under the glare of the giant Blockbuster Video sign.

"You want to ride with me, kiddo?" she asked as Pansy walked over to her. Her breath came out in giant clouds of vapor and I was glad I couldn't feel the cold. "No point in taking more cars than necessary and I mean, there's not a lot of room for anyone bigger," she laughed, jerking her thumb toward the inside of the car. Even with the crap lighting situation we were in, I could see that the entire back seat was stuffed with clothes.

"Never know when you're going to need a wardrobe change, you know?"

I stuck my head into the backseat, boggling at the mess. We would have been grounded for a month if our car had ever looked this bad. As I took inventory, because I was nosey, I noticed there weren't food wrappers or receipts or any garbage at all, really, just clothes. It wasn't even that there were a lot of clothes because honestly, you can't fit very much into the backseat of a Bug, but there were tank tops, baby doll dresses, leggings, scarfs, vests, and at least three different pairs of jeans with various flowers embroidered all over them. I knew she lived above her shop, so she wasn't homeless, but decided to mark this one on my list of *Mysteries To Be Solved At A Later Date.*

Shawn pulled in next to us, brakes squealing on his white Saturn as he came to a stop. Chandra was out of the passenger door before the engine had even completely shut down, bouncing around the rear of the car to meet us. Shawn rolled down the driver's side window and turned the heat up, holding his hands over the vents. Blake pulled in moments later.

"Sorry. I almost forgot my newest toy," he said, holding a 35mm camera above his head.

"Did you get the tripod?" Lumberjack Greg asked, leaning his head out the passenger window of the van and nodding toward the camera.

"Yes. And the filter. We'll give it a try tonight. The film was freakin' twelve dollars for twenty-four exposures so let's hope we catch something."

"Infrared film," Chandra told Pansy, noticing the confused look on her face. "We're going to see if it's more sensitive to spectral happenings than regular film." I gave the camera another glance, wondering if I would show up. Maybe we could test it out if I could position myself to be in the right spot at the right time. Chandra jogged back around to the passenger side of the Saturn while Blake loaded himself and his bag of camera equipment into the back seat. Pansy got into the Bug with Summer and we were off.

I floated directly over the van as it led our motley caravan toward a Saturday night adventure. I was excited and more than a little nervous; it was that same feeling I used to have before going on stage for an Elementary School Christmas solo. What if the house really was haunted? What if whoever was haunting it was mean, or sadistic? Or, what if he or she was just lonely and wanted to follow me around and talk to me for all of eternity? I wasn't sure which would be worse.

We traveled northeast for about ten minutes before turning off the main road. Homes were further apart out here, each property having two or three acres of mostly wooded land between the main road and the arroyo. Eventually, we came to a break in the pines and crossed a small wooden bridge. Continuing up a gravel driveway, I saw a two-and-a-half-story white farmhouse in a small clearing, light pouring out of the windows. It looked like every light in the place had been left on for us.

Illuminated by the three sets of headlights cutting through the darkness, the yard looked tidy enough. Although three inches of snow generally made everything look clean, I could see that the shrubs lining the porch were neatly trimmed and the house looked well-cared for. There was a detached two-car garage a few yards from the house and a rusted swing set in the side yard. It all looked very normal and there was nothing that immediately made you think that it was even creepy, let alone haunted.

The front door opened as everyone was turning off their engines and the family emerged, all three wrapped up in coats, scarves, and mittens. The taller woman, who I assumed was the mother, Maryanne McAllister, walked toward the wide graveled space between the house and garage where Randy was getting out of the van. After a brief discussion, she handed him a set of keys and then herded her two children into the garage. By the time everyone else was out of their vehicles, the family Outback was pulling out of the garage and with a wave, they started down the driveway.

"Hotel?" I asked.

"Where are they going?" Pansy asked for me as the group gathered in front of the van.

"They're staying at her mother's house tonight," Greg answered. "It's hard to get sleep when you have a bunch of strangers stomping through your house videotaping everything. Plus, it creates a cleaner investigation scene if we know where everyone is. If the house is really haunted then it shouldn't matter who's in there."

I felt like that wasn't entirely true since I could only specifically haunt my sister, but it wasn't like I could call him out on that. With a shrug, Pansy turned to help schlep equipment out of the back of the van to where they were lining it all up in the dining room. The dining room/command center already held two 13" TV monitors, a big plastic box with lots of buttons, whose purpose was completely lost on me, and what seemed like miles of cable. I watched in fascination as Randy opened a small tote that held more AA batteries than I'd ever seen in one place outside of a store display. He checked flashlights and passed out spare batteries to everyone.

"An actual phenomenon will drain the batteries from your flashlight, your camera, or your pager," he explained to Pansy, pointing to the beeper sitting snugly in a black pouch attached to his belt. I hadn't noticed that I'd been able to drain anything. Apparently, I didn't ghost very well.

After the last of the equipment had been brought in, coats and scarves were unceremoniously dumped onto the living room couch and everyone's shoes were fitted with little shower cap-looking things to keep the floors clean. As everyone else started running cables, wires, and extension cords throughout the house, I went to work snooping. There are very few perks to being dead and I fully intended to exploit every single one that I could find.

5

My joy at being able to snoop through someone else's stuff unimpeded by guilt or, more accurately, a fear of being caught, was dampened almost immediately. The ability to peer into any closet or drawer turned out to be completely useless as long as that drawer or closet was still dark. I didn't give off an otherworldly glow, couldn't hold a flashlight, and my ghostly self, much like my human self, couldn't see in the dark. Dejected, I found Pansy on the stairwell running a length of cable from the second floor. Eyes narrowing as she noticed me, she mouthed the word, "What?"

"I can't see anything."

"What?" Alarmed, she reached out for me, her hand halfway there before she remembered. Pulling her hand back, she looked around to make sure we were alone. "Has everything gone dark or is it fuzzy? What's going on?"

"No, dork. I mean, I can stick my head into any cabinet or closet but I can't see what's inside because it's still dark."

Rolling her eyes she exhaled, loudly, before continuing to reel out more blue cable. "Of course, you can't. Did you think you were going to gain supernatural night vision or something?"

"Well, I mean, I got excited thinking I was going to finally be useful, and wham! I'm still useless."

"You're not useless."

"Who's not useless? Giving yourself a pep talk there, kiddo?" Chandra came around the corner from the living room and before I could move she walked through me on her way up the stairs. "Wow, it's chilly in here. Do you feel a draft?"

"Uh, yeah. I sure do. I'll check the front door and make sure that it's closed all the way after I get this cable to the dining room."

Pansy shot me a wide-eyed look as Chandra continued up the stairs.

"Why didn't you move?" she hissed once the other woman was out of earshot.

"I didn't see her coming," I hissed right back. I'd been too busy whining about how much being dead sucked. "There aren't any ghosts here, by the way." I could contribute that much, at least.

"Unless they're hiding in a closet," I heard her mumble as she nudged the cable against the wall with her foot.

I stuck my tongue out as she continued down the hallway to the dining room. *Way harsh, Tai.* Trying to stay out of the way, I examined the living room where the foot traffic was light. The lamps on the end tables flanking the blue-and-white checked couch, currently piled high with coats and scarves, gave off plenty of light. Framed school pictures hung on the wall, a testament to braces and an unfortunate side ponytail for Kaitlyn, and a three-year stretch of bowl haircuts for Josh. *Poor kid.*

Their television perched on a black stand made of particleboard and stuffed full of videotapes—the bottom layer of tapes standing upright with more crammed sideways on top. The bookcase, also particle board, its shelves bowing in the middle, also held VCR tapes on the bottom three of its five shelves. Paperbacks lived on the second shelf and the top held an almost complete set of Encyclopedia Britannica from maybe the seventies, judging by the condition of the spines.

Finally, after almost thirty minutes of the Perth Paranormal Society rushing throughout the house setting up cameras and microphones, everyone gathered in the dining room. The room was small, more suitable for family breakfast than a dinner party, and barely held everyone and the equipment. And the apples. Which were everywhere. Ceramic apples on shelves, framed prints of apples on the walls, fake apples in the fruit bowl. Baskets of apples were printed on the curtains and wallpaper, and ceramic salt and pepper shakers, shaped like, you guessed it, apples, sat on the dining room table and had been pushed to the side to make room for the video monitors. Randy stood near the kitchen entry checking off something on his clipboard before addressing the crowded room.

"Okay, folks, Blake has set up his camera in the attic where the source of most of the noise is coming from. We've got a standard video camera next to it doing continuous filming and another shooting video from the other end since it stretches the length of the house."

Already bored, I made my way straight up, not sticking around for the rest of his directions to the troops. I floated through the floorboards and joists, through the electrical and plumbing systems and up to the attic where the overhead light was, thankfully, still on. The attic was practically empty but ran the entire length of the house.

I spotted the 35mm camera on a tripod near the door that led from a narrow stairway into the attic and floated in front of it, not sure how it worked. Was it motion activated? If so, it didn't seem to be doing anything. I waved my hand in front of the lens but didn't hear any clicking noises or the sound of film advancing. Maybe someone was going to sit here and push the button manually all night.

The video cameras looked new and seemed to use the smaller tapes that required an adapter to play in a VCR. *Fancy.* Turning, I ran a critical eye over the few boxes in the attic and noticed that one of the totes had what looked like stress cracks in the plastic lid, like something heavy had once sat on top of it. Maybe an old television set or microwave or something.

I closed my eyes, trying to sense any kind of supernatural presence, but didn't feel anything that creeped me out. Then again, I couldn't feel heat or cold either, so what did I know? Another ghost could have been standing right behind me and I probably wouldn't even know it. *Useless.*

I was halfway to the second floor when I heard footsteps on the stairs. I waited where I was, half in the attic, half in what I thought I remembered was a bedroom below me, to see who was going to be the first to investigate.

"Blake has the infrared film loaded and set on a timer so every thirty minutes it will take a picture. We'll start our session up here and see if we get anything."

Shawn led Pansy through the narrow doorway, ducking to avoid cracking his head on the unfinished rafters stuffed with pink insulation. Pansy was nodding and looking around, probably wondering where I'd wandered off to. "If you notice, this video camera next to the film camera is pointed down the length of the attic and I'm going to move those boxes over to the side so that they don't obstruct our view." He pushed the two stacks of totes over into a corner and they slid easily on the wooden plank floor. "This camera over here on the other side has a view of the door so we'll know exactly who enters and exits the room at all times."

"Makes sense," she said.

"Now, do you remember what EVP stands for?"

"Electronic Voice Phenomena."

Nodding, he pulled a mini-tape recorder from his pocket and pressed a button with his thumb. "This is Shawn Bailey of the Perth Paranormal Society. We're on-site at the home of Maryanne McAllister at 12 Briarwood Lane. The time is now 8:05 pm on Saturday, November 11th, 1995. I and our newest initiate, Pansy

Bellafini, are here in the attic of the home where most of the activity seems to be occurring." I could hear the click from across the room when he stopped recording.

"Now, the theory here, and they've been doing this kind of experimentation since the seventies, is that the voices of the spirits will be picked up on the tape, even though we can't hear them with the naked ear."

"Like the voice on the tape last night."

"Yes, exactly. We run a lot of tape doing these things and then we'll split them up and listen to them over the next few days to see if there's anything there. Anything that shouldn't be there, I should say. There's normally hours and hours of tape, so it gets pretty boring. These tapes will hold about four hours of footage," he gestured toward the video cameras, "so we'll have to change them out later, put in fresh batteries, that kind of thing. We'll probably only be here until about three. If nothing has happened by then it's probably not going to."

"Do you normally have more activity around the witching hour?" Pansy used the term we'd heard Summer use the night before. *Witching hour, my butt.*

"Well, no, not normally."

"Have you guys started asking the entity questions yet?" came Summer's voice from the stairs.

"Not yet, I was just explaining the setup. Did you want to join us?"

"Sure. Greg and Randy are down in the basement looking it over and starting with EVP's down there. Blake is starting in the boy's bedroom."

"Chandra watching the monitors?"

"Yep, she's taken up position in the dining room. If she spots something on the monitors she can direct a team to go look into it." She explained to Pansy. Bored, again, I decided to make a pass in front of the video cameras to see if anyone raised an alarm. Pansy's eyes widened when she saw me emerge from the floor and come into the light cast by the single naked bulb in the middle of the room. I sauntered toward the video camera, doing a full-on runway strut which isn't nearly as satisfying when you can't hear your heels clicking on the floor.

Despite my best RuPaul impersonation, I didn't hear anyone yelling or screaming that there was a ghost in the attic and no one seemed uncomfortable except for Pansy. Shawn, oblivious to my presence, turned his recorder back on. There was a click followed by a whir as the spools began to turn.

"If there is a spirit on these premises, what is your name?" Hunching his tall lanky form like a bad Quasimodo impersonator, he slowly turned in a circle, the recorder held out at arm's length. I listened and could tell Pansy and Summer were doing the same, but there was no answer to the question, at least not that any of us heard. "What do you want here?"

I wondered if my voice would show up or if this was complete and total bullcrap. Getting as close to the recorder as I could, I sang, "Hello, is it me you're looking for?"

Pansy started to laugh, but quickly changed it to a cough, thumping the heel of her hand against her chest.

"Dusty," she offered as an explanation.

"How long have you been here?" Shawn was still asking questions, circling around and around with the recorder, hoping to catch something on his tape. Wiggling my fingers goodbye to my sister, I pinched my nose between my thumb and fingers and descended through the floorboards like I was sinking underwater. It was time to go see what everyone else was doing.

Blake was still on the second floor. He'd moved from the boy's room and was now sitting in the hallway, his back against the wall and legs splayed in front of him, shining a flashlight around in the dark like that was going to help him catch a ghost. *Did he plan on tripping it?* I heard a click as he started his recorder. "Why are you moving the photos in the hallway?" He was silent, allowing the 'spirits' time to answer. I rolled my eyes. "Are you upset that there's a house here or did you live here?" If anything answered I didn't hear it.

Overhead, I did hear Shawn's footsteps as he continued revolving, presumably still asking questions. I continued back down to the first floor where Chandra was settled in at the dining room table, drinking coffee from a giant 7/11 travel thermos and watching the monitors. Twirling her fingers around a tendril of her cranberry hair, she didn't look anxious or like she was trying to rewind anything to get a better look at my form as it floated across the screen. I figured it was safe to assume that all of these cameras didn't actually catch anything useful.

Unless maybe a ghost could become visible if they really wanted to. Although, since I hadn't met any other ghosts, maybe I was the only one. Maybe every other person that had ever died had immediately moved on to wherever they were supposed to be and I was too stupid to figure out how to do that. Was that even a possibility? I mean, I was of above-average intelligence, but I really hadn't noticed any obvious signs that would show me the way to whatever came next.

It occurred to me that maybe I should visit my grave. Surely a graveyard would have ghosts if there were any more out there to meet. But what if they could only be seen by their loved ones like I could only be seen by Pansy? What if the world was actually overrun with ghosts but we couldn't see one another? And what happened if two people died together? Were they ghosts together? At this rate, I was adding questions faster than I could ever find answers.

After watching the monitors for a few moments more, being careful not to accidentally float through Chandra and set off her internal ghost sensor or whatever, I saw that Greg and Randy were still downstairs in the basement. They were examining the small ground-level windows that allowed sunlight into the basement with a flashlight and magnifying glass, looking for any signs of tampering. Those windows were much too small for a person to fit through, even a little kid, and it looked like they were wasting their time, to me.

I spent the better part of the next hour floating up and down through the house, checking on each group, back and forth, until I finally went out to the yard to snoop around. Ghost hunting seemed to be ungodly boring work and I didn't know if I had the patience for it.

The detached two-car garage only had room for the Subaru as the other bay was packed with big plastic totes and random sports equipment. Apparently, the attic wasn't full of crap like every other home because it was all out here. Less stairs, I guessed, shrugging. Enough light spilled through the windowed garage doors from an outdoor security light that I could make out the outline of skis and what looked like an old basketball hoop stuck behind the totes. There was no tool bench, no oil cans, or any of the stuff that our dad kept in our garage. Outside, a large, extendable ladder hung horizontally across the rear wall. There were a couple of five-gallon buckets and a coiled water hose stored under the ladder, all of which were now frozen to the ground. Glancing up at the house I figured that cleaning the pine needles out of the gutters must be a full-time job.

Towering Ponderosa pines crowded all sides of the small backyard and I watched for a few minutes as their ice-encrusted branches waved in the wind, their shadows, cast by the moonlight, danced across the snow. I supposed that enjoying nature's beauty without freezing my butt off could be put firmly in the 'good things' column of my ghost checklist.

By the time I floated back into the kitchen, the clock on the stove read two-thirty and I figured Pansy would be ready to pass out by now. She was one of those people who considered ten o'clock to be 'late.' I went to find her, noting that Greg was now at the dining room table, hunched forward with his bearded chin resting on his thermos as he stared at the monitors. Over his shoulder, I could see Summer and Chandra in the kids' bedrooms asking questions. Chandra was holding a recorder out in front of them, and they seemed to be asking the same kind of questions Shawn had been asking earlier. I figured you could only do so many of these 'ghost hunts' before you started asking the same things over and over again by rote. I mean, how many different things could you possibly ask a ghost? What's your sign? What's your favorite color? I guess you could get more specific if you thought you knew who the ghost had actually been, like did they miss their wife or husband or kids, or whatever. Good luck getting answers to any of that.

A second check of the monitors showed Randy and Pansy down in the basement waving some sort of plastic box near the electrical outlets. Randy was pointing to the LCD screen on the box, explaining its use to Pansy. I wasn't sure how much longer they could 'investigate' the house, but I had to give them credit for doing a very thorough job of it. My instincts, however, said "Not Haunted," and I figured that everyone here was just wasting their time. Including me.

6

Pansy rode back to Sycamore Plaza with Chandra and Shawn since they had to bring Blake back to his car, too. It was a little before four in the morning and the parking lot was lit only by the dim yellow glow of the street lights as all of the shopping center lights had been turned off at ten when everything closed. Even Canyon Lanes, the bowling alley in the corner of the L-shapped plaza, closed at ten o'clock. There was no such thing as a nightlife in Perth.

"Ghost hunting is crazy boring," I said as soon as we were alone.

"My head hurts and I'm tired but, like, wired and wide awake, ya know?" I nodded before floating into the back seat where she could hear me but wouldn't actually be able to see me in the dark as I bobbed up and down through the upholstery. I figured as long as she was talking to someone she wouldn't fall asleep on the short drive home.

She started the engine and the radio sprang to life with a commercial about a tree farm, jarringly loud in the otherwise silent night. I waited for her to get the volume adjusted and the CD pushed back in before distracting her with questions.

"So, was it everything that you thought it would be?"

"Well, honestly, no. I really thought that we might see something more, well… ghostly," she shrugged as she looked both ways before pulling out onto the completely deserted four-lane that ran through the middle of town.

"What, holding little machines next to electrical outlets isn't exciting?"

"I don't know." There was a sigh and some hand waving while she struggled to find the right words. "Maybe I'm jaded since I know for a fact that there was a ghost standing next to him and the needle on his little machine didn't waggle even a little bit."

"That may sway your opinion. Just a little bit."

"Maybe they'll find something on the tapes. That would be cool."

Since it was our first case, we hadn't been assigned any video or audio recordings to review, though Summer had invited us to come over to the shop the next day for some lessons on what to look for when reviewing tapes.

"I hate to be the bearer of bad news, but I don't think there was another ghost anywhere near that house. I didn't feel anything, or see anything."

"That would be disappointing, but we don't even know if you can see or hear another ghost."

"I was actually thinking about that tonight. What do you think about going to see my grave?" Her eyes darted to the rearview mirror to look at me, momentarily forgetting that I didn't have a reflection. "If we make a list of all the things we don't know about my current state and if 'Can Gerri see other ghosts?' is at the top of the list, then what better place to test it?"

Saying the words out loud made me think of what other things I might find there. *Was I ready for that?*

"Never mind," I said before she'd even formulated a response. "Scratch that idea. What if that's where my door is? You know, so that I can move on to heaven or nirvana or be reincarnated… whatever it is that you do next? I don't want to do that. I'm not ready to leave you."

"Well," she paused as she flicked on the turn signal before turning into our subdivision even though we were the only vehicle on the road. "Couldn't you decide to not walk through it?"

"What if it sucks me in?"

"What if 'it' doesn't even exist and you're only being ridiculous? What if there's another ghost there that you could meet and maybe give you some tips?"

"Like, *Being Dead for Dummies*?"

"Well, if the shoe fits. Do you have a better plan?"

I watched the familiar houses of our neighborhood scroll past the back window as I thought about it. "I think, for now, that we should stick with haunted houses. Or houses that have the possibility of being haunted. Like, by maybe one ghost and not a whole cemetery of dead people. That would be too overwhelming. I mean, my whole existence is one big unknown right now, I'm not ready to tempt fate yet."

She gave me a noncommittal sound as she navigated the final turn onto our street. I studied her, my view of her only available in brief glimpses between the street lamps, like a strobe light as we drove. She was concentrating on something, either the question or the road or maybe both.

"What about the bridge? What if your door or whatever is there?"

She didn't have to say which bridge. For the rest of her life, 'the bridge' was only ever going to refer to one bridge.

"I don't know. We could try that, maybe. There would have to be less dead people there than at the cemetery, right?"

"I don't know. I mean, lots of people wreck there."

"Yeah, but most don't actually die. And those that do? Well, surely not everyone dies right there on the spot, right? Some of them have to die in the hospital or in the ambulance on the way."

"Okay, but you're not there, so why would they be? You died there, you appeared there, but then you left." She had a point. I still thought that a hospital would be a good test. With my silence, I let her know that I was done with this part of our conversation. Besides, we were almost home.

The quarry that employed most of the town's residents had experienced several periods of growth over the last century. As a result, the need for quickly built, affordable, housing had boomed with each wave. When our neighborhood had been created in the seventies, the developers used three basic house plans, along with the flipped version of those same plans, punching out house after house like they were making Christmas sugar cookies. Twenty years later, it was the paint colors and landscaping that really set each house apart from its neighboring structures. Ours was a creamy yellow two-story with an attached garage on the left-hand side of the house.

Pansy clicked the garage door opener as we pulled into the concrete driveway and maneuvered around Dad's truck. She remained quiet as she concentrated, squeezing the large SUV into the tight space while leaving enough room to open her door. I almost floated right through her when she paused at the door that led from the garage into the laundry room. She turned back to look at me.

"I meant to ask you earlier, but when Chandra walked through you, did you feel anything?"

"Not really. Why?"

"Well, I was thinking about what you said, that she seems to be able to feel you and when she walked through you I was afraid that you might, I don't know, possess her or something."

"Wow, I hadn't thought about it, but no, I didn't feel anything weird."

"But, it got me thinking. Do you think you can do it? Possess someone?"

"How would I know? The question is do I want to try, and the answer is no."

"Why not? How are we ever going to know what you can do if you're too afraid to try anything? I don't even know what you have to be afraid of, you're already dead." She opened the door with one hand and clicked the garage door button on the wall with the other.

"What do I have to be afraid of?" I asked, indignant as she closed the door while I was still floating across the threshold. "Possess Chandra? My God, Ross and Rachel just kissed. What if I get stuck inside of someone and can't get out and miss the next episode of *Friends*?"

"I'm sure she watches it too," Pansy said, and I could tell she was trying not to laugh.

"That's not the point. What if I make her sick, or get stuck and can't get back out, what then? Are you going to call a priest and exorcize me?"

"Well, no. Don't get your panties in a bunch. I was simply throwing out suggestions of things we should try."

I like that she said 'we' even though it was my eternal life on the line.

Pansy remembered to lock the interior garage door like we'd learned on *Unsolved Mysteries*. Mom was at the top of the stairs as we rounded the corner, making both of us jump.

"Did you have fun, sweetie?"

"Yeah, it was interesting. I'll tell you about it in the morning, okay?"

"That's fine. I just wanted to make sure you made it home alright. Brush your teeth before you go to bed."

Oral health was no longer a consideration for me. *Score one in the perks column.*

Once Pansy's teeth were properly cared for and she was ready for bed, she grabbed a notebook from the nightstand. Tapping her troll ink pen against her chin, the neon green hair attached to the small doll on the end flopping back and forth, she started scribbling.

"Shouldn't you be getting some beauty sleep or something? It's almost four."

"I'm still too wound up. I think we need to make a list of all of the things we don't know if you can do or not and then start testing them."

A list full of things that we were probably never going to be able to check off. Sure, why not?

"So, number one. Can I see and talk to other ghosts?"

"Assuming there are others out there, yes. Number two on the list should be if you can move objects. Every good ghost movie we've ever seen could move things if they concentrated hard enough."

"I actually spend every single night trying to make that glass move." I pointed to her water glass on the nightstand. "That one is a no."

"Maybe you have to actually try to touch it. Ya know, with your hand, not just mentally."

"I've tried that too and it didn't make any difference. I can't."

She wrote the words, 'Not now,' next to item number two.

"Okay, so what else? We know you can walk through walls and can't see in dark closets. Oh, number three should be if you can possess someone."

"Great." *Yeah, I was never trying that one.* "Oh, I know one. Remember what the PPS said about ghosts being able to drain batteries? Where did you leave Dad's flashlight?"

"On my desk."

Floating over to the desk, I put one hand through the flashlight where I knew the batteries were lined up and then tried to move a pencil with my other hand. "It's not working. Come turn it on."

"What? Like, you think you need to be charged up to be the Energizer Bunny of ghosts?"

"Good grief, turn it on already. Then we can put it down as number four on your list and mark it off."

With a sigh, she got back off the bed and came to turn the flashlight on. "If you drain Dad's batteries he's going to be mad at me, just so you know." His batteries were safe though, putting my hand on actively working batteries didn't make any difference at all. She arched one eyebrow at me before turning it back off.

Flopping backward onto her bed, she sent one hand under the pillow, pulling out the all-knowing Magic 8 Ball.

"Oh, all-knowing Magic 8 Ball, will Geraldine suck at being a ghost forever?" She closed her eyes and gave it a good shake before rolling over onto her stomach to check her results. "It is decidedly so. That's it, Sis, you're doomed to suck for all eternity."

When Monday rolled around we were, or, at least Pansy was, supposed to meet Summer at Wild Harmony which was the small store-slash-yoga-studio that she owned which was only a block away from The Firefly Café in downtown Perth. A family-owned hardware store that was celebrating its 70th year in business—according to the red vinyl banner strung across the front of the building—snugged up against one side, while the store next door was empty. The vacant building had housed the Spin Time Records store until it had moved into Sycamore Plaza about three years before, with a For Lease sign on the door ever since. The large plate-glass windows facing the street had been plastered with newspapers to shield the casual viewer from the naked interior.

Most of downtown Perth had been constructed at the turn of the century, with facades taller than the actual two to three-story buildings, but constructed of enduring granite with little curlicues and carved details to make each one a little different from its neighbor. While some store owners had painted their facades in shades of white or cream to protect the stonework from the elements, Summer had caused quite a stir— and even some talk down at City Hall about writing up some historical preservation laws—when she had purchased the two-story structure and proceeded to paint it a vivid lavender with black and white glossy trim. Pansy and I, of course, immediately loved it although our mother had never let us go inside.

The afternoon sunlight was playing across the display windows, full of sun-catchers and wind chimes made of colored sea glass, and reflecting a rainbow of light across the sidewalk when we arrived. A little bell tinkled as Pansy opened the door, alerting the occupants to our presence. Or, Pansy's presence, at least.

"Smells like sandalwood," Pansy whispered after a few test sniffs of the smoky air.

Besides offering the only yoga classes in a fifty-mile radius, Wild Harmony sold a little bit of everything ranging from average hippie fare to the mystical. Which is exactly why our mother didn't want us in here. I didn't know if it was the gossip caused by the paint selection, or the incense, or the crystals, but our mother had gotten into her head that Summer was a witch and that we'd suddenly become corrupted if we stepped foot inside of her store. Which reminded me.

"Umm, did you tell Mom where you were going today?"

"Sure did." The sudden need to futz with her daisy hair-clip overcame her, which prevented her from looking me in the eye.

"What, exactly, did you tell her?"

"That I had some work to do with the PPS and that I was going over to my friend Summer's house."

I paused, trying to decide which side of the moral line that fell on. Summer lived above the shop, so, as a statement, it was all true. That was, like, good. But what's the phrase, lying by omission, or something like that? Which pushed it firmly over onto the wrong side of that moral line. If Mom had understood who Summer was then she would have freaked out and forbidden Pansy from going. But I didn't think Mom needed any extra stress in her life right now, and Pansy definitely needed to get out and be more social. I decided not to be a pain about it.

The store wasn't particularly wide, but it seemed to stretch toward the back quite a bit. On the left side, next to the heavy oak counter where the cash register was manned, sort of, by a bored young woman who greeted us without looking up from her magazine, was a bookshelf crammed to bursting with various heavy tomes. The shelves bowed under their weight and I browsed the titles which seemed to cover everything from tarot and crystals, phrenology, palm reading, and even kite making. Racks in the center of the store held hemp purses and colorful silk scarves and there was a round shelf display of various wooden sculptures, several styles of buddhas, and some sort of blue Hindu goddess with multiple arms that each held a candle. *I need that candle holder in my life—I have to work on convincing Pansy to buy it.*

I started to turn to see what Pansy was looking at when I caught movement out of the corner of my eye. If my heart had been beating, it would have stopped again when what I thought was a particularly ugly orange scarf sitting in the window display chose that moment to stand up and stretch. To further my shock, it eyed me up and down, which was weird to say because he only had one.

"There's a one-eyed cat over here in the window and he seems to be able to see me."

"Really?" Pansy was so excited that she forgot to whisper, and hustled over to stand next to me. We both stared at the cat, waiting to see if he or she would glare in my direction again, but it promptly rolled back, lifted a hind leg into the air and began licking its bits, ignoring us both. When it became evident that it was not going to participate in our experiment, we continued looking around.

We had reached the selection of incense holders— the source of the sandalwood smell—when we heard clattering behind us. "Oh, hey, Hun. You ready?" Summer was pushing through a beaded curtain painted with a lotus pattern that separated the front space from whatever was in the back. Today, her dreads were pulled back with a red handkerchief, making her look like some sort of hippie version of Rosie the Riveter. She wore thick rainbow-striped socks with her Birkenstocks and a long sweater cardigan over her paisley-patterned sundress. The sheer combination of colors and patterns was enough to give anyone pause, but Summer seemed comfortable and completely unconcerned about what anyone else might think of her appearance. I had to admit that I admired that about her.

"Sure am!" Pansy was all but jumping with excitement.

"I don't know what you're so excited about—I already told you that there aren't any ghosts there." My words fell on deaf ears as Summer motioned for Pansy to follow her into the back room. We entered a dark, windowless room, a floor lamp providing the only light at the moment. A spiral staircase took up most of the left side of the room while Summer's desk took up most of the right. I noticed several cardboard boxes stacked haphazardly around the room and assumed this space was used as her office as well as a spot to stash her extra inventory. I also assumed that if she ever died it was going to be because she'd tripped over something in this room and broken her neck.

Without pausing, Summer continued through a second beaded curtain, this one with several strange symbols painted on it. The wide-planked wooden floors that ran throughout the building were the prominent feature of the room, the afternoon light streaming through the clerestory windows along the back wall making them glow like honey.

"So, this is our yoga space," Summer said, waving a hand around the room.

"I've never done yoga before," Pansy volunteered, her eyes taking in the silk hangings that lined the walls. "Is it hard?"

Summer chuckled as she pulled a second chair over to a table she had set up in the corner of the room. "It's only as hard as you want it to be. I offer beginner classes if you're ever interested." She sat down, patting the empty chair beside her. "Now have a seat and we'll get started. Sarah will man the front for the next few hours and I don't have a class until seven. We should be able to get through at least one of these tapes in that time." She selected one of the videotapes and popped it into the adapter case before pushing it into the TV/VCR combo. Pansy was still staring at the beaded curtain, her face all scrunched up as she was trying to figure out what the symbols were.

"Isn't it gorgeous? I found that at a yard sale a few years back."

Well, it was certainly colorful. "It's very… unusual. What are these symbols?" Pansy asked.

"Oh, those are the seven chakras. I refer to them a lot in my yoga practice. They represent the centers of spiritual powers found in the body." She motioned to the top of her head, then forehead, then throat. "Like the crown, the third-eye, and the throat. While we practice, we try to align and cleanse the chakras, removing the negative energies. I have some books on it if you're interested in that sort of thing." Satisfied that Summer wasn't practicing witchcraft like our mother swore she was, Pansy sat down at the table as Summer hit play.

My sister and her new mentor spent the next three hours watching the tape from the attic—the one from the recorder that had faced the door. If there was an Academy Award for the most boring movie ever, this would win, hands down. Pansy and Summer both had their noses inches from the screen while Summer would point out what seemed to be variations in the shadows, but after much rewinding and watching the same things over and over in slow motion, they both agreed that there wasn't anything there. The only spot of any interest, to me, was a blurry spot near the beginning of the film that I was about eighty percent sure was caused by me waving my hand through the camera. I tried to make a mental note to have Pansy add that to our list of things to experiment with later.

After debating for several minutes over one particularly troublesome orb, which they finally agreed was dust, Summer hit the 'pause' button and turned to Pansy. "Have you ever taken a Physics class?" We both nodded, unsure where she was going with this. "Did you ever study electricity and the conservation of energy?" Again, we nodded. "Okay, so, like, energy can't disappear, right? It can be changed, it can be stored, it can be moved, but you can't create it and you can't destroy it."

Summer leaned forward in her seat, warming to her subject. It must have been a pet theory of hers that she didn't get to tell very many people. "Okay, so if you think about the human body, it's really just an electrical storm encased in a skin suit, right?" Pansy's mouth began to form an 'o' as her brain tried to process that, but Summer was on a roll now. "Every part of us is controlled by an electrical impulse. Our organs are these complex systems, but they run on electricity. Even our blood is mostly saline, because electricity conducts better in salt water, right?" We both nodded again, but slower this time.

"And if the brain—which you could compare to the main control panel of your home's electrical system—stops working, no matter the reason, then everything stops and you die." I wasn't certain about the accuracy of her comparison, but if I ever came across the ghost of a brain surgeon I planned on asking them about it. "Once you're no longer sending out all of those impulses, your body stops. Your heart can't pump the blood through your lungs to pick up oxygen, not that you'd have any anyway because the body isn't getting the impulses that tell it to breathe. So, immediately you start to decay. But where does the energy go?" She gave a dramatic pause here while I was picturing the live, beating heart that we'd watched on a video in Health class a few months before. *Gross.*

"But not only where does it go, where does it come from in the first place? If you can't create energy, how do you create a child? Does it steal part of the mother's energy?" I thought my mother might agree that it did, but decided not to volunteer that tidbit.

"Sorry, these are some of the things that I think about while I'm lying in bed at night." Summer needed a boyfriend. Stat.

Pansy was still mulling it over, though. "So, you think that ghosts exist because the energy that makes a human body a living person can't simply cease to exist?"

"Yes, exactly. And what if, when we die, our energy is absorbed into the next fertilized egg that's waiting for that spark to become a person?"

"I've never thought about it like that before." I hadn't either and trying to think about it was making my eyes cross.

Summer glanced at the large sun shaped clock on the wall. "My students should start trickling in here in a little bit so we'll stop here. Same time tomorrow?"

Pansy eagerly agreed while I groaned.

"Well, do you feel like you learned anything?" I asked, the little bell above the door tinkling behind us as we left Wild Harmony and headed toward the bus stop.

"My eyes are burning so I guess I learned that I should blink more often. And my head hurts, but that could be because now I'm thinking about this whole other world of energy and ghosts and how maybe reincarnation could be a thing if we're recycling the same energies over and over." She did look a little dazed.

"I'm not sure how accurate any of her theories are, although I have to admit that we should be able to test it better than most people. But I meant did you feel like you learned anything about how to look for ghosts on a video tape? I told you, there weren't any ghosts there."

"Actually, I know for a fact that there was a ghost. I even knew when and where to look for her since I can plainly see her except when she's being videotaped, apparently."

"Oh." She had a point.

"Yeah, oh. I was looking hard for a sign, any shadow, a reflection, a sparkle of light, anything that would give an indication that you were there and I didn't see a single thing." She sounded aggravated as she stomped toward the corner.

"Well, maybe tomorrow. You never know." But she was on her own because I was not spending another second of my eternity watching boring videos in a yoga studio.

8

Pansy spent every evening that week at Wild Harmony going over the tapes with Summer. Meanwhile, I had spent my days and nights alternately trying to make things move, trying to make Mom hear me, and haunting the McAllister's house. I called it haunting, but all I really did was hang out, try not to see anyone naked, and avoid running into anything that would make noise if I unexpectedly gained a ghost superpower and started making things move. However, even after all the hours I'd logged there, I never saw anything out of the ordinary. I hadn't even heard any of them wake up in the middle of the night, although the boy did talk in his sleep. I also never witnessed any vermin living in the attic. I began to suspect that the family had faked the whole thing so that they could have the PPS investigate, although I couldn't fathom what their motive may have been. Likewise, Pansy told me she hadn't seen anything abnormal on any of the tapes they'd watched. The whole thing was weird.

The benefit of doing all this floating back and forth was that I'd lost my fear of going too high. Instead of traveling along close to the ground, mimicking where I'd been walking my whole life, I was now going higher and higher as I got used to this new method of travel. My sense of direction and geography were improving and I wasn't as afraid of getting lost. Besides, it was really fun pretending that I was a bird, flying, literally, through the trees.

Friday afternoon, I checked the clock on the VCR at the McAllister's house and noticed that it was almost time for school to be out. I practiced my loop-de-loops on the way home, because I could, and arrived at Casa Bellafini a little after three. I was surprised to see Mom downstairs. She was in the kitchen doing the dishes with the cordless phone wedged between her ear and shoulder. She was actually dressed, wearing a pair of jeans and a black CU sweatshirt, the sleeves pushed up to her elbows.

I was ready to turn for the stairs, not wanting to eavesdrop on her conversation, when I heard her say, "I think he's having an affair, Bev," which, of course, stopped me in my tracks. "He just called to tell me that he was going to be late for dinner and that's been," she paused to reach for a paper towel, her wet hands soaking it before she managed to blow her nose. She must have been crying for a while because her eyes were red and her voice was hoarse. "That's been the norm for the last month, at least. He's always coming home late and doesn't want to spend any time with the family. Robbie's coming home for Christmas break next weekend and, oh, God, Bev, he's going to know that something is wrong. Pansy doesn't seem to suspect, but he's going to know."

She backed away from the sink and seemed to deflate, sliding down the front of the refrigerator as plastic fruit-shaped magnets clattered to the floor. I watched as her butt hit the linoleum, the phone falling with a thud beside her, my Aunt Bev's voice still squawking from the other end. Mom began bawling into her hands and my short-lived elation at flying was crushed under the weight of her tears. I was stunned, but if my dad was cheating I had to find out, for all of our sakes. I didn't know how I could stop it, but I had to know. He didn't seem the type; he'd always been a great dad and never—although we were definitely in the minority in my school by still having our original set of parents together—never had it occurred to me that they were anything short of perfect for one another.

I heard the brakes of the school bus squeal as it pulled up out front and watched helplessly as Mom pushed herself off the floor, dashing the tears from her eyes. She rushed, putting the magnets back on the fridge, and grabbing the cordless, telling Aunt Bev that Pansy was home and that she had to go before tossing it onto the kitchen counter. She was scrubbing dishes like nothing was wrong by the time my twin barged into the house.

"Hi, Mom."

Mom mumbled something that sounded like, "Hi, honey," and Pansy shot me a look with her eyebrows raised high, no doubt surprised that Mom was actually up and out of bed. I gave her my, "I know, right?" look. Grabbing an orange from the fruit bowl on the kitchen table, she headed upstairs, her book bag thumping against each stair tread as she pulled it behind her. I waited for a minute to make sure Mom was going to keep it together before following her up.

When Mom continued rinsing and drying and showed no sign of a relapse I followed Pansy up to our room.

For the first time in my life, I was going to keep a secret from my sister. She didn't need more misery and I decided that I wasn't going to tell her anything about what I'd overheard until I could confirm it for myself. I had only managed to open my mouth to tell her that I wasn't going to go to the PPS meeting tonight when she started flinging books onto her desk.

"I swear, these teachers get together and plan to assign all of the homework at one time," she grumbled as she pulled book after book from her bag. "I have two essays and a crap ton of calculus to do by Monday, plus a science worksheet. I mean, what are we, five? Who assigns 'worksheets' to seniors? One more week before break. Maybe they thought everyone would be useless next week." She grumbled some more while she pushed the books away from the edge of the desk and plopped down into her chair. I decided to keep my mouth shut and stay out of the way, so I floated over my bed while she started writing with a fury, the pencil lead making the only noise in the room. I finally requested the radio to be turned on, but was told 'no,' which was a first but really, what could I do about it other than annoy her until she turned it on? I considered it as a viable option, but figured I'd better lay low since she was probably going to be upset when I told her that I wasn't going to the meeting. So, she wrote while I tried to remember every evening that Dad had come home late, anything he could have said or any weirdness at all that would indicate that he was having an affair. Yes, he was late, and yes, he seemed upset and withdrawn, but I'd attributed that to sadness, not to an affair. Was I being naive?

Mom had called out for pizza and by the time the delivery dude rang the doorbell Pansy was finishing up her first essay. "Okay, one down, then dinner, then the meeting at six."

"I think I'm going to skip the meeting."

"What? Why? You were all gung-ho about going last time." And she didn't want me to go then, but now she sounded miffed.

"I thought I'd go hang out at the McAllisters' tonight and see if I can figure out what is really waking them up." Now I was lying to her, but she didn't know that I'd already been there today and she certainly didn't need to know where I was really going. "If anyone spots anything useful on any of the tapes or recordings or anything, just let me know tomorrow and I'll go back to check it out."

"Well, that doesn't make any sense. Why wouldn't you go tonight, find out for yourself if anyone found anything suspicious, and then go out there tomorrow? Why make two trips?" She glared at me while I struggled to come up with a plausible lie. "Is this about the radio? You're mad because I wouldn't turn it on?"

"What? No. I mean, would I have liked to listen to something other than you mumbling to yourself, yes, but I'm not mad about it. You seemed to be a little stressed so I figured you needed some peace and quiet."

"Then I don't understand, why don't you want to go?"

"You mean, besides the fact that it's boring?"

"Oh, I'm sorry it's not exciting enough for you. Correct me if I'm wrong," *Oh Lord, here we go*, I thought, "but I was under the impression that the only reason that we joined this ghost-hunting group is because we were trying to help you. You, ya know, because you're a ghost and all. So, I'm sorry if the search for answers isn't straight out of a Goosebumps story. This isn't going to all be resolved in under an hour; you may have to actually participate."

"Um, excuse me? Correct *me* if I'm wrong," two could play this game, "but I was under the impression that spending every single one of my evenings spying at the McAllister house was, in fact, me participating. I'm over there trying to help these people and what are you doing? Watching The Joy of Dust Orbs?" I noted with some satisfaction that her face was turning a lovely shade of red. Hopefully, I had her riled up enough that she wouldn't ask me any more questions about where I was going tonight. I'd rather her be mad at me for an evening or two than to ever have this idea that our father could be unfaithful rattling around in her brain.

"I, I just… ugh." Shaking her head in disgust she stormed out of the bedroom door and I took the opportunity to make myself scarce. Round two could wait until morning.

I knew that Dad supervised Area 12—not that I had the vaguest idea what that meant—but I knew the general area to search and started floating in that direction. I left as the dusk to dawn lights started to come on across the neighborhood, flying straight up, the world around me falling back smaller and smaller. I headed east, across the arroyo and slightly north until I was over the quarry. I found our father in the fifth office trailer that I looked in, alone at a desk filling out what looked like insurance paperwork. There was a picture of the family on one corner of his desk—taken when Pansy and I had been about six—but not a lot of other personal touches. A World's Best Dad mug held a few ink pens and a calculator that he used frequently as he worked. I sat there for an hour and during that time he took exactly one phone call, which seemed to be work-related, and did a lot of paperwork. His job was even more boring than watching dust on videotapes.

By seven-thirty Dad had straightened up the paperwork on his desk, and packed his empty thermos and lunchbox into his truck. I followed him until he took the last turn into our neighborhood, watching as his truck pulled into the driveway where he continued to sit for a few minutes before leaving what I imagined to be the warm confines and stepping out into the chilled darkness to make the ten steps to the front door. It was full dark now, and the wind pushed dry

leaves across the road, scritching across the silence.
Since I was feeling restless and didn't want to sit in the
house watching my parents not speak to one another, I
headed back to the McAllister house. I may have
wasted the entire day, but at least I wouldn't be a liar.

9

"So, Pansy, tell me about your ghost group. You actively go and look for ghosts, correct?"

"Well, I've only been that one time but we're going again tonight to a different house. I don't know if I'd call it looking for ghosts, maybe looking into what people think are ghosts and trying to explain what they think they're seeing or hearing. From what I understand, most of the time it's rodents of some kind or a faulty electrical system."

"So, do you believe in ghosts?"

Well, that was a loaded question. It was probably best to not sound crazy in front of your therapist, though. Pansy, still sitting on the chair in front Dr. Noonan looked over at me. Deciding to be as helpful as possible after we'd declared a truce earlier that morning, I struck a pose, doing my best Vanna White impersonation and showing off the Doc's fine collection of Beanie Babies that he kept in a glass curio cabinet. She laughed, of course, and waved off the doctor's question.

"Ghosts? No, I don't really think that's possible, you know?"

"Then why the interest in the paranormal?" He was eyeing her like she was a specimen to be studied, and I guess in a way that was exactly what he was doing. I still wanted to hit him with something.

"I was thinking that it would make a great essay for a college entrance application. I mean, it's not something that every single kid is going to have, you know? It will definitely stand out from the rest."

He seemed surprised, but quickly jotted down her response. "And have you entertained any other aspects of the occult or the paranormal? Tarot cards, Ouija boards, Dungeons and Dragons?"

Was this guy for real?

"Uh, no. None of those." Pansy gave me a quick skeptical look before resuming her serene pose. Peering over the doctor's shoulder, I could see his statements started with words like, "Patient claims…" this and that. Was he not buying anything at all about this? What were our parents paying him for anyway?

"Sometimes, and this opinion is formed from my experiences, traumatic incidents in the lives of young people can give rise to feelings of helplessness, a loss of control, if you will, and they seek other means to lose that control, or to give that control up altogether. Do you drink? Do any kinds of drugs? And remember, whatever you tell me is confidential between the two of us, I won't tell your parents anything."

"Yeah, buddy, she's cut back to only two lines a day."

"No, sir. Nothing like that." She avoided making eye contact with me that time.

"So, what do you do for fun, other than this ghost group? Do you have a lot of girlfriends? Boyfriends?"

"Uh, no. I mean, I have one or two friends, but mostly I stay home and read." Yes, she really was that boring.

"So, no boyfriend."

"No, sir."

"And what do you read? Do you like romance novels, murder mysteries?"

"Science fiction, actually. Neal Stephenson, Bruce Sterling, things like that."

He gave a noncommittal nod and wrote down the names with question marks next to them. Obviously, sci-fi wasn't his thing.

Thankfully, the therapy sessions were only for an hour. Unfortunately, Mom drove her there and back, stopping for lunch on the way home, so it was quite a while before we were safely back in our bedroom and able to talk about where we were going that night.

"So the house we're going to tonight, that's out on Sepulveda, right? In the canyon?" I asked.

"Yeah. Do you remember Delores? From the library?"

Delores had been our favorite librarian as children, but she'd moved away in the late eighties when her husband had taken a job somewhere in California. She'd been replaced by a sour old woman who hated children.

"Yeah. What? Did she move back?"

"No, it's her mother's house. Or, it's her mother that called the PPS. I thought the name sounded familiar, but I asked Chandra about her and she said that she'd gone to school with Delores' daughter and knew the old woman. That's how Mrs. Garcia heard about us. Apparently, Chandra and the granddaughter still meet in a chat room every once in a while."

"Aww, I loved her." I was trying to figure out how ancient Mrs. Garcia must be if Delores was her daughter when I became distracted by Pansy fiddling with her earrings. "You're not going to wear that are you?" She had worn her own clothes for the therapist and looked like a total prep. Her Eastland's were clean and oiled, the ends of her laces spiraled up like the perfect curly fry—if you were into that kind of thing. She wore dark blue stirrup pants and a long white poet's blouse with sleeves that she always caught in the car door. Like, every time. A fake crocodile belt—at least four inches wide—circled her waist, its huge silver buckle gleaming. Her long hair was parted slightly off-center with a little daisy clip holding one side back from her face and small daisy earrings to match. I would have gone hoops—bird perches as our mother called them—but that was me.

"I'm certainly *not* going ghost hunting dressed like this." The 'duh' was silent.

She carefully checked her sleeves for ketchup stains before hanging it back in her closet, but kept the stirrup pants on. She pulled an old sweatshirt over her head and traded her Eastlands for my old Docs.

"So, the house is old, like, built during silver mining times old, and the grounds include several acres according to the briefing we received last night." While not going to the meeting meant that I had avoided the McAllister review and the big fat nothing found on any video or audio tape, it also meant that I'd missed out on hearing about tonight's adventure. I stood dutifully by her desk as Pansy pulled a few loose sheets of copy paper from her notebook before beginning her lecture.

"Okay, so this here," she unfolded the pages and shuffled one to the top of the stack, "is the layout of the house. Greg and Randy already went on a recon trip earlier in the week to figure out where we'll be placing the cameras." The hand-drawn diagram showed a traditional layout where the front door opened to an entryway with a hallway and the staircase. The living room, or parlor, was in the front on the right side of the house, the dining room was to the left, the kitchen behind it. I couldn't tell what the room behind the parlor was used for on their map. There were two floors of living space and an attic.

"Greg said that Mrs. Garcia complained about hearing noises coming from the attic. She says that it sounds like footsteps, human footsteps, you know, one step followed by another distinct step and not the rustling you might expect from an animal. And not only that, but what sounded like a ball or something round will hit the floor and bounce across it at all times of the day."

"Dude, did Greg and Randy check to make sure there isn't, like, some homeless ski bum living in her attic?"

She frowned at my interruption. "I'm sure they did."

"And did they hear any of these noises while they were there?"

"No. Or, if they did, they didn't mention it and I'm sure that would have been the first thing they told us if they had. Anyway, Mrs. Garcia says that she'll lay things down and when she goes back later they'll have moved and be lying somewhere else. And, get this, she'll leave a room that is perfectly clean and by the time she comes back there will be a mess. Books thrown onto the floor, her balls of yarn strung out all over, things like that."

"So, what do the guys think is going on? Do they think it's haunted?"

"Well, they didn't say that. In fact, I honestly think they're leaning more toward her losing her mind. She does have a hearing aid in each ear and they said that she laid her TV remote down and 'lost' it three times while they were there."

She shuffled through the rest of the papers, a list of previous owners that Blake had put together, and some notes from the guys' recon. "Looks like she's also been keeping a record of every time she's felt an earthquake. She claims her house randomly shakes, but when she calls the police they tell her that she's imagining it, so she's been keeping a record."

"So, she might have an inner ear infection making her dizzy, or maybe she really is just losing her mind." Even though I had never met the woman, I hated to think that, let alone say it aloud. My loyalty to her daughter, the woman who had pointed me toward *Nancy Drew* novels as a child, made me want to solve the Case of the Haunted Attic, or the Case of the Senile Old Woman, whichever it turned out to be. Either way, I had plenty of time on my hands to figure it out.

10

The Garcia house was south of town near the canyon, or as close as privately owned property could get to the canyon as most of it was owned by the Feds. It was Saturday night, the sixteenth of December, and the sign in the bank parking lot registered twenty degrees as the Perth Paranormal Society drove past. The PPS had, once again, met at Sycamore Plaza before moving out like a modern-day wagon train down Main Street, turning right by the bank onto the Sepulveda Highway as Main Street curved to the east, and headed south over the bridge. The bridge. That bridge. *My* bridge. It was far enough outside of town that I had successfully been able to avoid it until now.

I came down, floating above the lead van as we approached the area. A Loaf 'N Jug squatted on the Plains side of Sepulveda as you came to the bridge, the last stop for southbound travelers before endless miles of desert. There were no street lights this far out of town, but the bright lights over the pumps reflected on the ice-covered rocks and low shrubs across the street, as well as the very end of the concrete bridge. I had a moment of anxiety as headlights came toward us in the other lane, but the driver was moving slowly and ended up turning into the gas station as the rest of our team drove across the bridge, oblivious to my presence or my distress.

I held there for a moment, looking left and right out across the arroyo, but could see nothing in the dark.

The moon was waning, a small sliver still visible, and I couldn't see the bottom of the arroyo. It was a black pit that could have held hundreds of other ghosts… or none. I didn't sense anything strange, I didn't hear any disembodied voices, I couldn't see anything that didn't look like it belonged there. I promised myself that I would stop being afraid and come back tomorrow in the daylight. Surely nothing bad could happen at noon on a Sunday. In fact, maybe I'd also take a run by the cemetery and see if there was anyone there.

My resolve wavered as I approached the other end of the bridge with its gaping section of guardrail that had not yet been replaced, but I pushed the anxiety down—deep, deep down—and continued on my way. The group was ahead of me now, but their headlights slicing through the night were easy to spot and I floated high above them as we traveled along for another ten minutes or so. The vegetation was sparse here—no one had taken the initiative to sew non-native grasses to make their yards look picture perfect. There were no trees planned, planted, and irrigated to create a fake oasis in the desert. Out here—where there was little to no protection from the winds that scoured the desert plains—rocky soil and crouching shrubs ruled.

The Garcia house sat a good ways back from the road but the ground was so flat and barren you could still see it in the daylight. It was painted Pepto Bismol pink so it was actually hard to miss. I had always wondered who would live in a pink house, and as I followed the rest of the crew across the gravel driveway, I figured I was about to have an answer. The front door was a massive dark oak affair with stained glass sidelights that opened into an open hallway. My first impression was that an old lady lived here, which I already knew to be the truth, but the house was such a cliché. When Pansy was old I was going to have to insist that she have more style than this. Which assumed that she lived to be a ripe old age and that I would still be haunting her. Neither thought was something I wanted to dwell on for too long.

The furniture in the overly-decorated parlor—where Randy was setting up a table for the monitors—looked stiff and uncomfortable. Floral wallpaper in shades of burgundy and forest greens covered the walls, a colorful background for the mishmash of art prints in heavy gold-leafed frames, decorative wall sconces, and framed photographs. It was enough to make your eyes cross. I was wondering why Randy didn't just use the dining room table until I drifted into the dining room and saw that the table was set for formal service; chargers, wine glasses, vases of fake flowers, the whole shebang. I noticed a layer of dust covering the whole setup, so Mrs. Garcia must have seen a similar display in Better Homes or Good Housekeeping and decided she liked the effect. No wonder Randy wasn't messing with it.

I continued through to the kitchen, which showed the age of the house more than any other room. The hunter green cabinets looked like they were custom built from plywood, the chipped and worn layers of paint so thick that the doors no longer closed properly. The refrigerator was covered in children's artwork, interspersed with various business cards and flyers held up with crocheted flower magnets. The white Formica countertops were cracked and stained and covered in their own crocheted artworks that concealed every small appliance. I identified the toaster which was disguised as a black and white spotted cow, the blender was dressed as a rooster and what was maybe a breadbox hid under a pink pig with a black pipe cleaner curled up for a tail. *Dear God above, why?*

The unidentified room on the map behind the formal parlor was Mrs. Garcia's TV room and looked like it was where she spent most of her time. She was sporting what my grandmother called a housecoat. It looked new, clean, and was covered in a pattern of roses, of course. She was sitting in a threadbare recliner that was pulled entirely too close to the television while Chandra was speaking to her.

"Now, Mrs. Garcia, I understand that you don't plan on leaving while we investigate, so we're just going to set up our monitors here in the front parlor, is that okay?"

"That's fine, dear. I'll turn my hearing aids down and I won't even know that you're here." Loops of yarn flew around a long needle as she talked and I noticed a basket of multi-colored yarn balls next to her recliner. A folding tray had been set up on the other side of the chair, its surface covered in magazines and paperbacks. Who knew what went on when she was at home with her hearing aids off if she spent most of her time camped out in this room. Chandra left and Mrs. Garcia fiddled with the hearing aids before turning her attention back to the television, its closed captioned text scrolled across the bottom of the screen as she watched a nature special.

Even though I was now unable to smell or taste anything, I thanked whatever was above or beyond for allowing me to retain sight and hearing. This would be an even more miserable experience if not. What happened to older people who became ghosts? Did they have to wander around blind and deaf? Did you get to take your glasses and hearing aids with you as a ghost? That didn't seem likely, although I was wearing clothes so what exactly were the limits? None of this made any sense. Maybe when you became a ghost everything was reset to factory condition. Maybe if you were eighty-five, deaf, and had cataracts when you died then you'd be able to see and hear again. One could only hope. Although, since there'd been a definite lack of other ghostly presence in my after-life to this point, maybe everyone else just knew how to die properly and I was the only fool still goofing off down here on earth. Or up here, or wherever I was in relation to whatever came next.

Brushing off my ever-growing list of questions, I decided that it was time to explore the upstairs rooms. "Get the flashlight," I told Pansy as she lugged in the last tote of equipment.

"I like how you don't have to carry anything or do any work, but think that you could blow the case wide open if you could only carry a flashlight," she muttered under her breath as she went to one of the other totes and located a flashlight. We made our way up the staircase, the wooden treads stained so dark they appeared black. Almost every square inch of stairwell wall space was covered in framed photographs and I recognized some as Delores as a child and assumed that the other children were her sisters. Pansy had already made it to the top of the stairs and located the light switch for the hall by the time I was done looking at the family photos.

The first room we looked in had been converted into a sewing room. There were quilt racks set up against one wall with a half-finished quilt on them and the fanciest sewing machine I'd ever seen on the other side of the room with multiple spools of thread attached and lots of buttons and levers. The wood floors were covered in colorful rag rugs and white lace curtains hung from the windows.

"Any ghosts?"

"Nothing but dust bunnies, so far," I replied.

The next bedroom we entered looked like a florist had thrown up in it. The walls were bisected by a rose patterned border, the top half painted a dusky pink, the bottom covered by white wallpaper with a tiny rose-patterned print. The lampshade had hand-painted roses on it and there was a backlit curio shelf hanging on the wall full of Lenox porcelain flower sculptures.

Dust catchers, my mother would call them. The polyester bedspread had a different floral pattern, although its main theme seemed to also be dark pink roses, and the carpet was, of course, rose. If I'd ever needed an example of too much of a good thing, here it was. I was thankful that I couldn't smell anything, as I was imagining Bengay and rose water.

The third bedroom appeared to be a guest bedroom, also rose themed but to a lesser degree. Judging by the thin layer of dust covering everything it wasn't used very often. A single bathroom rounded out our grand tour of the second floor.

The attic access door that had been marked on Pansy's diagram was at the end of the hallway. It was half the size of a normal doorway and opened to reveal a steep set of stairs which led to the third-floor attic. The swing of Pansy's flashlight revealed a hanging chain near the door and she gave it a tug, the lone light bulb casting serious shadows over the contents of the attic. It was stacked high with cardboard boxes filled to overflowing with what looked like junk and I can't say that I wasn't disappointed. If you go into the attic of a possibly haunted house built at the turn of the century then there should be fabulous old steamer trunks and at least one dress mannequin with a huge, moth-eaten hat. All I saw in Mrs. Garcia's attic were some carpet scraps and crumbling cardboard boxes.

"Stop!" I yelled as Pansy made a rotation with the flashlight. "Go back." I pointed to the far corner of the attic where there was a cleared space. "In that corner." She turned, the beam of her light brightening the area and I gasped for a breath that I didn't need. "Do you see him?"

"See what?" The beam of light wavered back and forth as she searched for something she obviously couldn't see. But I could. He was sitting there, plain as day and naked as a jaybird, looking straight at me with a dumbfounded expression on his face.

"Pansy, where did you go? We've got to get these cameras set up," Greg's voice floated up the stairs and Pansy looked at me for direction.

"Go ahead, the overhead light will be enough. There's a boy over there, and I think he's a ghost too. You sure you don't see him?"

She shook her head, giving the area a go over once more with the flashlight. "No. Nothing. Are you sure you'll be okay?"

"Yeah, go ahead before they get suspicious. Make sure someone sets a camera up here though. Just in case their quackery actually works sometimes."

"What are you talking about? Who are you?" The boy asked, still looking at me like he should be afraid of me. He looked ready to bolt.

"Can you hear him?" I asked Pansy even as she was heading back down the stairs.

"Hear who? I don't hear anything." She sounded miffed like she was jealous of my newfound skill as a ghost detector. I would have traded her in an instant.

"Go. I'll handle this." I tried to sound confident even though I had no idea what 'this' was and if maybe I wasn't hallucinating. Could ghosts hallucinate? I was adding questions faster than I was finding answers. At this point, I didn't even know what I didn't know. But, maybe now I'd finally find some answers.

Once I was sure Pansy was heading down the stairs, I turned back to the boy who seemed to have sunk further into the floorboards. He was pale, even by ghost standards, with thick dark hair that curled around his features and the brightest blue eyes I'd ever seen. I figured that he'd been around seven or eight years old when he'd died, but who knew how long ago that was. "Uh, hi. My name is Geraldine. My friends call me Gerri. What's your name?"

"Can you really see me?"

"Is there someone else up here that I should be talking to?" His eyes darted around the room which kind of freaked me out so I also took a look around the room. He was still the only interesting thing in the attic. "So, do you live here?"

"Yes."

"Really? How long have you been up here?"

"I don't know."

"Okay. So, are you going to at least tell me your name?" Seriously, the kid was going to have to give me something to work with.

"How can you see me? Hardly anyone ever talks to me, anymore." Hardly anyone? That meant at least one someone did, right?

"Well, kiddo, uh… you know that you're dead, right?" I had a brief moment of fear that he didn't know and that I was going to have to be the one that broke the news, but he pulled his knees closer to his chest and nodded. "I'm dead too. No one else can see us. Or at least, I haven't met anyone special like us." Yeah, special, that's what we're going to call it. "Who else talks to you?"

"When did I die?"

"Well, I… I don't know. I know that I died last month." Finally, an actual fact that I could contribute. "Didn't you think that it was weird when people stopped noticing you?"

"I thought everyone was ignoring me," he mumbled, his attention focused on his hands which were twisting together what looked like a baseball card.

"How long have people been ignoring you? How many months or years have you been hiding up here?"

"I don't know, a while, I guess." I felt like I needed to sit down, which was ridiculous, really, but a deeply ingrained habit when faced with weirdness.

"You noticed that you could float through things? Right?"

"I don't know," he mumbled. He picked up another baseball card that was sitting next to him on the floor and tossed it toward a dented metal box sitting a few feet away. I heard it slide across the wood planks before pinging off the side of the box.

"Wait a minute, is that card real?" Was this kid really picking up something that was a real, actual, tangible object and moving it? Was this possible?

"I guess. I've been playing with them for a while. I can't find my Willie Mays card though. My Daddy gave me that card and he's going to be really mad if I've lost it. I've searched through this whole box and can't find it anywhere. Have you seen it?"

"No, sweetie, I haven't. Were these your cards?"

His face screwed up while he thought about it. "Yes. I guess so."

"You don't remember?"

"It's been a really long time." *A long time? Like, how long?* I wondered. It wasn't like he was wearing clothes that would give me some kind of clue.

"Have you ever left the house?"

"No." He gave an emphatic shake of his head before leaning closer to me with one hand cupped around the side of his mouth like he was going to tell me the world's biggest secret. "I can't find my shoes." Huh. So, butt-nakey wasn't the issue for him, shoes were what was keeping him in the house. Which made me thankful that I hadn't died in the shower. I mean, if you didn't at least have modesty as a ghost, what was left?

"So, is Mrs. Garcia your mom?"

"No. Who's Mrs. Garcia?"

"She's the lady that lives here. She owns this house."

"Oh. Her. No, she's not my mom. Do you know where my Mom went?"

This poor confused kid. "No, sweetie. What was her name?"

"Maggie. Maggie Fairchild." The name sounded familiar, possibly one of the names on the list of previous owners that Pansy had brought home from her meeting. I made a mental note to check.

"I'll look into it, okay?" Thinking about his mother seemed to make him depressed; he was literally melting into the floor. "Are you going to tell me your name or do I have to guess? Is it Rudolph? How about Blitzen?"

He giggled—an innocent sweet sound that was kind of creepy if you considered that it was coming from a ghost kid. "Sorry. My name is Christopher."

"Christopher, huh? Well, Christopher, why don't you give me the nickel tour?"

"The what?"

"Show me around the house."

"Oh. Sure." He hopped up into a standing position and we floated down to the bedroom that had been converted into a sewing room. "This was my room." He looked dismayed as he gestured around at the quilting supplies and lacy curtains. I noticed that while the interior of the room was reflected in the dark window panes, the kid and I didn't show up. Cameras had already been set up and I told Christopher to wave in case it could pick him up. If the kid could pick up real objects—a trick I was absolutely going to make him show me how to do—maybe he could also appear on film.

Taking a shortcut through the wall we entered the other bedroom. "Was this your mother's room?"

"Yeah, but it didn't look like this. This lady really likes flowers."

"Totally." *Understatement of the year, kid.* Chandra and Summer were running wires down the hallway as we crossed—oblivious to our critique of Mrs. Garcia's decorating skills.

"This was a spare bedroom when I lived here with my mom. When the lady, what did you say her name was?"

"Mrs. Garcia."

"Well, when Mrs. Garcia moved in, she had a husband then too, and three little girls. The two youngest ones shared this room." His face lit up when he talked about the girls and he looked like he was remembering happy times.

"So, you had already, uh, passed on, when Delores was just a kid?" Geez, that had to be at least fifty years ago.

"Delores. Yes, that was her name. She was the oldest. Then Delilah and Diane. They had a lot of fun, but they're all gone now." His smile faded for a second before he tacked on, "But sometimes they come back to see their Mom and they've got kids of their own now!"

He seemed really excited about having other kids in the house which added another layer to my depression.

We were silent for a moment as we floated down into the dining room. I could see Mrs. Garcia making a cup of tea in the kitchen and through the double wide arches that led from the dining room to the front hall and across to the parlor I could see Greg manning the monitors.

"So, are you going to tell me how you pick things up?" Hadn't the paperwork Pansy had brought home mentioned that the old lady kept losing things and that stuff was moving around by itself. I was ninety-nine percent sure that I'd discovered the reason why. I needed to find Pansy and let her know that I'd been here less than twenty minutes and had, in fact, already solved the case with the help of a flashlight.

"I don't know, I just want to and I do." Well, that was less than helpful.

We wandered across to the parlor so he could check out what Greg was doing and I decided to try again with a different line of questioning. "So, you mentioned that no one 'hardly' ever talked to you. If you don't mind me asking, are there any other dead people around that you know of?"

"Yeah, there's a boy who comes to see me every once in a while."

"A boy? Is he young like you or older? What's his name?"

"Thomas is older than me, but younger than you. He's an Indian."

"Indian like his parents are from the country of India or Indian like from a Native American tribe?"

"You know, Indian. Like cowboys and Indians. Whoo hoo!" He placed his hand over his mouth and started wailing out his pseudo war cry. Well, if ever any of these sensors were going to pick up something it was going to be now. I looked around, but Shawn was setting up a video camera by the front door and no one else seemed to have heard a thing.

"Can he move stuff too?"

"I don't know. I guess. Why? Can't you?" Was that a smirk I saw on his lips?

"As a matter of fact, I cannot." *You smart alec little twerp.*

"Maybe you just need to try harder." Well, isn't that what every single movie about ghosts had already told me? Maybe they were on to something and I should be asking myself how Tim Burton would solve this problem.

"Okay, you can help me practice later, right?" I asked as Pansy walked back into the room.

She was conferring with Greg about camera positions in front of the monitors and he was telling her about all of the fantastic things that could possibly be seen on the monitors, but weren't. I raised my eyebrows and pointed to the kid next to me.

"Can your fancy cameras see him?"

She shook her head no and was squinting with real effort about a foot over the head of the kid.

"He's down here," I said, holding my hand over his head.

"Hey, did you know that that girl over there looks a little like you?"

"Just a little, huh? Yeah, she's my twin. She can see me and hear me."

"Really? Wow." He studied Greg for a few seconds before turning back to me and whispering. "What's he doing?"

"Well, believe it or not, he's looking for ghosts."

"Why?"

"Because they are all part of the Perth Paranormal Society and Mrs. Garcia thinks that her house is haunted."

"But," he looked really confused. "You said that I'm a ghost, right?"

"Yep."

"So, then, isn't it?"

Before I could reply there were raised voices coming from upstairs and I could hear a beeping noise. Floating straight up I accidentally ran right through Chandra, who responded with a squeal.

"Oh my gosh, I felt a cold spot! Quick, Summer, bring the tape recorder!"

I was going to have to quit running through the poor woman before I gave her a complex.

I knew that the beeping sound was coming from a handheld EMF detector and it sounded like it had hit the motherlode, although, as the only two paranormal things in the house—as far as I knew—had both been downstairs at the time, I thought whatever was setting it off may be interesting enough to check out. I explained what was going on to Christopher.

"So, they're looking for electricity?" He pointed toward an outlet and looked confused as to why they needed a machine to spot it.

"Well, sort of. Think of it as looking for extra electricity. They think that ghosts give off a strong signal on their meters."

"Do we?"

"Not that I know of."

"Oh, then I bet it's that box that those guys left here a few weeks ago."

"What box? What guys?"

"Well, there are these two guys that come into the house every once in a while. They've been coming in a lot lately, but the lady, uh… Mrs. Garcia, they hide from her. It was, uh… well, it must have been a weekend when they came the last time because she always has someone come and pick her up on Saturday mornings so that she can go down to the Foodarama and do her shopping." *Nothing like a routine to make it easy for someone to break in*, I thought.

"How do you know that's where she goes on Saturdays if you don't leave the house."

"Because she comes back with bags of groceries and the bags say Foodarama." Now he was looking at me like I was the stupid one.

"Fair enough. So what did these guys do?"

"Well, they put a box under her mattress. It's dark under there so I couldn't see what it was." I was momentarily thrilled to know that he couldn't make himself glow like a human torch or something and was equally as handicapped by a lack of light as I was.

"Hang on," I said, holding up my index finger and sinking back to the first floor in search of my twin. Luckily, she was still in front of the bank of monitors. "Hey, Sis, I need you up in the master bedroom for a minute."

Her eyes widened because Greg was mid-lecture about something boring and I pretended to tap my foot. "Make up an excuse. Like, now," I said quite loudly and went back up to the rose-strewn bedroom where Randy and Shawn were convinced that the bed was haunted.

Christopher had followed me. "How big was this box?" I asked him. The kid gestured, indicating something smaller than a breadbox, but bigger than a calculator. Super helpful.

Pansy appeared in the doorway, Greg right behind her. "I think I saw that orb right over there," she said, eyeing me the whole time. Crap, no, this wasn't about real ghosts. I didn't want them to get their hopes up that the place was really haunted. I mean, it was, but something else was going on.

"No, look under the bed, move the mattresses or something. Christopher said two men broke into the house and put a metal box thing under the bed a few weeks ago."

"Oh," she said aloud, and without further comment or any explanation for why she was doing it, she squatted down and lifted the full size mattress—bedspread, pillows and all—pushing it off the other side and into the floor. All three men stared. Smiling, she muttered a 'sorry' and then lifted the box spring, revealing a black box that had been taped to the bed frame with electrical tape. As Randy walked closer to get a better look the EMF detector's beep became a continuous obnoxious noise. Pansy stepped back as the three men converged on the box.

"What the heck is that?" Shawn asked as he bent over to peel the box from the bed frame. The mystery box was about four inches wide and maybe six long, with an LCD screen and a few knobs. Overall it looked like something that had been built with spare parts from Radio Shack.

"Judging by the way the EMF detector is freaking out," Randy said as he turned the EMF detector off, finally, "I'd say it's a signal generator. The question is, why is it here?"

"Well, high EMF does give some people a sense of unease," Shawn replied, still turning the box in his hands. "If someone was trying to make the old woman think the house was haunted then what better way than to make her so uncomfortable that she can't even sleep?" I seriously wanted to high-five Shawn.

"She sleeps downstairs in front of the TV," Christopher volunteered. He had a big grin on his face and looked fascinated by all of the commotion. How long had this kid been up here alone? He was going on my to-do list.

"The kid said she sleeps in the recliner downstairs so she may not have even noticed."

"Mrs. Garcia mentioned to me that most nights she falls asleep downstairs in her recliner, the poor old thing." Pansy offered. She should have kept her mouth shut because the initial wonder over the discovery was wearing off and suddenly all eyes were on her again. She practically shrunk under the force of the collective gaze.

"What on earth made you look under the bed?"

"Well, a ghost would move around, wouldn't it? They're not stationary, and it seemed to be concentrated right in that spot so I thought that maybe there was an electric plug on the floor or something that we couldn't see." *Good save, Sis.*

"Well, it looks like Mrs. Garcia is dealing with practical jokers, not ghosts. I'll let her know what we've found and see if she wants to see someone about setting up some kind of security system. I'm sure it's just kids trying to be funny." His brow furrowed and he turned back to Pansy. "You didn't tell any of your school chums where we were going to be tonight, did you?"

Pansy's eyes couldn't have gotten any wider. "No, sir."

He made a noncommittal sound and put the box in a plastic bag. "I'll give this to Mrs. Garcia if she wants to call the police and have them come take a look." He walked down the hall with the device and Randy turned the EMF detector back on. I heard the beeps as it reset but then stopped, the source of the crazy having been removed.

"Well, I'll keep checking, maybe there will be more of those things."

"There aren't. And they weren't kids," Christopher said to me.

"Did you get a look at them?"

"Oh yeah, they're here all the time."

I noticed Pansy looking back and forth between me and where I was looking at Christopher and realized that she was probably a little put out because she could only hear one side of the conversation.

"He saw two men break in about two weeks ago while Mrs. Garcia was doing her shopping. They were men, not kids." I turned back to Christopher. "What did they look like? Did they say anything about why they were putting the box in here or taking anything?"

"Well, one is big with dark hair that kind of swoops back, and the other guy is shorter, skinnier, and has red hair that's really short. Oh, and he wears glasses. They don't usually talk while they're in the house, but they did pull out a few rows of her knitting that day. She said bad words for a good long while about that one. They also moved some stuff around on the shelves in the bathroom. Sometimes they come in while she's watching TV and move things in the kitchen."

"So, the things around the house that are moving, that's not you?"

"Why would I want to mess with her knitting?"

"Umm… I don't know. Boredom?" He seemed to think about that one a little too long, like maybe he'd never considered aggravating the old woman, but maybe it sounded like fun. "Okay, so anyway, the old lady needs a security system, like yesterday," I told Pansy. "These two guys keep breaking in to mess with her."

"I wonder why?" she mused out loud.

"I don't know, but I'll add it to the list."

12

The number of people who needed my stealth-ninja-ghost skills seemed to be increasing daily. However, I hoped that the work the Perth Paranormal Society put into the search of Mrs. Garcia's house would allow me to mark her off the list quickly. Once the crew had been alerted that a live person, or persons were trying to mess with the old lady, they all went into full forensic investigation mode. A complete search of the house from top to bottom revealed three unlocked windows on the first floor—Mrs. Garcia hadn't realized that they were open—and two that were unlocked on the second floor. While no other electronic devices were located, several size-fourteen boot prints were found in the flower beds under the unlocked windows and a dirty boot print was discovered on one of the window sills.

Blake lost no time getting his camera out to take photos of the footprints and the signal generator before it was placed into an old plastic Foodarama bag as evidence. Randy had urged Mrs. Garcia to file a police report which she promised she would do the very next morning; she felt that it would be rude to call in the middle of the night. Because it was so close to Christmas—and, I figured because everyone thought the problems Mrs. Garcia had been experiencing were entirely man-made—the PPS had decided to take the week off and review the evidence after Christmas. I imagined that the videos and EVPs would not get the fine-toothed-comb treatment that the McAllister investigation had received.

After a solid ten hours of sleep for Pansy, and a lot of floaty pacing on my side, we spent Sunday morning continuing our own investigation. We had quickly located Christopher's mother on the list of previous property owners and it showed that the house had been purchased by Chester and Margaret Fairchild in 1946. It was then sold by Margaret Fairchild in 1953. There was no mention in Blake's notes about what had happened to Chester Fairchild or their child during that time.

"Can you call him and ask if maybe he found something and forgot to mention it. Maybe he didn't think it was pertinent?"

"I guess. Would that be weird if I called him?"

"It's not like you're asking him out on a date. You have questions about the investigation. But don't mention Christopher's name or he'll want to know how you found it. Be subtle."

Pansy rolled her eyes and gave me a 'well, duh' look before pulling the trusty yellow pages out of her desk drawer. Locating his listing she picked up the clear plastic digital phone on her desk with its brightly colored inner parts and looked at the keypad.

"Two. Four. Four. Seven. What does that spell?"

We puzzled for a moment, mashing the hot pink plastic hook—which matched the eight-foot long hot pink phone cord—down with her thumb when the dial tone stopped and the phone started beeping at us to hurry up and do something. Sure, she could have scribbled his number in her address book—the one with the basket of kittens on the cover—but we preferred to memorize any number that we could. Word association was the mnemonic trick that always worked best for us.

"BIGS?" I offered.

"I don't know. Blake is BIGS. That might work."

"It also might sound really weird if you say it out loud."

She grimaced before turning back to the phone.

"Okay, what else? Oh, CHIP!" Pansy finally said with a smile. Blake did look like the kind of guy that you might find some potato chip crumbs on his shirt if you looked closely enough. We'd totally remember that.

"Okay, so call him already."

Releasing the switch, she dialed the number and waited for him to answer. I had my face so close to hers that I could hear it ringing.

"Hello?"

Pansy jumped a little when he answered which of course made me jump too. "Oh, hi. Blake?"

"Yes."

"Hi, this is Pansy Bellafini. I, uh…I just had some questions about the previous owners of the Garcia house?"

"Uh, sure. Like what?"

"Well, like, I noticed the people who owned the house before Mr. and Mrs. Garcia bought it, well, they were a married couple when they bought the house but it only shows her name when it was sold. So like, did Mr. Fairchild die? Like, in the house, maybe?"

"Umm… no." There was some rustling of papers in the background like he was checking his notes. "No, the information I found said that they divorced, so I assumed that his name was removed from the deed. I didn't look up any of the divorce paperwork because I didn't think that it really mattered."

"You're probably right, I was just curious about what happened to him."

"So, you thought maybe he was dead and hanging around haunting old Mrs. Garcia?" He chuckled a little. "Nah, I figure we've got this one pretty much nailed down on the ghost front. I'd really like to figure out why someone wants to scare off Mrs. Garcia though."

"I know. I can't believe someone would be that disrespectful to such a sweet old lady. Well, thanks for letting me know what happened, I'll let you go."

"Anytime."

She hung up but continued to sit at her desk, her fingers tapping on her notebook as she thought.

"You should have asked him what year they got divorced. That would have helped narrow it down."

"I thought about it, but couldn't figure out a way to not make that sound weird, you know? What possible reason would I have for needing to know that?"

"True. Should we hit the courthouse tomorrow after school? Isn't that where they keep birth and death records?"

"I guess. It's as good a place as any."

The next day—the Monday of the final week of school before Christmas break—I decided to make myself useful while Pansy was in class and go hang out in the courthouse. My reasoning was that if I could figure out which office she needed to go to and maybe what paperwork we would need to fill out, then that would save us some time this afternoon. Unfortunately, after a few hours of lurking around—and learning more courthouse gossip than I ever wanted to know— I also learned that our local courthouse was a no-go for the info we needed. What we were looking for was called the Office of Vital Statistics and all of those records were kept in Denver. Mom was certainly not going to let Pansy go to Denver by herself and we needed Christopher's date of death in order to send in a written request, so that was a dead end. No pun intended.

Since my death, I had mostly avoided our high school. Knowing that I couldn't participate in classes, or clubs, or gossip depressed me. While alive, I'd worked hard, made good grades, took honors classes and where had that gotten me? I was never going to walk across the graduation stage, or go to college, or have a career. Unlike Pansy, I had actually enjoyed the socializing aspect of high school and it occurred to me as I stood across the street from the two-story red brick building waiting for the bell to ring, that maybe I was jealous. Whatever the reasons for my aversion, I knew that I wanted to sidestep this whole world of teenagerdom for a while. I had loved it. Well, except for maybe the smell of the cafeteria on the days they served sauerkraut and weiners. I wasn't going to miss that.

Even from across the street I could hear the three tones being broadcast through the school as the final bell rang. It signaled a human stampede as both of the steel front doors were flung open and a rush of students came barreling down the front steps. Seeing them all and knowing that part of my life was over made me want to cry. However, that was something else that I couldn't do. It reinforced my opinion that I should stay far away from all of these people and try to adapt in the best way that I could to my new life. After-life. Non-life. *Whatever.*

Pansy was almost to the street when I saw Bagel walk through the doors all by himself. I'd met Bagel in first grade when he'd accidentally stepped on my new shoes and scuffed them. I'd decked him and we'd been best friends ever since. He walked out slowly with his head down, his dark hair covering half his face from view. It made my non-existent heart ache to see him looking so sad. He tended toward the emotional and overly dramatic even on the best of days and I didn't want to have to hold him down and make him watch a *My So-Called Life* suicide special or anything. I met

Pansy halfway across Main Street and gestured back toward Bagel.

"We're going to have to tell him."

"Tell who?" She turned, spotting the 'who' instantly. "Oh. No. I can't tell anyone. If this gets out then everyone in town is going to think that I'm crazy." I looked Pansy over from tips of her tan suede Bucks to the top of her perfectly curled pigtails with big sunflower hair ties. She was wearing wide-legged jeans with daisies embroidered up the sides and a skin-tight tee shirt with a yin-yang symbol screen-printed across the front. She looked as normal as every other teenager coming out the door and I found it hard to believe that anyone was going to think that she'd lost her mind. Besides, I didn't want to tell everyone in town, only the ones that really loved me.

"But it's Bagel. Look at him—he looks miserable."

She turned, watching my BFF as he walked toward the student parking lot and I knew she was going to cave when her shoulders slumped. "Fine. When?"

"As soon as possible. I was his best friend, he has to know." I felt guilty that we'd already waited this long.

"Fine," she repeated.

"Go ask him to come over tonight after dinner. We've got to go to the library right now."

"I thought we were going to the courthouse?"

"Change of plans."

"Fine."

"Don't pretend that you're not as interested in this as I am. Now, go save my boy."

"Fine." She stalked off and I followed behind, giving her some room to talk to him. They'd never really gotten along well, although I suspected that Pansy had been jealous of our friendship. She had several girlfriends who would occasionally come over and hang out, but none that she would tell her deepest darkest secrets. I'd had that with Bagel and I think that had always eaten at her. "Dario, wait up."

Bagel's real name was Dario Ventura and Pansy had always refused to call him Bagel, saying that it was a ridiculous nickname. It was, no one could argue that, but he'd earned the name Bagel in elementary school because he had eaten a bagel—plain with pineapple cream cheese—on the bus every morning on the way to school. Bagel Boy the older kids had called him, and eventually, everyone had just called him Bagel. It was a stupid name, but he was probably going to be stuck with it for the rest of his life. Or at least until he graduated high school and moved out of Perth.

He looked suspicious that Pansy was speaking to him in clear view of other students—like he was waiting for someone to pop up and surprise him. Pansy approached, her pigtails bouncing as she walked and her pants swishing as the voluminous fabric brushed together. Bagel was dressed in what I liked to think of as his 'uniform,' Chucks, skater jeans and a Henley under his puffy Broncos coat. He didn't particularly care for the Broncos, or sports in general, but his dad had bought it for him last Christmas in an attempt at making his oldest son more sporty. Besides, it was really warm. His dark hair, shaved in the back and the left side, sloped to a point below his chin on the right. He looked anything but trusting as Pansy grew closer.

"Look, can you come by the house tonight after dinner? There's something I want to show you."

"Something of Gerri's?" Oh, God, the way his eyes lit up was killing me. Again.

"Yeah. Something I know that she'd want you to have."

"Can't you just bring it to school, tomorrow?"

"Umm…"

"Tell him you don't want him to be thinking about me while he's at school. It would distract him."

She shot me a look to express how dumb that would sound and said instead, "It's best to show you at the house, or I could bring it to your house. School isn't private enough, ya know."

"You're not going to try to seduce me or anything are you?" he looked repulsed for a second before he started cracking up.

Pansy shot me another dirty look. "Uh, no. Nothing like that. Look, can you come over tonight or not?"

"I guess."

He turned, resuming his walk across the lot to his Bronco while Pansy continued to glare at me.

"Do you even have a plan? How are you going to convince him that you're really a ghost and that I'm not just crazy."

"I don't know, I'll think of something, I guess. In fact…" I paused as I tried to decide how to verbalize the plan that was forming in my head. A plan that she wasn't going to like. "Look, can you do the library by yourself? If I follow Bagel home then I can tell him what he did after he left you. You know, tell him things that there's no way you could know and kind of prove to him that I'm real." As real as a ghost can be, that is.

"Which reminds me, why am I going to the library? What's wrong with the courthouse?"

"Well, I did some recon today and they don't keep that kind of stuff at the courthouse, it's all in Denver. But we only have a seven-year time frame to look through. You may not make it through all of the microfiches before dinner, but maybe you'll get lucky."

"We only have seven years of newspaper clippings to look through," she mocked and I looked around to make sure that no one else had noticed that she was standing here talking to herself. She realized what she was doing when she saw me looking around and began walking toward the library which was a block away. "I don't get lucky," she hissed over her shoulder at me. As she was the one walking away and I was the one floating, I could argue that point but decided to save my breath.

It wasn't like I could scroll through the microfiche myself so my presence was not going to be a value-add either way. Pansy would get over her snit as soon as she found something relevant to the case. I turned back toward the student parking lot and spotted Bagel's Bronco, its black paint marred by a passenger side panel painted primer gray. Yep, that was the right one. I caught up to him and floated along in the passenger seat, glad for a moment that I wasn't corporeal since his passenger floorboard was a mess of fast food bags and random clothing that probably hadn't been washed in a month. *Boys are so gross.*

He stopped at the Foodarama where he worked part-time as a bagger and grabbed a gallon of skim milk. "No, no, no," I said when I saw his manager walking toward him while he was waiting in line to check out. Of course, he asked Bagel to fill in for a no-show and work the evening shift and Bagel eagerly agreed, the thought of adding to his paycheck apparently winning out over whatever mysterious gift Pansy had promised. With a sigh, I decided that following him would be pointless because there was no way he was going to get off work until a time well after what our mother would allow a boy, even a boy like Bagel, into our room.

"Bagel isn't coming," I informed my livelier half as soon as she got home. "I followed him and we only made it as far as the Foodarama before he got suckered into working tonight. He's out."

"That's okay, we'll tell him some other night. Besides, look at what I found at the library." After a brief wrestling match with some papers that had been folded in half and then stuffed into her denim backpack purse, she waved them triumphantly in the air. Smoothing the wrinkled copy paper she began to read aloud,

---

"Questions have arisen in the disappearance of seven-year-old Christopher Fairchild and fingers are being pointed at the child's father, Chester Fairchild. Rumor has it that the couple were sharing custody of the child while the details of the divorce were being finalized, however, now it seems that the child has gone missing and Margaret claims that her ex-husband has hidden their son somewhere in an effort to hurt her further. According to the state police investigating the matter, Mr. Fairchild is the original filer of the missing person report and while he is currently a person of interest, they do not have enough evidence for any arrests at this time."

She laid the papers out, eight pages in all, across my bed so that I could read them at my leisure. "I printed every article that I could find that mentioned your little ghost friend or his parents. Basically, the gist of the story is, the kid went missing, the mom blamed the dad, the dad claimed that he was innocent, and two months after he went missing she picked up everything and moved to parts unknown."

"Well, that's super weird. Why wouldn't she stay here? How would he be able to find her again if she moved?"

"Well, we know that he couldn't have found her because he was already dead, wasn't he?"

"But she didn't know that, did she? And we know he died somewhere around that time, but it could have been months after she moved. Without a date of death to go on… which reminds me, how did you find these?"

"Why does that question sound like you didn't actually expect me to find anything?"

"Well, I knew you'd find them eventually, but not in under four hours. How did you narrow it down?"

"While I would love to regale you with tales of my research prowess, I actually just asked at the front desk. There was an older lady checking out when I asked the librarian if he remembered a local missing kid from the fifties or sixties, and she piped up. Her first child was born right after Christopher went missing and it scared her. June of 1953."

"Good work, Detective Bellafini."

"Looks like I did have good luck, after all," she said with a shrug. "Since Bagel isn't coming over, I want to grab something to eat and then let's make a Blockbuster run."

I nodded absently, still reading the articles she'd spread across the bed for my perusal while she heated up some leftovers downstairs. There really wasn't much to go on, the kid disappeared, no one claimed to have any idea where he went, and when he didn't come home Mrs. Fairchild sold the house and got the heck out of Dodge. There was no further mention as to where *Mr.* Fairchild had ended up.

I was still thinking about how Mrs. Fairchild must have felt, walking through town and everyone talking about her and her family as she passed. It was probably a lot like what happened every time Pansy walked by a group of two or more people. They'd smile, wave politely, and then start talking about the "horrible accident" amongst themselves as soon as they thought she was out of earshot. Pansy pretended not to hear them and I didn't bring it up.

After she'd been fed, I followed her to the end of the street, bundled up in her rainbow-colored scarf and fur-lined boots since the temperature had dropped another ten degrees now that the sun was down. We had timed our arrival perfectly, getting to the stop as the bus arrived so she didn't freeze to death waiting. Her earphones were in place and she was silently mouthing the words of a song—from her newest Mariah Carey CD—as we rode into town. Fifteen minutes later, we came to a jarring, air brakes screeching, stop in front of Sycamore Plaza where we departed with half the other bus occupants. I noticed that there was a line of people waiting outside the Taste of China despite the almost zero-degree wind chill, and we passed a pizza delivery boy weighed down with orders as he loaded them into his SUV. It looked like no one wanted to cook on a Monday night.

We went straight to the Comedies section, fighting through the crowded aisle and trying to make enough room to see what was available. Giving up on being nice, I floated right through people, not that any of them noticed. Pansy was stopped by no less than three of her school friends, but since we were rushed and they couldn't see me, I continued my perusal of brightly colored cardboard boxes. A black and white cover caught my eye. The title was spelled out in colored letters that looked like they had been cut out of different newspapers or magazines, *Clerks*. I'd heard people talking about this one. We had a winner.

"Pansy, come get this one, it's the last copy." Still talking to her friend Sarah, she walked over and deftly reached between a random dude who was reading a movie description on the back of a box and a middle-aged woman who was trying to wrestle the *Dumb and Dumber* box away from the kid on her hip. Pansy was still talking to Sarah about Mr. Mueller's exam on Friday when I spotted our friend Brandon Ortiz wiping off the counter next to his station. His electric blue polo practically glowed under the lights by the registers. "Hey, if you hurry up, Brandon will probably waive your late fee from the last time. It looks like he's getting ready to close out his register."

The thought of not having to pay a late fee put my sister's butt in gear and she weaved through the maze of stanchions up to his register. Ignoring the displays of movie theater-sized boxes of candy, she laid our choice on the counter. Brandon's dark eyebrows shot up when he saw the title.

"Are you sure that your mom is going to let you watch this?" He leaned forward to whisper, "They talk about sex and drugs."

Perfect, with Mom as distracted as she was she'd never notice. Pansy hadn't even looked at what I'd told her to get and her eyebrows raised to join Brandon's when she finally read the box. She recovered quickly.

"I think it will be fine, she's cool like that," Pansy said.

With a shrug Brandon retrieved the VCR tape from shelves behind the counter. He slid the protective clear plastic box past his barcode reader before stashing it in a plastic bag, his perfectly gelled hair never moving as he did so. Pansy had pulled her membership card from her purse and he hit the appropriate keys on the register.

"Oooh, you have a late fee," he said before a grin broke across his face and his dimple showed. "And… now you don't. Try to get this one back on time, okay?"

"Thank you, so much," Pansy told him, her own dimples showing as she paid him for the rental.

"Thank you for shopping at Blockbuster, and remember…" He pointed toward the sign by the door next to him with the cheesy smiley face on it.

"Be kind, please rewind," we all repeated in unison, not that anyone but Pansy could hear me.

Laughing, we left the store and headed home, our illicit purchase burning a hole in our oversized pockets. We arrived back at the house to find that Dad had arrived home from work while we'd been gone. Mom came to the top of the stairs to tell Pansy that they were going to watch TV in their room and to keep it to a dull roar. Pansy threw a bag of popcorn into the microwave and I stood there wishing I could help do something. I couldn't even fast forward the movie past the previews or pour our drinks. What could I possibly do to repair our parents' marriage? I briefly considered telling Pansy that Dad may be having an affair, but she still looked excited about the movie and I didn't want to ruin whatever happiness she could get.

Twenty minutes later I was free to laugh as loud as I wanted while Pansy was trying to muffle her snorts and giggles by hiding her face in a decorative couch pillow. All in all, it was just the kind of stress relief she'd needed.

She'd hidden the tape in her book bag to drop off after school the next day, and we'd talked about the movie characters until she'd finally gone to bed, the television in our room tuned to Jerry Springer for my nightly entertainment. I floated there for a while listening to Pansy snore, but I couldn't make my mind shut down enough to veg out. There were too many questions floating around in my brain and my overwhelming sense of being useless was weighing foremost in my thoughts. Maybe, instead of hiding out here, I should be out doing things. It was dark and I couldn't see, but there were street lights and I could literally go anywhere and no one would see me, even if the lights were on.

It wasn't like there was anything out there that could hurt me, right? I was already dead. I couldn't fall into the canyon, I couldn't get hit by a car or be attacked by a dog. I was safe from rapists or murderers or— murdering rapists—all of the things that our mother warned us about every time we left the house. But, what if there was something bad, like supernaturally bad, lurking out there? What if there were other ghosts out there that did know how to hurt me, or knew how to poof me to wherever ghosts went when they stopped haunting a place? What if someone poofed me and Pansy didn't even know where I'd gone?

Since I couldn't leave a note, I yelled in her ear until she woke up. It worked.

"What… what's wrong, what time is it?" she mumbled, pushing her long braid over her shoulder and she squinted at the alarm clock on her bedside table.

"I'm going out. I just wanted you to know that I was going to go exploring around town in case someone poofed me."

"In case someone… what?" She rubbed the heels of her hands against her eyes. It was two am, she must have been in REM sleep. *Oops.*

"Sorry. Go back to sleep. I wanted you to know that I was leaving in case I'm not here when you get up."

"Okay. Whatever. Goodnight." She snuggled back into her pillows and was asleep again before I had even straightened back up.

Squaring my shoulders with my new resolve to take on the world, or at least my tiny piece of it here in Perth, I went straight up through the roof, my journey made surprisingly easy by the reflection of the moon on the snow, and the numerous street lamps that lined most of the roads close to town. I'd been dead for almost two months and had so far only met one ghost. Surely there were more out there.

If I had been a ghost for years and was bored with everything, where would I go? Where would there be lights on and people around twenty-four seven? My first thought was that gas stations and convenience stores were open all night, but after watching *Clerks,* who knew what kind of late night freakiness I would see there? That was fine in a movie but I didn't want to experience any of it in real life. I thought about the Walmart, but that was thirty miles away, and while I was feeling adventurous I wasn't feeling *that* adventurous. It would be my luck to take the wrong road and be lost in the desert forever. No, thank you. The local drug store was open all night, and as I made my way downtown, not sure what I'd find, I noticed another building where all of the lights were on—the police station.

Having never seen the inside of the police station in Perth, I imagined it would be busy and exciting , like an episode of Law and Order. There would be perps sitting in chairs giving their statements and there would be cells full of people yelling about their rights and that they needed to make their one phone call. I entered through the front door and my excitement was quickly dashed at the silence that greeted me. There was one guy behind the front counter reading the newspaper, his feet propped up on the counter in front of him. I could hear a coffee pot percolating somewhere down the hall and found a woman in uniform leaning with one hip against the counter, her empty coffee cup in hand, waiting for the machine to finish its death throes before she could get her next fix. Exciting stuff.

There was a jail cell, but it was empty, and as I wandered up and down the deserted hallways I thought this must be a bust. No excitement, no story to tell Pansy about here. I found an office with two men in it. The younger man was sitting at the desk facing the doorway, forcefully punching the keys of a word processor with his index fingers. The other man was wearing a long brown coat and sitting on the corner of the desk with his back to the door. He looked like he was reading the other man's report upside down.

I'd already turned to leave when I heard someone say, "Hey, what are you doing here?" Surprised, I turned to see the man on the edge of the desk coming toward me and I noticed two things immediately. One, he was floating, not walking toward me. Two, the long brown coat was made of threadbare terry cloth and had a belt. He was wearing a bathrobe, not a coat. It seemed that I had found exactly what I had set out to find, and now I was shaking in my boots.

"Uh, I was just wondering if anything exciting was going on." I smiled, trying to look friendly. That was me, Gerri the friendly ghost.

"Exciting? Here? Hey, aren't you that Bellafini girl that died recently? Gertrude or something?"

"Geraldine," I replied, my initial fear quickly replaced with irritation. "I go by Gerri," I said without thinking and instantly regretted it. I should have told him that he could call me Miss Bellafini. That had a more grown-up ring to it. He eyed me up and down and I wondered if his scowl was a permanent fixture.

"How old are you, kid? Weren't you still in high school?"

"Yes. This was our senior year."

"Our? Oh, that's right, you had a twin didn't you?" Such a charmer. I gave him a dose of his own medicine and looked him over, from his scuffed slippers to his wrinkled, coffee-stained, blue-and-white striped, *Leave It To Beaver* pajamas. He was really old, maybe in his sixties, and his long oval face was heavily lined and chapped. His cheeks and nose were redder than the rest of his skin, which could have been from either too much skiing or too much drinking. Maybe both. His hair was still thick and full, a silvery gray parted on one side with a few dark strands still showing through. He looked like he would have been short, maybe five-foot-six.

"Who are you supposed to be?"

"Who am I?" He sputtered. He seemed genuinely shocked that I didn't know him so I guessed that he was *someone* back in his day, whenever that was. I couldn't judge how long he'd been dead based solely on his clothing. "I'm Lee Bradley, Investigative Reporter for the Perth Gazette."

"Really? You know that went out of business a few years ago, right?"

"I am well aware, yes," his icy tone made me think that he was taking the loss personally.

"Well, so like, do you hang out here all the time?"

He continued to stare at me for a few minutes, apparently still not over the fact that I didn't know who he was, but finally caved and answered me.

"Not all the time. I go on ride-alongs when I get bored." I guess he'd decided that conversation with me was better than nothing.

"Oh, well, there doesn't seem to be a lot going on right now," I swept my arm, indicating the quiet hallway.

"Well, it's below zero out so no, there's not a lot of crime when it's too cold to get into trouble. Just the occasional drunk."

I, however, had other options and didn't have to converse with him. "Look, I'm going to cut right to the chase—you're only the second ghost I've found so far, not that I've really been looking that hard, but do you know if there's anyone else in town? Is there a place we all meet, discuss things that we've found? The naked little boy I met could pick things up and I can't do that yet. Do you know if there are more things that we can do?"

"Which boy? Christopher? Is he still haunting that old house?" I didn't like the way he snarled his nose like Christopher's inability to leave the house made him beneath this world-weary old man. *Jerk.*

"Yeah, Christopher. I'm trying to find out what happened to his parents. I thought that maybe if he found them he'd… I don't know, move on, or something."

"Move on? Move on to where?"

"Uh… like, heaven, I guess."

He seemed to find that hilarious and I wanted to kick him in the shin.

"Kid, listen, it's going to take you a long time to learn how to move things and no, there aren't any meetings. There's no Ghosts Anonymous, we don't have reunions. There are only three, four now, here in town. There are always more in the bigger cities but we have no answers. We don't know why only some are still here and others have, as you so quaintly called it, 'moved on.' We don't know any more than you do."

"Okay, but who are they? The other ghosts, I mean. Where can I find them?"

He looked thoughtful for a moment before shaking his head. "Nah, you've got all of eternity to find them. I wouldn't want to make it too easy for you, now would I?" Laughing, he went past me, disappearing into the front of the police station where two officers were dragging an uncooperative man into the cell. On my way out the door, I noticed that one of the officers was covered in chunks of what looked like vomit and for a brief moment I was really glad that I couldn't smell anything. Like, eww.

I was still fuming over Mr. Jerkface when I left the police station and had started in the direction of home when I remembered that everyone there was sleeping and I would have nothing to do. My investigation of the police department had only wasted half an hour of my time, judging by the giant digital clock over the bank, however, the visit had put an idea in my head. I decided to go talk to Christopher and try an experiment. Once I left downtown there weren't any street lights and my way was lit only by the moon and its reflection on the snow. I had a moment of doubt but I knew where I was going and the road south soon became a dark ribbon against the eerily lit landscape thanks to the DOT and their snow-removal-vigilance. I was at the Garcia house with little-to-no fuss and walked through the front door, employing my living manners once again.

"Christopher, are you home?" I shouted up the front stairs. His reply came from the den so I made my way to the back. Sure enough, Mrs. Garcia was in her recliner, her features lax as she snored softly in the flickering light of the television set. The set was on "mute" with the closed captioning scrolling along the bottom.

"Did you come to watch television with me?" He looked excited by the prospect of company so soon after my last visit.

"Well, I actually came to talk about some things with you. Would you like me to visit more often? I don't have anyone to talk to besides Pansy and she's asleep right now. You must be really lonely."

"Oh, gosh, yes. If it wouldn't be too much trouble. I don't have any friends that I can talk to." Those vivid blue eyes shot me the saddest puppy dog look.

"Well, I'd be more than happy to come and talk to you at night while my sister is sleeping. My sister has been helping me during the day, we're trying to find out where your parents went." Actually, we hadn't even started on that part yet but it was on the list.

"Really? Do you think I could go live with them?"

"Um, well, I guess you could, but I don't think they live together anymore. Do you remember when they got divorced and your dad moved out?"

"I… I don't remember a whole lot about them." He whispered this to me like he was sharing a secret. "I remember there were a lot of people after, though. After I'd, you know…"

"After you'd died?"

"Yeah. There were a lot of people here. Policemen. They thought I was playing hide-and-go-seek with them at first. But they kept looking and I kept trying to tell them that I was right here and no one listened to me. I didn't understand why no one would talk to me at first."

"Well, I know that you went missing and people thought that you'd been kidnapped. Your mom and dad were in the middle of a divorce and they each blamed the other for stealing you away and hiding you. Then, a few months later, your mom sold the house and moved, but I don't know where she went after that."

"Oh, Aunt Kitty came and helped her pack. She said she was taking her home to…" his face scrunched up as he searched his memory. I'd almost given up on him coming up with the name when his dark eyes popped open and he grinned. "Niceville! They were going to have a real nice time in Niceville. I remember Aunt Kitty telling Momma that."

Great, where was that Rand McNally when I needed it? "I'm so proud of you for remembering, sweetie. Uh, have you ever been there?" A girl could hope, right? He shook his head, eyes wide.

"Do you even know where Niceville is? Is it like, on the top of the map, or close to the bottom, or near water?" Again with the head shaking. I looked around Mrs. Garcia's den but didn't see an atlas anywhere.

"Well, I'll have Pansy find out. We'd need a map and I can't move things like you can." Of the couple hundred things running through my brain, one thought stood out. "When your mother left, why didn't you follow her? You could have floated along in the car and gone to live with her." Couldn't he? Was he somehow spiritually tethered to the house? Could he really not leave it?

"But I can't go outside, Silly Goose. I'm nakey."

"Dude. You're a ghost. No one is going to notice."

"No. My mom says I'm not allowed to go outside without shoes on."

Well, this answered one question—apparently time did not make for more mature brain development. "If your mom was still here we wouldn't be having this conversation, now would we?"

His little kid mind was searching for something clever to say, I could see the gears grinding in there but I decided to cut him off. "So your mom's name was Maggie Fairchild and she moved to Niceville in 1953. Pansy and I can hit the internet cafe in town tomorrow and see if we can find anything about her online." Which assumed that his mother was still alive and still living in Niceville, wherever the heck that was. That also assumed that she hadn't remarried or changed her last name back to her maiden name. I hadn't considered that possibility.

I noticed he was looking at me with a weird expression on his face. "What?"

"How are you going to find her on a line? What kind of line?"

It took me a second to catch up. "Oh, no. Not on a line, online. On the internet. There's these things called computers and you can get lots of information on them. Maybe we can find something there. Do you remember what your mom's maiden name was?"

He looked at me like I was speaking a foreign language. "Okay, do you remember where your grandparents used to live?"

"Yep."

Maybe if I could track down her parents, I'd find her maiden name in case we needed it. Or rather, Pansy could find it, I was still useless. "So, where did they live?"

"Florida."

"Great." Even deaf and asleep Mrs. Garcia should have heard my sigh. "Both sets?"

"I didn't ever meet my Daddy's parents. I don't think he had any."

We sat for a moment in silence while I contemplated the best way to proceed with our search and Christopher went back to watching the black-and-white western on the television.

"Hey, by the way, I met another ghost tonight. He was a reporter or something when he was alive."

"Mr. Bradley?" He asked without looking away from the screen.

"Yeah, he said he knew who you were. What do you think of him?"

"He's okay, I guess. He came around after I died."

"Really? He acted like I should know who he was, I wouldn't have thought he'd been dead so long."

"No," he said, shaking his head. "He was still alive when he came here. He was asking Momma a lot of questions about me and scribbling things in his notebook."

"Oh, you mean he was reporting on your kidnapping?"

"I guess."

"Well, what about after he died? Did he ask you any questions about what happened when you disappeared? Like, who took you and where did they take you?" I wasn't sure if it would be rude to ask him if he knew where his body was.

"He came by a few times and tried to make me answer his questions, but I remembered that he made my Mom cry so I wasn't going to tell him anything."

"Oh." That made sense to me, I couldn't imagine Mr. Jerkface having a great bedside manner with a grieving mother. He probably outright accused her of killing the kid. Which, knowing next to nothing about what really happened was always a possibility, I guess.

"Well, what do you remember? Where did you go when you disappeared?"

"I don't really remember. I was getting ready for my bath, and when I woke up I was still in the bathroom but nothing was… real anymore? I could float through things and couldn't put my clothes on. I hid before Mom could see me and raise a fuss."

When I'd returned I'd been at the bridge where I'd died but three days had passed. Where I'd been for those three days I had no idea. I remembered the accident though. Remembered the fear, the pain, Pansy's screams, and the thunk-thunk-thunk of the windshield wipers in the silence afterwards. I wasn't likely to ever forget that. And then I was just there, floating next to traffic with no idea what was going on. We continued to sit in silence as I pondered the strangeness of my overall situation. If Christopher had appeared in the bathroom, did that mean he'd died there? Had he drowned? Had it been an accident?

"Okay, enough about your past, have those guys come back to try to scare Mrs. Garcia?"

"Yeah, they came and were rattling the windows last night, but Mrs. Garcia had her hearing aids out and couldn't hear them."

"I can't wait for her to get the security system guys out here. Those jerks won't know what hit them."

"What does a security system guy do?"

"Well, they install a security system. It's like, if someone moves any of the doors or windows when it's turned on then it'll set off an alarm, with, you know, like, flashing lights and a big siren. Hopefully, she'll get one that will call the police too. I would guess that they'll also install some motion lights outside so that if anything moves it'll light up the yard. Even if she can't hear them pounding on the glass, she'll notice a big light going off in the yard."

"Maybe," he looked skeptical. "She sleeps like a rock."

"Well, if it goes off, you need to go wake her up. Can you shake her awake?"

"Yeah, I can do that, I think. I heard her talking on the phone with some people about an alarm. She scribbled something and hung it on the fridge. That must be what it's for."

Curious, I floated across to the kitchen, the kid right behind me. Amongst the wallet-sized pictures of family members and child crafted magnets made from popsicle sticks and pom-poms, there were several business cards and some hand-written notes. The Patriot Plumbing card had their phone number on the card with the last four numbers spelled out as CLOG, which gave me a chuckle. The card for Touchstone Realty was 0937. The 0 threw me since it didn't have any letters, but after a moment of working out the other three on Mrs. Garcia's phone with the giant buttons, I finally realized it would spell yes O YES. Giggling while mouthing the words, "oh, yes" in my best Harry Meets Sally impersonation, I found the piece of paper for the security system install, which was scheduled for Friday. Their phone number was 7796 and, after wasting approximately thirty seconds, I realized I was never going to be able to spell anything with those lousy numbers and gave up.

"According to this quote it looks like this is going to be a complete system that ties into her phone line. Once the men come and install the security system, if Mrs. Garcia gets hurt or falls and can't get up, you can break a window and it will call the police, okay?"

I could tell by his facial expression that this was not going to be an option for my little rule-following ghost friend.

"Break a window? On purpose? But what if I get in trouble?"

"Kid, we've been over this. You are beyond getting into trouble. Just throw something at the window or hit it hard enough to break. It'll set the alarm off and help will come." He still looked unconvinced so I decided to give him options. "Look, can you lift the phone off the hook?"

"Phones are not toys," he said, sounding like he was repeating a warning from his mother.

"I know, but this is important." I pointed to the bright orange sticker that had been plastered above the notepad hanging on the wall next to the phone. It showed the numbers 9-1-1 with the caveat that the number was only for emergencies. "Do you remember when you were alive your mom probably had the number for the police and fire departments hanging next to the phone?" I waited for him to nod but he gave me a blank look. Good grief, there had probably been a live operator on the line back in his day. "Well, a few years ago, the phone company set up this new phone number and you can call it and they will send someone out. Police, fireman, ambulance, whatever you need."

"Oh, like a party line."

"Uh, no. Or, I don't think so, anyway. If you dial it, they'll know who's house to go to, and if you leave it off the hook they'll send someone to come find out what you need, okay?" He nodded. "Now, try to pick the phone up off the hook."

"Phones are not toys."

Was it possible for one ghost to throttle another

"This is serious, Christopher. I'm not asking you to play a game, it may save Mrs. Garcia's life if you can dial the phone for her."

He nodded with a grim expression on his face while he processed that. "Okay," he said and reached for the receiver. He had it almost up and off the hook when his hand slipped through it, falling back onto the hook. I held my proverbial breath and waited as he tried again. With success, he managed to remove it on the second try. It may have been my imagination, but the effort to hold it up seemed to make him glow a little brighter than his normal super pale complexion. I made a mental note to see if Lee also glowed when he stressed himself.

"Do you want me to dial the numbers now?" I was thankful Mrs. Garcia had upgraded to a push-button wall phone instead of a rotary like my Mom still had in her kitchen. I didn't know how touching things actually worked, but surely pushing a button would be easier on his little ghost fingers than having to dial it the old way.

"Oh, no, sweetie. We don't have an emergency now, we're just working out a plan of action, okay? The security installation guys aren't going to be here until Friday, so if you see the bad guys coming again, you call that number right there on the big orange sticker, okay?"

"I could save the day."

"Yes. You absolutely could."

He seemed satisfied by this and returned the receiver to the hook.

"Time for me to go home, Pansy will be up soon and I have to tell her about everything I learned while she was asleep."

"But you'll come back, right?"

"Sure, kiddo. Same time tomorrow night?"

"That would be great."

"It's a date."

He giggled.

I was floating over the end of my bed when Pansy's alarm went off, causing her to groan and smack her hand on the snooze button. Ignoring her intention to sleep for another ten minutes, I quickly filled her in on my nightly adventures and then pointed to three of the eight articles she had pulled the day before.

"See, Lee Bradley, his name is on the byline, right here."

"But he doesn't know what happened?"

"He wasn't exactly talkative, or helpful, or even nice in general, really."

"And Christopher doesn't remember anything?"

"He says he doesn't. He woke up in the bathroom with no clothes on and the ability to float through things."

"But that might mean…"

"Yeah, if it works the same for him as it did for me."

"So we'll go to Connekt after school today. Maybe we'll get lucky and find a listing for one of his parents."

"Maybe." I wasn't convinced it would be that easy. We knew that Maggie had moved, but maybe Christopher's dad could still be living here in town. Had the kid's death been an accident? Why report him as missing if he'd drowned in the tub, unless you were afraid you'd be blamed. Or maybe she should have been blamed. Why had his body never been found? Or had it actually been found years later and Christopher didn't know about it because he never left the house. We might have to go through a gazillion years worth of microfilm to find something. I'd only been on the case for three days and if Christopher or Jerkface hadn't figured out what had happened or who had killed him, then who knew how long it would take me to figure it out. However, judging by how long they'd both been hanging out as ghosts, apparently I had plenty of time.

15

After confirming our plans to meet after school so we could go to Connekt, Pansy bundled up and headed out for school. I decided that since I had some time I'd go spy on Dad so I took off toward the quarry, no scarf and mittens required for me, thank you very much.

Dad was settling into his office when I got there—putting a pot of coffee on before switching the electric typewriter on his desk to 'on,' sending it through its series of beeps and clicks as it aligned the printer ribbon. The office was sparse and the only thing I noticed that was different from the last time I'd been there was a notepad on his desk with the top page full of phone numbers with labels like 'attorney' and 'insurance agent.' Justin Woodbridge's name was also written there and caught me by surprise. Justin was the man responsible for our car wreck, and it occurred to me that Dad was dealing with all of the legal aspects of my death by himself, and doing it here where Mom wouldn't see any reminders. Surely a man this careful to not upset his wife wouldn't cheat on her? Would he?

The coffee pot was gurgling away and Dad was halfway through some report when the phone rang. I had already zoned out and the shrillness of the ring made me jump a little. I moved closer to the handset so that I could hear the voice on the other end since I already knew that my father wouldn't notice if I accidentally touched him. The call was about a dump truck that needed some new part and I quickly lost interest in the conversation.

If this were a movie, I figured that I would find a lacy red garter hanging from the rearview mirror of his truck, but I'd already been in his truck and there was nowhere to hide anything like that in his office. I concluded that unless I hovered over him all day and happened to catch him calling another woman, then my best bet would be to follow him on the way home and see if stopped somewhere else before arriving at our house.

It was still early in the morning and the rising sun had caused a thick fog to roll through the streets of Perth. There was little traffic since everyone was already at work or school and with no clear direction in mind, I wandered through town until I came to Wild Harmony. The little bell over the door made no sound as I entered and I felt self-conscious—like I was sneaking around behind Summer's back. Summer was behind the counter, helping a customer decide which deck of tarot to purchase, so I floated around for a bit before finally making my way over to the shelves of books which seemed to cover every subject that could ever be listed under the heading of the spiritual or occult. There were books detailing ancient vampiric beliefs, herbal remedies, and phrenology. I'd never believed in vampires before, but I'd also never believed in ghosts and look how wrong I'd been there. Maybe werewolves and Bigfoot were real, too. One shelf was filled with nothing but books about ghosts—*Ghost*

Stories of the Midwest, Ghost Stories of the Apache, Ghost Stories of Atlantic. There were books on how to avoid ghosts, how to detect ghosts, and how to call forth spirits in a seance. There was one particular book on general ghost knowledge that I made a mental note to have Pansy pick up later. Evidently, all of your ghost problems could be solved on one shelf. I also spotted a book on Colorado's most haunted places and decided that we could potentially go check some of those spots out once the weather warmed up and the roads weren't so bad. I certainly wasn't going without Pansy, you know, on the off chance I got poofed.

A yoga class had started filtering in while I'd been reading book titles and Summer's assistant, Sarah, had taken over the front of the shop. I followed a pair of women wearing jewel-toned spandex through to the back area where the rest of the group had spread out their yoga mats on the hardwood. I'd never tried yoga before and had the bright idea that it could be a fun thing to try. As it turns out, my ghostly spirit body, or whatever you wanted to call it, was no more flexible than it had been in real life. After five minutes, I wasn't sure if my lack of gravity and balance was helping or hurting me, but I was super grateful for my inability to sweat. This was not a beginner's class that I'd walked in on. No, it was definitely some sort of advanced pretzeling. Everyone in the room worked to the best of their abilities and Summer was an excellent teacher; she always kept up a positive attitude and was constantly correcting people's postures so that they wouldn't hurt themselves. The music was soothing and eventually, I gave up trying to fold my body like origami and floated there listening to the music. It was the most zen that I'd been in days and decided that I'd totally found my new favorite spot to hang out.

In fact, I spent the rest of the afternoon there. Summer kept the music going even between classes and I watched two more yoga sessions and eavesdropped on people's conversations as they shopped. Were there other things I could have been doing? Sure. Would they have added more things to my lists of questions? Probably. When three o'clock rolled around I went down the street to meet Pansy and of course kept an eye out to see if my Bagel was anywhere around.

"He wasn't at school today," Pansy said when she noticed me looking around. She knew exactly who I was looking for.

"Was he sick?"

"I'm sure I don't know. He doesn't normally call me to let me know these things." *No, but he used to call me*, I thought as she walked down the sidewalk without me.

The internet café on Main Street, Connekt, was around the curve from the school and across the street from the police station. As we walked closer I wondered if Lee Bradley stayed in the station all day every day or did he ever leave to go 'investigate' cases. Would he see us across the street and wonder what we were doing? After such a relaxing day with Summer was he going to come over and ruin it?

The café was in a relatively new building, only about thirty-years-old, with floor-to-ceiling windows all across the front. The windows were tinted with some kind of reflective film that kept the patrons inside from being blinded by the sun while also preventing the people on the sidewalk from seeing in. I hoped that it would be enough to keep Jerkface from spotting me if he decided to get some fresh air.

Pansy walked up to the counter and paid for the minimum, half-an-hour to start. We chose a computer terminal and found one that was already booted up. Connecting through Netscape, Pansy tapped her foot impatiently as we waited for the sounds of the modem dialing out and the subsequent beeping and squealing to stop as it connected and the browser loaded. As soon as half the page was visible on the screen Pansy entered the name Chester Fairchild into the search bar and pressed the enter key. We waited. Twenty-three results were found, but none were local.

"I wonder if we can ask to see the court records from the divorce?" Pansy muttered aloud.

"Nope, the courthouse basement flooded in 1972 and they lost all of the records," I replied with certainty. "I heard the clerks tell at least five people that the other day while I was hanging out there."

"Dang it. Well, let's see if we can track down Niceville."

"Sure, finding Grandma and Grandpa No Name in Niceville USA should be a breeze."

My sarcasm was not appreciated and our search came up positive for Niceville, Florida. And Wisconsin. And Oregon. We found multiple listings for variations of Maggie's name—Maggie, Margaret, Meg, Peg, and Peggy Fairchild in both the Florida and Oregon locations. The local phone company in Niceville, Wisconsin did not have their telephone directory online yet.

"What was the aunt's name?"

"Christopher called her Aunt Kitty, but, who knows? It could be Catherine with a 'C' or with a 'K', or Cathy, or Christina, or it could be a nickname totally unrelated to an actual name."

"Well, I don't know where to go from here."

"It would be nice if everyone would put all of their old records online and make this kind of thing easier." I glanced at the clock. "Our half hour is almost over anyway. Back to square one with this for now."

Pansy caught the bus back home and I floated ahead, eager to see if the answering machine was flashing, hoping that maybe Bagel had called while we were out. After dinner, when Pansy still hadn't heard back from Bagel and refused to call him because she was convinced that telling people that she could see me as a ghost would ruin her life forever, I went over to stalk him. Haunt him. Whatever.

I floated over the blocks of cookie cutter houses in our neighborhood, three streets over to where a large quantity of my life had been spent since the age of about eight. Mrs. Ventura was in the kitchen, cleaning up after the family meal, and Mr. Ventura was in the living room, smoking a cigarette while watching the nightly news. It felt weird not knocking and saying 'hi' before running up the stairs to Bagel's room in the back. There was a hand-painted sign on the door with his name, his real name, Dario, that would always slap against the door when I closed it. It didn't budge as I floated through it this time.

My first thought upon entering the room was, thank goodness he had clothes on. I loved him, don't get me wrong, but there were some things that I didn't need to see in my life or death and his junk was definitely on the list. I hadn't caught him in the process of getting dressed or undressed for bed or a shower or anything like that. Disaster averted.

My second thought was that if my heart was still beating it would be pulverized to dust watching him now. He'd started a painting of me, a huge canvas on the easel by his bed, the paints dried on the palette. He'd started it, but it had obviously been in this state of half finished chaos for a while now, and he was laying on his bed, staring at it, crying. This is why I had stayed away, why I hadn't spied on him sooner. The grief of my family was heavy enough, I couldn't take on more. I was sure that some people may revel in seeing family and friends mourn their loss, may think of it as some sort of prize, collecting sadness like gold stars, but not me. I felt so, so... guilty. I was the cause of his obvious grief and there wasn't anything I could do about it. At least, not without my trusty interpreter who refused to come with me.

I floated closer to him and tried to put my hand on his arm despite the fact that I knew it would pass right through him. He flinched. I did it again and he flinched again. I thought about tapping him, the old 'shave and a hair-cut,' two bits routine, but figured I would probably scare him to death and without Pansy here to tell him what was going on and that he wasn't going crazy, well, crazy and sad weren't a combination I'd push on anyone willingly.

I sat there with him, watching him stare at my half-finished portrait for a while until his mom yelled up the stairs that it was time for him to take a shower. That was my queue to exit.

16

Christmas Break brought our brother Robbie home from his sophomore year at college in Greeley. Before I'd died, he'd always come home bearing loads of dirty clothes and lots of crazy stories that Pansy and I couldn't wait to hear. He'd been home last for the funeral, taking only a week off before returning to his fabulous dorm life and leaving Pansy here with me and our parents who barely spoke to one another.

Robbie came home after dinner on Friday, the fifteenth, for winter break. I was standing in the front hallway when he came in the door and dropped his duffel bags in the entryway before removing his Docs. There was no walking on Mom's carpets with shoes on. Stashing his boots in the coat closet, he grabbed his bags and went straight to his bedroom, taking the steps two at a time and not stopping in the living room to speak to the 'rents or even look into the kitchen where Pansy was making no-bake cookies. This was unusual for Mr. Sociable.

I followed him up to his bedroom where he tossed his wallet onto the dresser before sitting down with a heavy sigh on the edge of his bed and holding his head in his hands, elbows firmly planted on his knees. His dark hair looked unwashed and stringy, the shoulder-length mass falling over his face and hands. I stood in front of him, hoping he would be able to see me, but it was no use. He looked incredibly sad, but since this wasn't a play and he didn't give a soliloquy, I didn't know if it was about me not being there or something else. After a few more minutes with both of us sitting, unmoving in the dark, I went back down to oversee cookie prep.

"It's Christmas break, shouldn't you be making sugar cookies or those little wedding cookie things?" I asked as she checked the candy thermometer.

"I like oatmeal and chocolate," she answered in a low voice. She didn't want the parents thinking that she was even crazier than they already did. "What are they doing?" She nodded toward the living room. I floated straight through the stove, mostly to freak Pansy out, and into the sunken living room where both of my parents had claimed a separate end of the sectional and were watching reruns of *Walker: Texas Ranger*. They made no conversation. Dad had a crossword puzzle sitting on the arm of the chair and I noticed that he would pick it up, give it a brief glance, look back up at the television, and after a moment set the folded newspaper back on the arm of the recliner. He did this three times in the five minutes that I floated there. Mom was working on a cross-stitch pattern, her hands moving automatically with occasional glances at the pattern. I could see her mouth move as she counted the stitches in each row. Her eyes kept returning to the television, but I knew if asked she couldn't have told you what program was on.

"How much wine did she have at dinner?" I asked Pansy as I went back into the kitchen.

"A bottle, more or less," she muttered, scooping the last dollop of chocolatey oatmeal goop onto an oiled piece of wax paper that she'd laid on the counter.

"We're going to have to buy stock in a vineyard or something." Nothing like a parent self-medicating. "Do you think we should tell them?"

"We?"

"Well, you of course. Maybe I can learn to make stuff move like the kid can and then we can dazzle them with our paranormal powers."

"I think they'd be less dazzled and more freaked out."

"They seem so sad right now. I can't stand it."

"I know."

"You know what?" Robbie said as he came into the kitchen, immediately grabbing for a glob of cookie and burning his fingers as the molten sugar oozed over them. With a yelp, he hustled to the sink to wash his hands off. Pansy cracked a dish towel at his denim clad butt.

"Stay out, dork. I just scooped them out, it's going to be a while before they set up."

"Fine. Who are you talking to? I thought you must be on the phone." An idea hit me then, the perfect disguise when the parents were in the room, she could hold a phone up to her ear and talk to me normally, they'd never know.

"No one. Myself. I'm the best company I have around here."

Hey now. "What about Robbie, we could at least tell him," I said. Pansy shook her head.

"What's your therapist going to think about you talking to yourself? How's that going by the way? You don't seem to be any different than… well, than before."

"It's going fantastic if you think spending big bucks for some dude to ask me over and over again if I'm sure that I'm not drinking or doing drugs. Because apparently, that's all that teenagers do."

"I miss her." He said so quietly that I almost didn't hear him. He worried the dish towel between his fingers and looked out the kitchen window. I waved at his reflection, but even I couldn't see myself in the window so there was no chance he would see me. "I don't know if I can stay here without thinking about her."

"Tell him that I said, as soon as I learn how to move things I'm going to get a razor and get rid of whatever that crap on his face is." He was obviously trying to grow a goatee, but the sparse and random hairs weren't shaping up to be anything impressive.

Pansy snorted, a smile breaking across her face. Robbie, offended, snapped back, "Why is that funny? You don't think I loved her too?"

Holding both hands up in front of her Pansy shook her head vehemently. "No, no. Not that, that wasn't what was funny. Ugh. I…"

"Tell him. You need to tell someone, why not him? He can keep it a secret, he's not going to tell Mom and

Dad and have them lock you up in the looney bin or something."

"Fine," she said, looking at me before turning back to our very confused and hurt brother. "Look, if I tell you something, you have to promise to keep it to yourself."

"What?"

"Upstairs, now. We've got something to tell you and they," she jerked her thumb toward the living room, "aren't going to be able to handle it yet."

"What?" He repeated, but Pansy grabbed him by the shoulder and shoved him from behind toward the hall and the staircase heading up to the bedrooms.

He was still sputtering as she pushed him the final few steps into our bedroom before closing the door behind her. "Okay, go ahead and sit down, because you're not going to believe me."

"I can tell him exactly what he did when he got home, and you wouldn't know that," I volunteered. We could do this. Robbie would believe us.

He was still standing in the middle of our room. "Like, seriously. Sit down." She waited for him to sit on the bed, I thought the frame would break, he sat down so hard.

"Okay, I'm sitting, what's going on? Are you pregnant or something?"

"What?" Okay, she totally screeched there. "No, I'm not pregnant. What I want to tell you is that I can see Geraldine. And I don't mean in a see-her-everywhere-

I-look, kind of way, I mean she's standing right here. Or, her ghost is, anyway. And she's really not digging that pathetic excuse for a goatee." If I could have given her a high-five I would have.

Our brother sat on the bed, mouth slightly agape, but no words were forthcoming.

"Tell him that when he came home he put his boots in the closet, went upstairs, put his wallet on his dresser and then sat on the bed with his head in his hands."

"Really?" She asked, looking at me now. I nodded. "Well, yeah, no wonder you wanted to tell him, that's just sad." She repeated his itinerary and his mouth fell further open. After a moment of silence, she took a seat on the other twin bed across from him and waited while he processed this information.

"Is this why they've got you going to a shrink? Because you're hallucinating?"

"I'm not hallucinating. I can see and hear her. It's not like it's a memory of her playing on repeat, she follows me all over the place and is as obnoxious as ever."

"Hey! Who else am I supposed to follow?"

"Be quiet," she waved her hand in my direction and Robbie turned, eyes squinting like he might be able to make me out.

"I…" He started and then stopped. Clearly, he wasn't convinced.

"Get my playing cards off the desk and have him look at one where you can't see it. I'll tell you what it is."

"Good idea." She got the cards and handed them to Robbie. "Here, pick a card and look at it. Gerri will tell me what it is."

"What?" Poor guy still seemed like his brain wasn't rebooting.

Pansy sat back on the end of my bed cross legged, waiting for him to get with the program. After a moment of him staring at the cards in his hand he pulled the one off the top. "Three of clubs," I said.

"Three of clubs."

"No, that was the card on top, that's not fair, you could have planned this." Pansy rolled her eyes as he shuffled the cards four times and cut them twice. "There, now you can't possibly know." He picked up several cards, and fanned them out.

"She said to move the ten of spades a little, she can see that the card under it is a red six but she can't see the suit." Cursing, Robbie dropped the cards like they were on fire.

"Are you for real?" He asked, looking for a mirror or reflective surface behind him that she could have possibly seen his cards in.

"Dead serious," she said, smiling at her pun.

"This isn't funny, Pansy. I don't think your humor is called for, at all."

"Look, I've been with her since conception and apparently she wasn't ready to leave me, although we haven't yet figured out why. There doesn't seem to be a lot of other ghosts running around, so far we've only found two, so we really don't know what's special about our Gerri."

"'Cause I'm a super special snowflake."

"Oh, you're a special snowflake alright," she smirked at me. Robbie jumped up like someone had set his pants on fire.

"Oh, my God, was she sitting next to me?"

"Well, yeah. How else did you think she was going to see your cards? I mean, she's a ghost, not psychic."

He had that blank look on his face again. "Go get the boy some chocolate. I think his brain shorted out. He needs cookies."

"Fine." She opened the door and I could hear her steps on the stairs. Robbie stood right where she'd left him, although he'd started shaking his head back and forth like his common sense was trying to talk him out of believing what we were putting out there.

"We're losing him," I told Pansy as she came back in with a saucer filled with cookies which she handed to him. He accepted it, staring at the cookies while he continued to gently shake his head back and forth.

"Okay, what do we have to do to convince you?" Pansy resumed her seat on the end of the bed.

"I don't know. What am I thinking right now?"

"Dude, ghost, not psychic," she said.

He took a bite of a cookie, chewing thoughtfully, assuming the eye squinting meant he was thinking and being thoughtful. "Okay, so wait, you said you'd met another ghost?"

"Yeah, I joined a ghost hunting group and we did an investigation last weekend. Gerri found a kid in the attic. She can see him, but I can't. Apparently, she's the only ghost that I can interact with. Anyway, this kid can move stuff. Gerri can't yet, but she's still a new ghost." He flinched at that, way to keep it smooth, Pansy. "Gerri's been trying though."

"Trying." He sat down on the end of Pansy's bed again and started on a second cookie. "Okay. Tell me everything." Pansy started at the beginning, going through the first night I'd shown up, how our parents had been ignoring one another ever since the funeral, and detailing all of the ghost investigations. We heard our parents go to bed sometime around eleven, completely oblivious that their oldest child was even home.

"That's… unbelievable," he said when Pansy finally ran out of words.

"Tell him to hold his hand out."

"She wants you to hold your hand out."

"Why? What's she going to do?"

"Just do it." He complied, looking uncertain like he was afraid he was going to pull back a bloody stump. I laid my hand in his and hoped for a reaction. He didn't flinch. "Why is my hand out?"

"She touched you, some people feel it."

"I didn't feel anything."

"I can't either, although Dario apparently does."

Was she seriously still jealous of Bagel?

"Okay, so assume I believe you. Why on earth did you join a ghost-hunting group?"

"Well, we were hoping that they were going to be able to answer some questions for us because we have a lot."

"But they suck," I added.

"Yeah," she nodded, "like a Hoover. They think the first house was haunted even though we didn't find any ghosts, and they think the second house is vandals, but there really is a ghost there."

"So, the second house has vandals and a ghost?"

"Yeah. He's just a kid. He won't leave the house because he's naked. I think I'll keep working on their investigations, though. It is kind of interesting."

Robbie had started shaking his head again, some sort of internal struggle was being waged here and it looked like we may be winning.

"Tell him not to tell Mom and Dad."

"You were literally the one telling me to tell Mom and Dad half an hour ago."

"I changed my mind."

"Fine. Gerri doesn't want you to tell Mom and Dad. She thinks they'll go even crazier than they already have."

"That's a distinct possibility. I mean, she's kind of dead, but kind of not."

"I'm standing right here."

"Well, he can't see that you're standing right there, so get used to being spoken of in the third person. I already feel like Whoopee Goldberg in *Ghost* here."

"Oh, Lord. Okay. I think I almost sort of believe you. It does explain why you're not crying your eyes out every day or slashing your wrists or something like a normal teenager."

"Well, Gerri always says normal is boring."

"So does this mean she can snoop anywhere? She can read other people's answers on tests and tell you about them. Oh, or better yet, look at the teacher's copy?"

"Yeah, I guess, if I suddenly wanted to sink that low. But she could only see the teacher's copy if it was laying on the desk. She can't see into dark places and can't carry a flashlight."

"Yet."

"Yet."

"So how has the moving things worked out?"

"Well, we've only known it was a possibility for a week, so she's not like, killin' it yet, or anything."

"I also suck."

Pansy nodded but didn't repeat my sentiment.

"Tell him that since he now knows your big secret that he has to tell you what's up with him. Why is he moping around? Or is he still missing my smart mouth?"

"Gerri wants to know what's up with you. She said we told you our big secret, now it's your turn."

"Nothing as exciting as your news. My girlfriend was cheating on me and I found out right before I came home."

"Oh, well, that's not good."

"I was planning on bringing her home for the break and having her meet the parents. Guess that's one less social interaction I can avoid now. How about you? Do you have any boyfriends that I need to scare the crap out of?"

"As if. None wanted, thank you. I've got college to plan for and no time for some guy trying to grope me in a movie theater."

"Uh, huh. One day you'll want some guy to grope you in a theater, but keep in mind, if any try it when you don't want them to, point me in their direction."

"Deal. And next time you have a girlfriend that you're so sure of that you want to bring her home, have Gerri spy on her for a few days."

"Oh my gosh, yes! That would be so much fun, like Private Investigator stuff but I don't have to worry about being spotted."

"See, she's all over that idea."

Robbie turned to the door still chuckling. "I'm going to take a shower and go to bed and try to process this. If she somehow figures out how to move things during the night, hide the razors, okay? I've been working on this goatee for a month."

"I can make no promises. Your face has mange, bro."

"Whatever," he mumbled as he closed the door behind him.

"Well, that went well," I said.

Pansy nodded.

17

By Saturday night the snow had melted off most of the yard, and it was a balmy 43 degrees according to the big sign over the bank. I had checked up on Christopher, the security guys had fascinated the boy and he wanted to show me where each and every contact for the windows and doors were for the alarms, which he then imitated for my entertainment because they had tested them before leaving. He assured me that even Mrs. Garcia couldn't sleep through that much racket.

My family was nestled, snug in their beds, and with nothing else to do I decided to follow up on the McAllisters since I hadn't been there in over a week. As soon as I arrived I knew that something was different. The ladder that I had previously noticed hanging on the back of the garage was now propped against the side of the house and expanded to reach right to the decorative vent that led into the attic. The slats had been removed and there was a hole just big enough to fit a man through if he wasn't worried about looking graceful getting in. I figured that for whoever was doing this, grace wasn't a concern.

Going straight up to the attic, I saw a dude with a flashlight sitting on the end of a tote. From the sounds of a slosh, followed by a gulp and a sigh, it sounded like he was drinking something. Unfortunately, he had the flashlight pointed away from his face and I couldn't see who it was. He sat like that for quite a while, drinking from the bottle and occasionally mumbling to himself. I wondered if I had been wearing a watch when I'd died if it would still work. I was zoning out, thinking about the hows and whys of my own state when he finally stood up. I heard the scrape of metal on metal as he screwed the lid back onto whatever it was he was drinking, I figured it probably wasn't lemonade from the way he stuffed it into his back pocket and stumbled toward the door that led to the lower levels of the house.

What did he think he was doing? More importantly, what did I think I was doing? I couldn't even turn a light on, how was I going to stop him if he planned on hurting someone? Setting my questions aside, I followed him down the narrow stairs, marveling as he left handprints all over the walls while wallowing from side to side down the narrow staircase. He reminded me of a bowling ball thrown by a kid using the bumper pads. While the rest of the world had spent the summer glued to their TV sets watching the OJ Simpson trial, learning all about latent prints and DNA evidence, this guy had obviously been under a rock, somewhere. He wasn't even wearing gloves for goodness sake. What kind of criminal was he?

Still trailing his bare hand across the wall for support, he stopped at the first bedroom and opened the door as quietly as a drunk man could. If I'd had a pulse it would have been pounding, fear was absolutely something my brain could still process and I was ready to fly back to Pansy to call 911 as quickly as I could go, although explaining how she knew to call would be an interesting lie to come up with.

I was poised, ready for flight, but he didn't do anything but stand there in the doorway, silhouetted by the security light coming in through the windows. Floating through to the other side I could see we were in Kaitlyn's bedroom and she was snoring softly, one arm thrown up over her head. I realized that I knew the guy standing there. *In fact*, I thought, squinting at a framed picture sitting on top of the dresser, I was about 90% sure that the man standing at the door was her dad. Well, if that didn't up the creep factor, I wasn't sure what would. I didn't know the whole family story here, but if he tried anything I was willing to try to use her body like a meat suit and run for it. I still didn't know if possession was possible or not, but we could add it to the list.

He continued to do nothing for a few more moments before turning and closing the door behind him. Going across the hallway, he repeated the process with Josh's room, and honestly, I started to feel bad for the guy. He must miss his kids an awful lot to go through all of this trouble to see them while they were sleeping. Did our parents ever come to our rooms at night to check in on us? They certainly hadn't since I'd become a ghost. I was less tense now that my fears that this guy was here to cause trouble were somewhat assuaged by my conviction that he was just a divorced dad who wanted to see his kids. Apparently getting drunk, climbing a three-story ladder and breaking into the house was the best plan he could come up with to do that.

Well, this explained the dark figure in the doorway, the strange bumps and the cold spot caused by opening the door to the attic. I marked this one off my list. My part here was done, I'd need to tell Pansy in the morning so we could let the family know. Somehow. I'd come up with that plan later. He finally closed the bedroom door and I thought he was going to climb back up the stairs to the attic but instead he removed a picture from the wall and, leaning it against the wall, picked up another framed piece of wall art on the opposite wall and, as I watched in fascination, switched them.

Why on earth? Unless he wanted to screw with his ex-wife and make her think she was going crazy, and honestly, bravo because that was a great way to go about it. I stood there, mouth slightly agape and watched him saunter back down the hallway and up the stairs. He tripped on something once he was up there because I heard a thud and scrape which must have woken the boy up. From the hallway, I saw a sliver of light appear from under the bedroom door as a lamp was turned on. I went through the wall and the kid had the covers pulled up to his nose, all body parts tucked firmly into the center of the bed and nothing sticking out for a bogeyman to grab. These kids were going to need therapy.

I went upstairs to the attic to watch the spectacle of Mr. McAllister scrambling back out of the vent feet first, flinging his foot around in the air until it connected with a rung on the ladder. I tried to move the ladder, I really did, but no matter how hard I concentrated I couldn't connect.

He scrambled down the ladder without breaking his neck, much to my surprise, and picked the ladder up, carrying it upright and wavering in the breeze until he was behind the garage. It was obvious the ladder had been oiled but it still made considerable noise and I realized that he extended and lowered it back here where the noise wouldn't be heard from inside the house. Apparently, he'd been smart enough not to do any of this while there had been snow on the ground because he would have left an awful mess of footprints that even a blind man would have been able to follow.

I started to leave but then realized that I had no idea where he'd parked his car, so I waited and followed him as he turned into the tree line. I followed him through the pines. Once we were clear of the house, he turned the flashlight back on and we followed a deer path around the side of the hill to where it met up with the main road. All in all, this trip could have been made in about three minutes in the daylight, in the dark, with the ground slick with melted snow and mud, and with him drunk and cursing as he walked into tree branches, it easily took twice that. I could see his Toyota truck parked off the side of the road there, gray with a black stripe down the side. *Good information to have*, I thought as he piled into the driver's seat of the truck, pulling the bottle back out of his pocket and taking another swig before starting the ignition. Fantastic.

I went back to my room and pretended to lay on my bed, disturbed by the knowledge that nothing I was watching on Springer could match the weirdness of what I'd just witnessed.

The first week of Christmas break passed and I'd like to say that we made groundbreaking advancements in our cases, but nothing interesting happened. No one tried to break into Mrs. Garcia's house, my dad never stopped anywhere on the way home except the gas station and the grocery store, and Robbie and Pansy spent evenings visiting their friends or playing board games together in the living room while the VCR played all the classic Christmas movies on loop. My parents, while happy to have Robbie home, continued to ignore one another for the most part.

Christmas morning dawned on a cold and wet Monday. The temperature was barely above freezing and the rain was soaking everything, so there was a good chance everything was going to freeze solid and the electric lines were going to be snapping tonight. It added an extra layer of tension for everyone. Mom had been up since four A.M. when her sleeping pills had worn off and had been baking up a storm ever since. I don't know how Pansy or Robbie could sleep through all the noise she was making down here: the mixer going, the racks of the oven clanging as things were put in and taken back out, the pots and pans being tossed with no great care into the sink where she'd washed them twice. She was on a roll today.

Finally, when every flat surface was taken up with cookies, muffins, pies, or some sort of quick bread she went to get the paper. She poured what had to be her fourth cup of coffee and sat down at the table to read the paper. I noticed that she forgot to turn the pages. It was like the energizer bunny had run out of juice and she couldn't go anymore. I heard footsteps on the back stairs and saw Dad come down. He was dressed in jeans and a flannel shirt, untucked with no belt, and didn't say a single word as he surveyed the damage. Reaching into the fridge he pulled out some eggs and a flat of bacon and started making breakfast. Mom never looked up from the paper, but did finally turn a page.

Again, I thought that if anyone needed therapy it was these two. Sure, Pansy had lost her twin sister, but she still had me in a different way. Even Robbie seemed happier now that he knew that I was still available in some sort of capacity. It was less like losing me and more like an intense game of hide-and-seek where I was the undisputed champion.

But these two. Ugh. I didn't know if breaking the news of my ghostiness would do more damage or help them to heal, or if they'd commit Pansy to a mental institution and never look back. It was too risky, and Pansy would never forgive me if they put her in a straight jacket. Like, can you imagine being in a straight jacket and having to scratch your nose? That would be the worst torture of all. If you weren't already crazy you'd get there, quick.

The Christmas tree was packed with presents, my parents obviously trying to make up for the space created by only buying for two children instead of three this year. I sighed looking at it. I had no idea how to help them through this.

"Come and eat," I heard Mom yell up the stairs followed by a thump a few minutes later as Robbie rolled his butt out of bed. I went up to make sure Pansy was going to play the part she needed to play in this crazy train downstairs. Her eyes were open, but she was staring at nothing and mostly unresponsive as I came toward her.

"Hey, you've got to put on your big girl panties and go take care of Mom today. She's been baking since four this morning. Compliment her, tell her how wonderful it all looks, tastes, smells, whatever. I think she's losing her mind."

"Really, Sherlock? You're just now noticing that she hasn't been able to pull herself together? That she physically recoils every time she sees me because I look like you, and I'm the reason you're dead? You think I haven't noticed this?"

"No, that's not what I…" Actually, come to think about it, no, I hadn't noticed, but maybe Pansy had a point. "I don't know. Maybe." I mean the physical appearance thing made everyone at school uncomfortable, I hadn't even considered that my own parents would need to be reminded of what I looked like to miss me.

"Maybe we *should* tell them. About me, how I am now, I mean."

"They won't believe us," she said, flinging back the covers and stalking out the door and down the hall to the bathroom. I didn't follow her. I mean, there had to be some boundaries, right?

She came back through the door and I heard Mom yell again. "Just a minute," Pansy yelled back and we heard Robbie coming down the hallway. She reached through the open doorway and yanked him in as he passed by. "Look, Pansy said Mom has been up since four baking her heart out and that we need to act appreciative and be as nice as possible before she finally cracks up." He looked around the room like he was looking for me and I waved, not that that was going to help anything.

"Baking what? Did she make blueberry muffins?" Pansy threw her hands up in the air and looked to me for an assist.

"Yes," I answered, "and there's still a cheesecake in the oven." Cheesecake was Robbie's weakness.

"She said yes, and something special for you in the oven, so be nice."

"Cool." He started to turn to go but must have seen the worry on Pansy's face because he turned back, and in a completely un-Robbie-like move, pulled her in for a hug. "It'll be okay. I'll work on her."

"Thank you," I heard her muffled reply from the depths of his armpit where her face was now buried. He patted her on the head and looked around the room again.

"Tell Gerri that I'm going to savor every bite of blueberry muffin knowing that they're all mine and I don't have to share with her."

"She can hear you just fine," she said, extricating herself from the hug and turning to look at me. "And she's flipping you off," she giggled.

"Ah, some things never change." He waved in my general direction and headed down the stairs. Pansy got dressed, changing out of the tee shirt and Looney Toon boxers that she actually slept in and putting on a pair of long-sleeved pajamas that Mom had bought last year for Christmas. They were bright red with little white snowmen printed all over them. Mine were green with white pine trees.

Breakfast was eaten, compliments were passed around like butter and Mom actually smiled. Everyone at the table sighed when it happened, like a bomb had been diffused. Who knew how long it would last but she felt loved and it was getting through to her that her other two children still needed her and loved her, so I felt like I could relax a little.

Presents were opened, mostly clothes, so many clothes, and new Chucks for both of them. Then it happened. Dad pretended that something was missing, it hadn't been opened, where could it possibly be? As he walked out to his car to get whatever "it" was, Pansy looked at me and I shrugged. I had no idea what the surprise was.

Dad came back from the garage carrying a white paper shopping bag. As he bent over to push the torn scraps of colorful wrapping paper off the coffee table, I saw the logo printed across the side. Cellular One. Omigosh, we were getting a cell phone! Our very own cell phone. Everyone at school was going to be insanely jealous. If my feet had been able to push off the ground I would have been jumping up and down like Pansy was doing now as Dad pulled out a box and opened it.

"Now, I've already got it charged up and ready to go for you. Here's the instruction manual. I've already programmed home on your speed dial as the number two. See here," he showed her on the phone where to push to call home. "You've got one hundred minutes a month, so if you want a three hour long phone call with your girlfriends, do it upstairs on the house phone, understand? This is for emergencies only. If you're going to be running around at all hours of the night with those ghost hunting people then I want to know where you are. If either me or your mother calls, you answer it, do you understand?" We both nodded, even though I wasn't going to be able to even hold the darn thing, but I was still too excited to care.

"Call me, someone call me!" she yelled, pulling out the antenna on the top of the phone. It wasn't as long as the one on the house phone and looked like it was coated in black plastic instead of the chrome-colored antennas we were used to. So exotic. "Wait, what's my phone number?"

Robbie, having bought his own cell phone the previous year with his leftover scholarship money, laughed and went to find the cordless house phone.

"The phone number is written across the top of your instruction manual there," Dad replied, sitting back in his recliner and laughing at the sheer joy that was still emanating from my sister.

Finally locating the cordless under a pile of sweaters, Robbie dialed the numbers as Pansy read them off and we heard the electronic tones of the newest gadget ring. It was so exciting.

"Hello?" she answered the phone, still giggling.

"Why, hello, is this Miss Bellafini?"

"Why, yes, yes it is."

"I'm calling to inform you that you've won the Publishers Clearing House!"

Dissolving into laughter, the pair collapsed backward onto the couch, neither bothering to hang up the phones.

"Umm, you're using minutes, you know," Dad said, nodding toward the device Pansy had clutched to her chest.

"Oh, no. Sorry."

"I foresee a thousand-dollar cellular bill in your future," Mom said from her post on the end of the couch, her feet tucked up underneath her and her fluffy maroon robe, she toasted him with her coffee cup and laughed.

It was really nice to hear her laugh about something.

"Oh, no Mom. I promise. I'll be really careful. Thank you, thank you both, so much."

"You know that you're only going to have reception up on the major highways, right?" Robbie said, his arm still around her. "There's like this twenty-five-mile stretch once I leave I-25 where there's no service at all. It should be good in town, as long as you're within range of the tower though."

"I don't think they investigate things that are outside of town, not too far anyway. If we do, I'll let you know."

While traditionally our family packed up after breakfast and headed to Grandma's house in Red River, Mom's mom since Dad's family lived outside of Phoenix, this year was different. Mom and Dad had begged off from making the two hour journey and honestly, although I know our Aunts and Uncles loved us, I imagine that they were relieved to celebrate the holiday without a reminder of grief. Instead, we laid around watching *A Christmas Story* as it played on repeat all day long and stuffing ourselves with desserts. If anyone missed having a traditional Christmas dinner they didn't mention it.

Pansy made some calls on her new cell phone so that her friends would have the number, in case of emergency, of course and she and Robbie played card games. By the end of the evening, Mom and Dad were cuddled together on the loveseat in front of the fireplace that took up one corner of the living room. Maybe it was a Christmas miracle, but for the first time in weeks, I felt hopeful. It looked like everything might work out okay without Pansy and I having to expose our secret.

That hope was dashed the next morning. The day after Christmas was a regular working Thursday for

Dad, and he'd left at six as he normally did. By eleven, Mom was still in bed.

"Look, at your next therapy session you've got to tell Dr. Noonan to trick Mom into coming in or something. She needs someone to talk to other than Aunt Bev."

"I think you're right. What's she doing now?" I went to check, for about the fourth time that morning, but there had been no change. She was still laying in bed staring at the closed blinds on the window. She'd been in the same position for hours. I sighed, hope crumbling. Mom was still firmly on my list.

19

Since Pansy was out for winter break and had nowhere that she had to be, we decided to go to the Plaza and spend some Christmas money at Spin Time. The temperature had continued to rise, melting the thick ice from the electric lines, and everything outside was a wet, soupy mess. Pansy dressed in a new sweater, pulled on a pair of long johns under her wide-legged jeans so that she wouldn't freeze to death—those things were drafty—and added a pair of low-heeled, fur-lined ankle boots that she'd received for Christmas. She made it out to the bus stop and we waited for her friend Anne to join us from down the street. Anne arrived just as we heard the rumble of the bus coming around the corner and the three of us, whether Anne knew it or not, left the depression of the day after Christmas at home and went out.

Spin Time was located at the far end of Sycamore Plaza and tried very hard to cover every type of musical genre. Our friend, Amber, was behind the counter looking bored out of her mind, but perked up when she saw Pansy and Anne walk in the door.

"Hey guys, what's up?" she asked, flinging one side of her waist length blonde hair behind her shoulder. There was no dress code at Spin Time, no polo shirt with a logo that the employees were required to wear, so Amber was dressed in a KISS concert tee that was probably older than she was, and a pair of faded jeans. Her standard attire.

"Grandma sent me some money for Christmas, I'm going to waste some of it."

"And get away from our mother for a few hours," I added, although only for Pansy's benefit. Spin Time was set up with rows of wooden racks holding stacks and stacks of CD's on one side, and a wall of cassette tapes on the far wall for those who hadn't upgraded to the newer technology. For those that were way, way behind the times, there was a back room with a neon sign over the entrance that flashed the words, "The Vinyl Lounge."

Pansy and Anne separated, and as they were the only two people in the store, would occasionally hold up a CD and shout out a yay or nay as they browsed the racks. Tired of not being able to flip through the music myself, I'd started reading all of the notices of local music events, musical equipment for sale, and lost dogs that were posted on the giant cork-board by the register. I tested Amber, brushing my hand across her shoulder, but she didn't seem to notice or even look up from the book she was reading which, judging from the cover and the page she was currently on, looked like vampire smut. Interesting.

I tried reading along with Amber but she was halfway through the book and I was hopelessly confused about the plot, so I turned to my phone number game for some time-wasting entertainment. I started in the top left-hand corner of the cork-board. I found WORM and FORK and YOUR, but when I got to 0YES, I stopped. I'd already found that number once before, at Mrs. Garcia's house. But there it had been on a business card for something, I didn't remember what, exactly, but I didn't remember it being for the mining company on this particular flier advertising for jobs. Marigold Mining. No, I would have remembered that. *New opportunities are coming to your area soon.* Mrs. Garcia wouldn't have needed a flier advertising mining jobs.

No, now I was going to have to go back and see what the business card had been for or it was going to drive me crazy. Might as well go now. Going over to where Pansy was digging through the discount bin, I let her know that I was going to go check out a hunch at Mrs. Garcia's house. She nodded without looking up at me and I took off out the front of the building, going straight through the plate glass window in the front simply because I could. I was halfway across the parking lot when I spotted Kaitlyn McAllister walking out of the Chinese takeout place with an older woman that I assumed was her grandmother. Here was my chance. Turning, I went back in and got Pansy.

"I need you. Come outside right now, Kaitlyn's out there."

"Now?" She hissed.

"Now," I confirmed.

She sat her stack of CDs on the counter and asked Amber to hold them there for her for a minute. "I just saw someone that I need to talk to real quick," she explained as she rushed out the front door. Amber didn't look up from her book, waving her out the door before turning to the next page.

"Kaitlyn!" Pansy hurried toward her, waving her hand in the air as she hustled down the sidewalk.

"Pansy?"

"I'm sorry to, like, attack you in the middle of the parking lot and stuff, but I wanted to let you know about something I saw the other day." She paused, her hand over her heart as she caught her breath. "Okay, so like, does your dad drive a gray Ford truck with black stripes?"

"Uh, yeah… so?" Her grandmother was already in the car and sitting behind the steering wheel, looking impatient.

"Well, we drove past your house the other day and I saw your Dad's truck parked on the edge of the woods a little ways down the road from your house. I thought it was really weird, especially since when we were there investigating your house I thought I'd notice some holes in the ground under the vent that's up in the attic. You know, on the end of the house that doesn't have any windows?"

Kaitlyn looked embarrassed at the mention of the investigation, like she didn't want anyone knowing that her mother was crazy and thought her house was haunted. "Holes? What kind of holes?"

"Well, I didn't put it together at first, but then when we were reviewing the pictures and stuff I noticed a really big ladder behind the garage. You know we didn't find any real evidence of a ghost there in the house, but I know the others want to believe there is. I think someone is using the ladder."

Kaitlyn looked like she was processing the information slowly. Her grandmother started the engine, indicating that Kaitlyn needed to wrap this conversation up. "So you think someone is coming into the house through the attic vent and that maybe that someone is my Dad?"

"Well, I don't know for sure,"

"Liar," I said.

"But I thought it was really weird. You may want to tell your Mom and let her know, okay? I don't think your house is haunted by like, ghosts, or anything."

"Yeah, sure." She was nodding, still processing as she opened the passenger door of her Grandma's SUV and climbed in. "Thanks for letting me know," she said before closing the door.

"You think they'll figure it out?" She asked me as she turned around to head back into the store to continue her shopping.

"Let's hope. You did a good job of making it sound like it was a huge coincidence that you saw his truck. Right now though, I've got to go work on another coincidence."

"What's going on?" she asked, turning back to me, her arms wrapped around her body to conserve heat.

"One of the fliers in there is for a mining company and their phone number is the same as a phone number on one of the business cards on Mrs. Garcia's fridge. I don't remember what the card was for, though, and it's going to irritate me."

"Well, have fun with that. Tell Christopher I said 'hi' and be careful."

"Will do," I said before launching myself into the air like Supergirl.

20

Christopher was watching TV with Mrs. Garcia, as per normal, when I got out to the canyon house, and I greeted him politely before making a beeline for the fridge. I looked for the digits in question, searching all of the numerous business cards until I found the number on one for Touchstone Realty, Joe Shafer. There was no picture on the card, but there was an address and it was a familiar address.

"What are you looking for?" Christopher asked me, peering over my shoulder to see what I was staring at.

"I saw a flier for a mining company down at the music store that had the same phone number on it that one of these business cards had on it and I knew it wasn't for a mining company. I just wanted to see what it was."

"So what was it?"

"It was for this real estate guy. Has anyone been around trying to buy Mrs. Garcia's property?"

"Yeah, the guy with the dark swoopy hair. He was wearing a suit that time and knocked on the front door. He was carrying a folder with some papers in it and he told the woman that she wouldn't get another offer on a place like this." His voice dropped to a whisper like he didn't want Mrs. Garcia to overhear and be offended. "He told her that no one else was going to want to buy a house this far from civull… civaal…"

"Civilization?"

"Yeah."

"Interesting. The address on this card is somewhere near Wild Harmony. Maybe the empty store next to it. Do you want to go explore it with me?" I was really hoping that he'd say yes in case I needed some lights turned on. I remembered seeing the windows papered over with old newspapers so that people couldn't see in, but it would probably make it fairly dark in there.

"Go? Out there?" he waved his hand toward the back door and seemed to shrink three sizes.

"Yeah, I go out there all the time, it's okay."

"No, that's not what the boy says. He told me that there were things out there that could get me, and that I should stay inside." With all of the other projects I had on my list, finding this other mysterious boy hadn't even registered. I mentally added him to the list since the kid was either a jerk trying to mess with Christopher's head or I've been galavanting around the countryside in immortal peril. Either, or.

"Look, I haven't seen anything out there that can touch us. Heck, I haven't found anyone but my sister that can even see us." Unable to convince him, I left to explore on my own.

I flew over the tree line, across the sparse forest that covered this area of transition from high desert to mountain, I even spotted a few prairie dogs although they couldn't see me. I flew high above the town, landing right in front of Wild Harmony. 1502 Main Street. 1504 was indeed the empty storefront right next to it and the For Lease sign did have a Touchstone

Realty logo at the bottom, although there was a different phone number on that sign. Maybe I was on a wild goose chase and the phone number had been recycled. But the flier for Marigold Mining had looked new so I decided to snoop anyway.

Although it was a little past noon, it was so dark inside that I couldn't see anything. Surprise, surprise. I could see darker shapes against the darkness, like maybe sawhorses had been set up and they were doing work on it or something, but nothing definite. Upstairs there were blinds, old, beat up blinds that were missing more slats than they had, but they were open and let in enough light that I could see it was empty. Wherever that phone rang to, it didn't come to this place unless it was somewhere downstairs.

I tried three times to turn the light on downstairs with no success before deciding to see if Lee would be willing to help me. I figured it was a slim chance, he didn't seem interested in being helpful at all, but I was out of options. There was no way I was going to let Pansy get caught breaking and entering. Especially in an empty building that, more than likely, didn't even have any clues in it.

Crossing the street, passing right through the cars going down Main Street, I floated the two blocks to the police station and went in search of my only other ghost contact. He was standing behind a cop who was eating lunch at his desk, reading an open file over the other man's shoulder. It occurred to me that he was probably the most well-informed ghost in the tri-state area.

"So, whatcha reading?" I asked when he noticed me floating in.

"Some Lorena Bobbit wanna be. Looks like she didn't quite get the job done though," he smiled, tilting his head toward the file and I saw that it held glossy eight by tens, not paperwork. I so did not want to see any part of that.

"Fuuun," I commented, wondering why I was trying to align myself with some dude who had undoubtedly been a jaded, dirty old man in real life.

"Look, I'm trying to work out a mystery of my own, uh, nothing quite like that," I motioned to the guy eating his lunch and looking at pictures of a mostly dismembered, uh, member. How could he eat and look at that stuff at the same time? "But I'm trying to see if there are any clues in a building down the street here and I need help because I can't make things move."

"Clues, huh? Inside a building. So, you need someone to turn on the lights for you."

"Yeah. I do. Assuming that the electric is still on." I mean, of all the pathetic things to have to ask for. "So, uh… will you help me?"

"Depends. What kind of mystery are you trying to solve and why are you trying to solve it?"

"Well…" I launched into our investigation of the Garcia house and the subsequent multiple mysteries that had ensued but only made it about two minutes into my spiel when he stopped me with a raised hand, making the universal "stop" motion.

"Wait, wait, wait. You keep saying 'we.' Who is *we*?"

"Me and my sister, Pansy. My twin."

"So where is she? I thought that only one of you died?"

"Yeah, she's still alive. I don't know why she can still see me and hear me, but maybe it's the twin thing, we haven't figured that out yet, but I…" Again with the hand motions.

"Wait." Judging by his expression, he was properly shocked. "You can talk to her? And she can hear you and talk back to you?"

"Uh yeah. It's exactly like when I was alive, except for the floating thing, which really kind of freaks her out, ya know?"

He said nothing for a moment, he just stood there with his arms crossed and making tapping motions with one foot while he made some decisions or something. "So why don't you get her to turn the lights on for you?"

"Uh, because she's alive and other people can still see her. Obviously."

"So you don't want these fine folks hauling her to jail for a B&E." He said it as a statement, not a question.

"Exactly. It wouldn't look good on a college transcript." The old fart rolled his eyes at that one.

"Okay, fine. You may be helpful later with some other cases that I'm still working on, so I'd love to have you owe me one." I wanted to make some pithy comment about him being dead for thirty years or whatever and should have had plenty of time to solve these cases, but I decided to be grateful for the help and worry about the consequences later. I continued to fill him in on the whole story, about finding Christopher and that someone was trying to buy Mrs. Garcia's house and trying to act like it was haunted to scare her out.

"And you think that these two things are related?"

"Yeah, we do. I don't think that this Joe Shafer guy is really a real estate agent since that phone number is the same as the one I found on a flier for a mining company in the music store. I think he made fake business cards and they want something that's in Mrs. Garcia's house and are trying to get her out of it."

"Maybe," he looked like he was mulling it over and finally nodded, uncrossing his arms and motioning for me to lead the way. We left the building and headed back up the street to Wild Harmony where a group of women were leaving. A yoga class must be letting out.

"You see that woman there, with the red coat?" He was pointing to an older woman with her gray hair cut in a short bob, sweat-slicked and tousled now after the yoga class, bundled in a red winter coat that covered her from neck to knees.

"Yeah. What about her?"

"She has had three affairs and her husband has no idea."

"What? How do you know that?"

"Because I've been dead for a long time and have nothing better to do than to spy on people."

"Do you spy on everyone?" The old pervert.

"Just the ones that caught my attention back in the day when I was still on the beat. Rumors and speculation around them for one thing or another. I don't let those go."

"So, what about Christopher? He said that when you were still alive he saw you come to the house to interview his mom. That she cried and then you left. Did you ever solve that one?"

He looked surprised for a moment, I guess he hadn't expected anyone to ask questions about him. A quick shake of his head was the only answer I got before he stepped through the concrete block wall and into the dark downstairs rooms of the old music store. I was right behind him. We'd come in from the back, away from the street windows and I waited in silence while he searched for the light switch and managed to turn it on. Someone was still paying the electric bill. We were in what had been a small manager's office when Spin Time had been here, now it was an empty square with a six foot section of telephone line still curled on the filthy carpet. There were rows of dead bugs against the baseboards, obviously they'd been sprayed, and for a split second I wished that I could smell so I could determine if the bug spray was still fresh or not. On second thought though, looking at a trash can overflowing with pieces of carpet and tile and lots of used paper towels, who knows how bad it would smell in here.

"Can you smell?"

He had been looking around the room with a look of disgust that probably mirrored mine and seemed startled by the question. "No, of course not."

"What do you mean, of course not? I didn't think it was possible to touch anything and look at you, turning on lights and stuff."

"I guess that's a valid question. No, I cannot smell anything or feel hot or cold."

"Can you change your clothes? Ya know, like imagining yourself in something Victorian and becoming corporeal long enough to freak people out?"

"No." The look he gave me made me think that he was rethinking our association. I should probably keep the conversation on a more "normal" level.

"So, how do you make things move? I can't do it."

"It took me a long time, I'm sure it will you too." Great, that was helpful. He was already turning on the lights in the back hallway that led into what had once been the receiving area. There was a truck parked in the garage stall, and not an abandoned one. It was covered in mud and relatively new. The paint that was visible through the mud, mostly on the top third, was white and it looked like a utility truck, like you'd see the electric or gas company driving around in, with built-in toolboxes on the bed. There were no logos and no license plate on the back.

"Well, that's weird," I said.

Lee looked at me, stroking his white goatee before turning back to the truck. "Very."

He searched the glove box, which was empty, and I seethed with jealousy that he could open and close things. Ugh. I went to the front, which had originally been the retail space for the store, now partially lit by the light from the hallway. The things I had thought were sawhorses were, in fact, sawhorses, but had nothing on them. There was no glint from tools or drywall stacked on the floor like I had imagined in my head. There were still scraps of tile stuck to the concrete floor in places but it looked like most had been scraped off and dumped. Again, I wished I could smell to see if it was musty or smelled like cleaning supplies or glue remover. I hadn't realized how much information I took in with my nose before.

"Anything in here?" Lee asked, emerging through the wall. Hallways were too mainstream for him, I supposed.

"Not that I see. I don't understand. This is the address the realty card had on it and Touchstone is the company that is leasing this building, so those two things kind of go together, but there's no phone here."

"How long has that card been hanging on the old woman's fridge though? It may have been there for years."

"Christopher said that it had only been there for a few months."

"Christopher's ghost has been in that house for over forty years. He doesn't leave or even go outside—his sense of time is, doubtless, way off."

He had a point, one I hadn't considered. "You never did tell me what you learned about his death. Don't think I'm going to forget. I read the articles you wrote about him, after he died."

"You did? How did you find them?"

"Pansy looked them up in the library on microfiche."

"I didn't know kids even knew how to do that anymore. Don't you people use those little television sets now?"

"Computers?" I asked, laughing. Little televisions. I bet he thought they worked with magic and required little computer witches to make them work. He didn't seem to be amused so I pulled it together. "I mean, you can find information on a computer if someone has actually put that information online. Newspaper articles from the fifties aren't ever going to be online. No one is going to waste their time putting a bunch of old stuff on the internet." *I mean, get real.*

After turning off the lights downstairs, we began our search of the upstairs, although having a light on didn't reveal anything more than what I had seen before. There were no desks, half of the carpet had been ripped up and every windowsill was littered with the carcasses of dead bugs. Gross.

"So, did you ever figure out how he died?"

"Christopher? You mean, did I ever conclusively prove how he disappeared? Because we never found a body and I didn't know that he was dead until I died in 'eighty-three. So, in short, the answer is no." He opened a closet door, looked inside, and closed the door back. "Do I know who killed him? Because I don't think it was an accident. I'm ninety-eight percent sure that it was his father."

"His father? Not the mother, not some random stranger."

He chuckled, a humorless and rusty sound like he hadn't had much use for making that noise in a long time. "The incidence of random strangers breaking into a home and kidnapping a child are few and far between. That's why when it does happen it makes national news and people talk about it for years and pick it apart. No. When kids go missing it's because a relative or someone close to the family took them."

"So, like, the Lindbergh baby, or Adam Walsh. They're the exceptions."

"Exactly. Kids are reported missing or stolen every day across the country, and one can assume that at least twice that number go missing who aren't reported. Older kids usually run away from a bad home life, but the younger ones are most often taken by one of the parents. Divorce and custody disputes all over the place, fighting over their kids like they're property." He sounded disgusted and I was pretty sure this was the most words I'd heard him string together since I'd met him.

"But we know Christopher didn't run away and no one kidnapped him. He wasn't moved to some other state to live out his life there. We know he died."

"We know that now. At least, we," he pointed back and forth between the two of us, "do. The rest of the world still considers him a missing person case. When his mother moved out two months after claiming he'd disappeared, everyone thought that she'd stashed him away somewhere and was going to go get him and move him somewhere else. As his father was a local politician that no one liked, it wasn't looked into very thoroughly." His facial expression said it all.

"But you did, didn't you? You said you suspected the dad, not the mother, why?"

He turned the light off and motioned for me to follow him and we left by the back of the building in the alley. He patted the breast pocket of his robe absent-mindedly and I didn't know if he was looking for a cigarette or his reporter's notepad that I could imagine him using back when he'd been alive.

"Like I said, Mr. Fairchild was a local politician and he was involved with all of the mining big-wigs in this part of the state. He liked power and prestige. Now, Mrs. Fairchild was a pretty woman, but she was a housewife. He left her for some fancy arm-candy and the rumors before the divorce was finalized were that things weren't going his way in the custody dispute, that the judge was someone he'd screwed on his way up the power ladder and that Margaret was going to get full custody. Mind you, these were rumors that came up *after* the boy disappeared, no one here in town had any idea that anything was wrong or that they were even divorcing until this happened. They had big-city lawyers and were keeping it all hush-hush. People didn't get divorced back then, it wasn't done." He nodded his head like he was agreeing with that ideal.

"But when it was all said and done, Christopher stayed with his mother, right?"

"Not officially. Chester was granted full custody. Who knows how many people he had to bribe to make that happen, but don't think for a minute that the man actually wanted Christopher with him. No, he wanted custody so that he would have the upper hand in negotiating the alimony. With the offer of him giving that custody back to her, Mrs. Fairchild would have agreed to whatever terms he wanted. For all of his spit and polish, he was nothing but an over-educated thug. Never did like that man."

I figured that there was more to this story, but left it at that for now. Had Lee known Mr. Fairchild personally then? Sure seemed like it. They had probably been of an age, went to school together or something. I had plenty of time to work on that one though, so I put it on the back burner.

"I didn't see you accusing him of anything in your newspaper articles."

"Well, again, he was a lawyer and a politician. I had no evidence, no proof, just a gut feeling. I certainly didn't want a defamation or libel suit. The police looked at him briefly, so they could put it in the report but, as I said, everyone thought the Mrs. had hidden him, and no one could blame her, so after she moved they quit looking. Even I didn't know that the kid was dead until I found him up in that attic."

I couldn't even imagine what he'd been doing in the attic in the first place. Maybe looking for clues of his own? "Okay, so obviously someone is doing some work on this building and keeps a truck here. Who that person is, I don't know. The business card had this address on it and a phone number that actually belongs to another company, so I can assume that it's fake. But who does the truck belong to?"

"Maybe it belongs to the realtor who's trying to get this place fixed up to lease. I think you're making a mountain out of a molehill, kid." He once again patted absently at his breast pocket. Mumbling something about needing a smoke, he turned back toward the police station. "If you need me, you know where to find me." I started to thank him for his help and for being so forthcoming with the information, but I didn't want to remind him that he'd let the Jerkface persona slip.

I simply said, "Goodbye."

21

I found Pansy and Anne at Taste of China, finishing up their late lunch.

"Hey, I need you to call a number and see where it goes." I quickly filled her in on what I'd learned about the address on the business card. Anne was talking about a pair of shoes she wanted that her mother wouldn't pay for and Pansy was trying to nod and make sympathetic noises in the right spots while also listening to me.

"I just remembered that I need to make a phone call, can you excuse me for a minute?" She got up, snatching up her purse from the seat next to her as she went, and walked outside to the sidewalk.

"Star sixty-seven, right?" she was already typing it in so that her cell number would be blocked. "What should I say?"

"Say that you saw the flier and were calling to get more info for your brother. That's plausible."

"Good idea." I put my ear up against hers, my face partly in the phone, and could hear the tinny ringing sound coming from the speaker. It rang four times before the answering machine picked up. "You've reached Joe, leave a message."

"Hang up. That doesn't do us any good at all."

"Well, we know his name really is Joe."

"Or at least that's the name on the answering machine. I'm not sure where that's going to get us.

Now, try this other number, it's the one on the For Lease sign that's actually on the building." I recited the digits I'd memorized and she dialed. Again, it went to a machine, but this message was different. "You've reached Ernie Jenkins at Touchstone Realty. Please leave your name and number and I'll be sure to get back to you as soon as possible."

"Interesting. Where are you going to go now?" she asked, still holding the phone up to her ear like she was talking to someone on the other end and not me. She was really getting the hang of this.

"I think I'll go watch TV with Christopher. I kind of feel bad for the kid, being alone so much."

The next day we went downtown, stopping at Wild Harmony where we were surprised to find a live rooster in a wire cage on the counter. Summer was busy, her hunter green crinkled skirt with the big white magnolia's printed on it swinging all over as she hustled back and forth to help customers with their purchases. Sarah was at the register ringing people out and the soothing tones of Enya were playing over the speakers, punctuated by the occasional crow of the rooster.

We picked out five different books on ghosts and I swear Pansy sniffed every different scent of the incense sticks on the rack while waiting to check out. I was sure her nose was going to seize up for at least the next hour. Passing a display of wind chimes, I tried my best to make them move, taking deep breaths and trying to focus all of my energy. I heard the barest brush of the glass disc against a metal tube, and opened my eyes, convinced for half a second that I'd caused it. Then I heard the chime of the bell over the door and realized that it was a breeze caused by the door opening as one of the other customers left.

Pansy was staring at the rooster while Sarah rang up her books. The rooster was staring right back at her while it hopped from foot to foot.

"What's up, kiddo?" Summer asked after the customer she'd been helping had left.

"Is this for like, some sort of voodoo ritual or something?" Pansy asked, nodding toward the pacing poultry.

"Voodoo? I'm pretty sure no one in this area knows the first thing about voodoo. No, I found this guy on the side of the interstate coming back from Denver this morning. He looks like he's been doctored up for fighting, so I figured he escaped from the back of someone's truck. See how his waddle has been cut off?"

"So what are you going to do with him?"

"Sarah is going to take him home and turn him out with her chickens. He can eat bugs and live in a nice little chicken coop and not have to fight any other roosters since hers recently died of old age. You're going to be king of your own little castle, aren't you buddy?" She tapped the wire of the cage and the king in question tried to snap her finger off.

"Can I talk to you for a minute? It's about the Garcia case."

"Sure, it looks like the morning rush has died down, come on upstairs. I was going to make some tea."

We followed Summer up to the second floor of the building which she used as living space. It was mostly an open floor plan with two doors, one I assumed went to a bedroom, the other to a bathroom. She had almost as many books up here as she did downstairs for sale and the walls were hung with abstract florals in bright colors. I hadn't floated up here before, not wanting to intrude on her personal space, but thought it was lovely. She had several houseplants by the front windows that overlooked the street and provided most of the light. Since her building was pressed between two others there were no other windows, but there was a skylight over the kitchen area toward the back which let in more natural light.

Summer motioned toward one of the stools that surrounded a quarter circle bar that made up one edge of the kitchen. Pansy perched gingerly on the stool and Summer opened up a cabinet door and started pulling down tins full of herbal teas.

"Plain green? Pomegranate? Cherry? Apple spice? Lemon ginger?" She turned toward Pansy. "Do you have a preference?"

"Oh, none for me, thanks."

"So, what did you want to ask about?"

"Well, when we were at the Garcia house I noticed a business card on the refrigerator for a realty company and the address on the card is the address next door to this place. I was wondering if you've seen the realtor coming and going because the place next door looks deserted."

I was examining a carved wooden buddha, his belly gleaming from good luck pats and the fake flowers he held aloft were poinsettias. I imagined she decorated him for every season.

"Well, you're right, that's weird. I've seen the light on every once in a while over on the second floor if I leave and come home late, but I've never really seen anyone coming and going on a regular basis. There was a work crew over there a few months ago pulling out a few dumpsters of tile and carpet but they haven't been back. I wonder how long that business card has been on her refrigerator?"

"Well, that's why we wanted to talk to you, because if anyone would notice anything strange going on it would be you, right next door."

"We? Who else have you talked to?"

"Uh, just my friend Anne. We talked about it and decided that you would be the best bet for any info."

"Oh, well, I'm sorry to not have been any help." She took a sip of her tea and fluttered her eyelashes in ecstasy. "You have a really good eye for detail though, so I must say that I'm impressed. I never even noticed that card." We'd debated telling her that the phone number was the same as on the mining company's help wanted flier, but decided not to complicate the matter. It wouldn't make any difference and trying to explain the phone number game to an adult always made them look at you like you were crazy.

I followed Pansy down the stairs and as we made our way back out to the street I spotted Bagel going into the Firefly.

"Look, there's Bagel, go talk to him."

Pansy groaned and after a minute of some sort of inner struggle, she started walking in that direction.

22

Chandra was bringing out drinks to a table by the door when we came in and she gave Pansy a hug when she saw her. "There's my favorite junior investigator. Are you ready for the January cases? We have two lined up so far, one is the old hospital over in Middleton and the other is an old man out on Mountain View."

"Sounds exciting. I bet the hospital will take all night."

"I'm sure it will. We may have to recruit more people for it," she sped off toward one of the booths where an empty glass was sitting on the edge of the table and went back to work. After a quick glance around the room, the black-and-white tiled floor reflected in the chrome accents and mirrored walls was a little disorienting, she spotted Bagel in a booth by himself. He was, needless to say, surprised when Pansy dropped onto the bench across the table from him.

"What's up?" He said, looking at her suspiciously.

"Uh, nothing much," she said, adjusting her bag of books so that they didn't slide off the slick red vinyl and land on the floor. "You never came by the other day."

"No. Sorry. I had to work."

"Yeah, I heard." She was still fiddling with her purse and books and didn't notice the quirk of his eyebrow, but I did. "So, I really do have something important to tell you." She finally turned to face him head-on, but he was staring down at this menu, his hair in his eyes while he avoided eye contact.

"Like what?" he mumbled.

"Well, I don't think this is really the place to go over it. You might get upset and I don't want other people around if you do."

"Upset? What could you possibly tell me that would make me upset?" He looked up then, obviously irritated enough to get over his initial reluctance to look at my twin's face. "Wait, Gerri wasn't pregnant when she died or something, was she? Because I can promise you that we never..." Pansy leaned forward, slapping her hand over his mouth.

"No." Removing her hand, she sat back down with enough force to rock the booth seat. "Good grief, Charlie Brown, why on earth would you say that?"

"I don't know, it was the most upsetting thing I could think of," he mumbled.

"Aren't you gay?" She whispered to him, one hand shielding her mouth from the view of the rest of the restaurant.

"What? I am not! Wait, is that what Gerri said?" I absolutely had said that because it was absolutely true, and my dear friend Bagel was absolutely in denial. Which was fine—if he didn't want to admit it to himself that was okay—but I had, in no way, planned for Pansy to broadcast this newsflash to him in the middle of The Firefly Café.

Chandra chose this moment to come over, notepad in hand, and ask what she could get everyone. Looking up from her notepad she quickly noted Bagel's pissed-off expression and Pansy with her face buried in her hands and turned around and left with the grace of someone who'd been running a cafe full of teenagers for a good ten years. This wasn't her first rodeo.

"Look… you," she waved her hand in circles in front of his face, "are not what I wanted to talk to you about, but it does have to do with Gerri. She misses you and wants me to tell you that she's still here. Much against my better judgment," she qualified.

There was a pause, but he did finally look her in the eye. "What?"

"Tell him that I wish I had his camera to capture that stupid look on his face, forever."

"She says she wishes she had your camera to capture, and I quote, that stupid look on your face, forever."

"What?"

This was seeming to be a repeat of our conversation with Robbie.

"You see why this isn't the best place for this conversation?" She whispered back to him.

"Do you think I'm some sort of idiot? What are you trying to pull?"

"Okay, look… do you remember the movie, Ghost?"

He settled back against the bench seat of the booth and looked around the table, probably wishing he had something to drink so that he'd have something to do with his hands. They were currently tearing a paper napkin into little tiny bits.

"Yeah, I've seen it. What about it?"

Oh, he'd seen it. Umm, yeah, at least five times at the theater with me. *Seen it... pfft.*

"Okay, so you know the scene where Whoopee is talking to Patrick Swayze and trying to convince Demi that he's really there in the room with her?"

"Yeah."

"Okay, well that's what I'm trying to do here. She is my twin sister. I can still see her and hear her, and she can see and hear both of us, but you can't see or hear her. Got it?"

"Are you on drugs? I heard a rumor that you were seeing a psychologist, but honey, I don't think it's helping." He seemed genuinely concerned about her mental state and I started cracking up.

"Shut it," she said, turning to me.

"Wait, are you pretending that she's sitting right here?" He motioned to the spot on Pansy's left where I was hovering between her and the wall.

"Well, sitting is a strong word, but yeah, she's right here laughing her butt off. She said it's too bad you don't have pottery this semester or she could go full Swayze on you. She is obviously the one on crack," she muttered, rolling her eyes.

"Prove it."

"I'd love to, somewhere other than the middle of a restaurant."

"No. How do I know you don't have some sort of little gag set up at your house? You could have it rigged somehow. Prove it here, now."

"Sure. Why not? Can I order a sandwich first though? I'm starving." They waved Chandra over to the table and each placed their order, specifying separate tickets. Chandra laughed, probably thinking they were having some sort of lover's quarrel. Gag me with a spoon. They sat in uncomfortable silence, each avoiding making eye contact with the other until the food was brought out.

"Okay, I'm thinking of a kind of snack food, what is it?"

"What?" Pansy asked around a mouthful of turkey sandwich.

"What am I thinking?"

"How the heck am I supposed to know what you're thinking? We're not psychic. You'll have to do or say something where she can see or hear you and I can't. That's how we test this. Oh," she said before swallowing. "And Gerri said that if you're thinking of a snack food then it's Cool Ranch Doritos because you know she hates them and you can have every last one on earth as far as she's concerned."

"Lucky guess."

"Or she just knows you. Look, let's do this," she set the sandwich down in the little plastic basket and wiped the mayo off of her fingers with a napkin before digging into her book bag purse. "Here's a piece of paper," she pulled an old crumpled receipt from the bottom of her bag. "And here's an ink pen." It had a pink pom-pom on the end, but it would work. She slid them across the table before picking her sandwich back up. "Write a word, a sentence, draw a picture, a number… whatever. Cover it so I can't see what you're doing and Gerri will tell me what it is."

Wiping his own hands on a paper napkin, he picked up the pen and made a few circles in the corner of the receipt to make sure the pen was working. He took a moment to think before he started writing.

"Crazy. Really?"

"Lucky guess," he mumbled.

"Sure, keep believing that. Maybe you shouldn't be so predictable." He scribbled again. "Zombie? Good song."

"I'm not much of a Cranberries fan, I meant the living dead."

"Well, if you're talking about your former best friend, it's not exactly living. She's bored out of her mind, to be honest."

"Okay, tell you what, I'm going to go to the men's room, I'm going to whisper something to myself, and when I come back out you'd better be sitting right here and be able to tell me what I said."

"Fine. Wait, she wants to know if there are any urinals in there."

"Uh, yeah. Of course, there are."

"Well, she said she doesn't want to accidentally see anything she shouldn't, so make sure there's no one in there before you go in, and then she'll follow you in."

"This is the stupidest conversation I've ever had."

"Just do it."

"Fine."

I followed Bagel across the mostly empty dining room and waited until he had opened the door and looked in. "Come on," he muttered.

He walked to the double sink and braced his hands on the edge, looking into the mirror at himself. Since I already knew he could sense my touch, I brushed my hand over his shoulder and he instinctively reached up to brush it off. I left it there.

"Is that you? Are you doing that? I thought Pansy was crazy, but I really, really want to believe that you can still be here with me, because honest to God, Gerri, I miss you so much. I don't have anyone to tell my stories to, or make fun of other people with, or to watch old movies with. Every single day I see something and think I should tell you about it and then it hits me all over again that you're gone and I can't. I just can't."

I removed my hand from his shoulder and laid it over his hand, his knuckles white from his grip on the sink. "Are you touching my hand now? It's cold."

Deciding we needed some basic signal techniques, I tapped his hand twice.

"Twice for yes, once for no?" Again, I tapped him twice.

"Holy shit." I tapped him twice more. This could totally work. "Touch the other hand," he demanded. Like, whatever, dude. I grabbed his other hand.

"Okay, okay." He was talking to himself again and turned on the cold water as someone else came in. He was splashing water on his face when I left.

"We worked it out," I announced as I floated back to the table.

"What does that mean? Does he believe us?" She whispered.

"I think so."

It was another minute or two before Bagel returned to the table, the neck of his tee shirt soaked.

"Did you, like, go swimming in there or something?"

"I don't think that would have helped. I think I can feel it, you know, when she touches me."

"Two for yes, one for no," I told Pansy and she confirmed this with Bagel.

"Yeah, I don't… I don't even know what to think." He was staring at his half-eaten sandwich like he was waiting for it to do a magic trick.

"Yeah, well, how do you think I felt when she showed up in our bedroom three days after she died? It scared the crap out of me, let me tell you."

"So, you can really see her?" he looked up, examining Pansy's face, so like mine.

"Yeah, and I promise, she is loving the fact that no one else can. She makes faces at everyone and no one can see her or call her out on it. It's like a free ticket for her to be her most obnoxious self."

He chuckled and picked the sandwich back up. "Yeah, I can see her doing that."

"We also joined the Perth Paranormal Society. Gerri wants you to join too."

"What? Isn't that the group of crazy people who believe in… Why?"

"Because we're… I don't know. We thought that it would teach us something about ghosts, but all we've learned is that most people's problems aren't paranormal. And watch it, because Chandra is one of those *crazy people* as you want to call them," she nodded toward Chandra who was buzzing past with a tray full of sundaes. "However, due to someone's super impressive snooping skills, we've found out that we really can help people." She filled him in on the McAllister case and how I'd discovered that the person sneaking into the house was Mr. McAllister. "I talked to Kaitlyn yesterday and sort of mentioned that I'd seen the truck, which I didn't, Gerri did, and that I'd noticed some divots in the dirt, which I also didn't, but it's possible that I could have. Hopefully, they'll either lock the ladder in the garage or set up some security cameras or something."

"So, essentially what you're doing is a lot of lying."

"Well, yes." Pansy squirmed in her seat, her giant sunflower earrings bobbing back and forth. "I guess you could look at it like that. But I think once we figure out what's going on with Mrs. Garcia's house it'll be worth it."

"Mrs. Who?"

"Look, do you have to work this evening?"

"Yeah, I've got to be at the store in," he checked his watch, "twenty minutes."

"What time do you get off?"

"Eight."

"Then come over tonight and I'll tell you all about our current case and what we've done so far."

"And you think that I'd be helpful?" He was eyeing her suspiciously again, and I tapped him on the arm twice. "Fine, fine, don't double-team me. I'll be over tonight."

It took about two hours to explain everything to Bagel's satisfaction and either out of boredom or genuine interest in the paranormal, or maybe a mixture of both, he agreed to help us. Having turned eighteen in October, he didn't need a permission slip to join the group, and Pansy promised she'd call Greg in the morning to let him know that she'd be bringing a friend to the next meeting.

Pansy had started reading our new research books when we'd arrived home that afternoon and as soon as Bagel left we were back at it.

"It says here, painting the roof of your porch blue will keep ghosts away. Do we know anyone with a blue porch roof we can test that on?"

"Not that I know of, but that's interesting. I wonder what's special about blue?"

"I don't know, it just said it's supposed to ward off evil or restless spirits."

"Evil? I'm not evil. I guess I'm restless when I'm bored, though." I hadn't met anyone evil, at least, not yet. I mean, I know I'd only been dead for a month, but you'd think I'd have met evil if it was hanging around town by now.

"Here's a whole section on how to keep spirits away. Crosses, dream catchers," we both turned to look at the large dream catchers hung over both of our beds. "Seemingly not effective," she said, turning back to me with a shrug.

"There's a whole list of herbs in this chapter, including under what conditions you need to pull them up, like a new moon or full moon. Basil, thyme, onion… so basically the whole kitchen should send you running."

"Next."

"Iron. Apparently burying an iron knife under your house will keep a witch from entering, and cemeteries used to be surrounded by iron fencing to keep the ghosts in.”

“Interesting. To contain them, then, not to keep them out? Maybe they didn’t know that the ghosts start where they died, and not where their bodies were later moved?”

“That’s something to think about. Maybe they thought burying the body released the spirit or something? The cemetery may be the safest place around if you were running from an evil spirit.”

“Are you on the phone?” Mom poked her head through the door.

“No, just reading out loud so that I’ll remember it.” My sister was actually becoming an adept liar.

“Oh, okay. I needed to make a phone call and didn’t want to interrupt you. Was that Dario I heard earlier?”

“Yeah, he’s helping with a school project but he had to work late so he didn’t get here until after eight. We’re writing a paper on the paranormal. The teacher said we could write about whatever we wanted and I figured I could use some of my experiences with the PPS.”

“Oh,” she looked closer at the books littering the end of the bed. Her eyebrows drew together, making a little crater of concern. “Okay, honey. It sounds… interesting.”

“Oh, you have no idea,” she said cheerfully.

"Well, that's good, I guess, but you need to get ready for bed, it's late."

Mom's expression was full of concern as she pulled the door closed again.

"You know she's going to tell the therapist about this," I said, floating next to her on the bed and looking over one of the other books.

"Oh, well."

"What if he wants to read it?"

"Then I'll tell him that Mrs. Stratton never gave it back to me—that it was so well written that she decided to keep it."

I laughed and turned my attention back to the open books spread out in front of us. We'd make up something when the time came if we needed to.

"I think our best bet to find out ghost stuff is to talk to Christopher and Lee. They must know more than people who write books do. I'll ask Lee if he knows about the cemetery thing or where to find the other kid that Christopher had mentioned next time I stake out the building next to Wild Harmony."

Pansy yawned, stretched, and started putting bookmarks in books before stacking them on her desk.

"Are you going to go investigate anything tonight?"

"Honestly, I'm too tired of finding things that make me ask more questions. I think I'm going to stay home and watch infomercials. That's the maximum capacity I have for using my brain tonight."

With a nod, she went to brush her teeth.

23

While Robbie had been home, my parents had put on a reasonably good show of being 'normal' people. With the exception of the day after Christmas, my mother had dressed herself every day, and sure, some of those days were before breakfast and some days she didn't come down until after lunch, but she put a lot more effort into existing that week than she had in the previous weeks.

Robbie and Pansy had left early Friday morning to start their roughly five hour trip north to Winter Park where one of his college friends had a family-owned cabin. It was a mark of how little attention our mother was paying that the thought of seventeen-year-old Pansy in a cabin alone with a bunch of college students didn't send her into hysterics. She told them to be careful and have a nice trip. Like, for real, that's all she said. Pansy and I had exchanged a look, both of us fully expecting a litany of do's-and-dont's and more than a little shocked when that didn't happen.

Honestly, I moped a little. I'll admit it. We'd never been to Winter Park before, but I stayed home because I knew that seeing Pansy and Robbie have fun without me would only hurt my feelings. I also knew that they needed time together to escape the grief that suffused every corner of this house, but it still hurt.

Mom went back to bed after they left, Dad left for work, and I zoned out, Pansy had left the TV on for me so I watched morning talk shows and reruns all day. I could have gone to see Christopher, but didn't have any news for him, and if Pansy was taking some time off from the investigation then I should too. Besides, I needed to learn what to do with myself once we figured out our current mystery.

By five I was bored out of my skull, so when the phone rang I went to eavesdrop. I heard Mom saying that it was okay if he was late, that she wasn't planning anything for dinner anyway. Perfect, here was something for me to do. I left immediately, not having to change my clothes or bundle up had its advantages. I sped northeast toward the quarry, expecting to find my dad still sitting at his desk doing actual work, so it took a second for my brain to catch up when I passed him on the road, his truck heading south on the two-lane gravel road that wound down into the quarry. I stopped and turned to follow him, excited by the idea that I might actually catch him this time, and wanting to vomit at the idea at the same time. No, my dad was a good guy, he couldn't really be doing this. *Could he?*

He pulled into a gas station a little way up the road from the quarry entrance and went inside. I floated behind him, noticing for the first time how his once dark hair was now mostly silver, the fluorescent lights making it seem almost gold. He purchased a cup of coffee and left with less than a dozen words between himself and the cashier. He settled his steaming hot paper cup into the center console and started the truck, pulling out and heading east, away from home and out into the desert. As there wasn't anything out there that I knew of besides some scrub and the occasional cactus, I had no idea what the plan was. Dad seemed to know exactly where he was going and after what had to have been about ten minutes, he put on his turn signal even though there was no one else around for miles in either direction. There were no road signs and from the height I was floating over him I couldn't even see where he was turning until I moved closer. An unmarked, dirt road snaked through some scrub on the side of the road and headed up through a talus field, large chunks of broken rock and debris that had probably been here since the last ice age. There was a road—if you wanted to call it that—and I watched Dad's truck bump and bounce through it, hoping the lid on his coffee would hold. The road had several switchbacks and after a good five minutes he'd climbed to an area slightly higher in elevation than the surrounding desert floor, and, I had to admit, provided a spectacular view. I had a moment of panic when he pulled so close to the edge and I thought he planned on continuing right off, but he put the truck in park, turned the ignition off, and picked up his coffee.

He was facing toward the mountains, although, from this distance they resembled small lumps disrupting the otherwise perfectly level horizon. He sat in silence. I sat with him, and together, we watched the sun fall off the edge of the world. There was no snow on the ground, but the below-freezing temps kept the normal night sounds, cicadas and toads, from singing. The wind slightly buffeting the truck was the only thing I heard, even when I turned to see tears running down his weathered face. He took another sip of the coffee and wiped his face with his sleeve. He never made a sound and I could almost hear my own heart breaking. Why did he come out here to the middle of nowhere to grieve? Was he afraid Mom couldn't handle seeing him like this? Was he trying to be the strong one? That would absolutely be like him.

My sadness was overtaken by frustration. They needed to talk to each other, grieve together. And they both definitely needed to see Pansy's therapist. I mean, he was paying for it, someone should benefit from it.

He sat there for what seemed like another hour, his coffee long cold as he continued to take little sips of it. When it was finished, he started the engine and backed up to turn and make the trip back down to the main road. He seemed to know where every turn was, every boulder, and I realized this is where he went. He'd been coming up here for weeks for the peace and quiet so he could go home and be the strong one. Stupid man. If I'd been able to cry I think I would have.

Once I was sure he was turning into our neighborhood I decided to stake out the upstairs of the empty building on Main. I needed something to take my mind off of my parents and was hoping I'd get lucky and someone would show up and announce themselves, or at least turn on a light so I could see who they were. It started off hopeful. The white truck was missing, the garage space completely empty except for a grease stain on the concrete. After what seemed like twenty hours but was actually only three, I had done every yoga pose I now knew at least three times, had recited the alphabet backward as fast as I could go, and had tried to remember all of the words to the "She Walks in Beauty" poem by Lord Byron, I gave up. I was not good company for myself and the dark was starting to skeeve me out.

Opting for light and people, both live and dead, I headed down the street to the police station where I knew there would be movement and lights on and maybe something entertaining by way of a drunk guy talking to himself.

Lee was sitting at the front desk with the office guy that directed people to whomever they needed to see, looking over the man's shoulder as he typed up whatever someone was telling him over the phone.

"What's up, Hot Stuff?"

"Hot Stuff? Isn't that the chick on MASH?"

"What? Absolutely not. Sorry to burst your bubble, Missy, but you are certainly no Hot Lips Houlihan. What's got you up and wandering the town tonight?"

I explained my failed stakeout attempt, leaving out the part of the evening where I'd stalked my own father. I floated over to see what the living dude was typing.

"That's not failure, that's called uncooperative bad guys. Unless their habit is to go somewhere at a certain time on a certain day, or every day, which no self-respecting criminal would do unless they're part of the mob and think they're untouchable, well, you can't expect them to come to a place solely because you're watching it. Most stakeouts these guys…" he motioned around the station. "Actually, these guys haven't had a stakeout in five years, but in the big city, most stakeouts take endless boring hours with little results. Don't take it personally."

Since he seemed like he was trying to be helpful and friendly I didn't tell him this was far from my first stakeout. "Thanks. Anything new going on here?"

"Just the usual drunks, although yesterday we had a lost hiker in the arroyo. He got separated from the rest of his group and finally found his way out to 113. So, he found a diner and was eating dinner when he saw his own picture on the news. Turns out the rest of his group had returned to the parking area, found a payphone and called it in. Search and Rescue had already been searching for him for two hours when he called the station to let them know he was okay." He actually laughed and the rusty sound made me smile. What was it with these ghosts that didn't talk to one another? They were all so lonely.

"Well, at least he was safe."

"True. I've certainly found my fair share of bodies out in the canyon. Either lost or put there on purpose." I was mulling that one over and wondering what I could do to maybe reunite random bodies with living people who could identify and bury them properly when I remembered the cemetery.

My train of thought was interrupted by the ringing of the telephone at the front desk. The front desk dude went from bored to excited in about five seconds, asking lots of questions including, "Bear trap? Are you sure it was a bear trap?" before calling out the alarm over the radio and then calling next door for an ambulance. He gave the address as 12 Briarwood Lane and my heart sank. *Oh, no.* I heard people hustling out the back door of the station where the officers parking lot was located and the wail of sirens as everyone took off.

"You coming?" Lee asked me, looking back over his shoulder as he started through the front window.

"Wouldn't miss it for the world."

As we followed the flashing lights through the forested area toward the McAllister house, I had a sinking feeling that I knew what we were going to find. Apparently, security cameras or moving the ladder had not been Mrs. McAllister's solution to her ex-husband breaking into their home and sneaking around in the night. No, she'd had a much different train of thought on this one. Sure enough, we rounded the bend as the first of the caravan of police cars, an ambulance, and a freaking fire truck pulled into the gravel driveway, headlights washing over the family, all of whom were in their pajamas, standing in the middle of the driveway. Josh was in tears, Kaitlyn—her hair still in curlers—had a dumb look on her face like she couldn't believe what was happening. Obviously Mrs. McAllister had not consulted with her children on her plan.

I found the victim—he was very vocal and easy to find—one Mr. Jason McAllister, lying on the ground behind the garage, clutching his leg and cursing at the top of his lungs. The bear trap had been hidden under the pine needles behind the garage where he'd been sure to step on it when he reached for the ladder. The ladder in question was laying next to him on the ground and I hoped that his being caught red-handed would strengthen Mrs. McAllister's case. Because there was most certainly going to be a case after all of this. I floated back around to the front porch where I spotted Maryanne already speaking to an officer, he was holding a clipboard and writing furiously as she talked. The red and blue strobe lights reflected drunkenly from every surface, giving the entire scene a carnival-like atmosphere which may have contributed to my feeling of nausea.

"What on earth happened here?" I heard Lee say once the final siren was turned off, its piercing wails bounced around the trees for a few seconds before finally dying out.

"Oh. Well, my friend, do I ever have a story for you."

24

Pansy and Robbie returned on New Year's Eve with windburned faces, no broken bones, and at least ten new stories to tell. I laughed and smiled and pretended not to be jealous before dumping all of my adventures on Pansy who then repeated them back to Robbie. Pansy was properly shocked about the bear trap while Robbie thought that it was hilarious. But, when I told them about overhearing Mom on the phone, and that she thought Dad was cheating on her, and that Dad was actually either really working or sitting in the desert crying by himself, well, Pansy was furious.

"Why didn't you tell me sooner? How long have you known that Mom thought he was cheating on her?"

"Well, do you remember the last PPS meeting and I didn't want to go? It's because I was going to spy on Dad."

"And you didn't tell me? You let me be mad at you for not wanting to participate and kept this from me?"

"Kept what? What's going on? What did she say?" Still glaring at me, Pansy filled in our brother.

"Yeah, Gerri, why didn't you say something sooner?"

"What good would it have done? Everyone in this family has enough to worry about as it is. And besides, he isn't having an affair so it's all good, right?"

"No, it's not all good because now I don't know if there's anything else that you're not telling me."

"There's nothing else. This is the only secret I have ever kept from you in my whole life because you had school to finish up and I didn't want you to think that it could even be a possibility."

"She says this is the only thing she hasn't told me," Pansy said to Robbie, turning her back on me.

Robbie squinted and looked around the room, like that would help him see me, before pulling Pansy into a hug. "Look, you go back to that therapist in January, right? I think he needs to talk to them, like, a hundred times more than he needs to talk to you. You need to tell him about how crazy they're both being, okay?"

She nodded, her head still buried in his armpit and it wasn't until I heard her snuffle that I realized she was crying.

It was the Thursday after New Year's before my nightly visits to the empty store next to Wild Harmony proved fruitful. The white truck had never made a reappearance and I had begun to worry that they were gone for good, but around ten that evening I heard a truck in the alley. I was working on my Warrior Three pose, or Virabhadrasana Three, when some dude came waltzing in the back door like he owned the place. Which, maybe he did, who the heck knew? He immediately started flipping on lights as he made his way around the empty saw horses to the front door and gathered up all of the junk mail that had formed a nice little pile under the mail slot. Lee and I had already gone through it earlier in the week only to find that there was nothing from a real person, just ads for used car lots and the Foodarama circular, as well as a special offer from the Franklin Mint, all addressed to "current resident."

Mystery Dude was a big guy and would have made a good linebacker. I noted that he was wearing a dark blue polo shirt and khakis under his navy knee-length wool coat. Not your standard burglarizing attire. The overhead fluorescents made his black hair gleam—it was longer and gelled back in a wave straight up and off of his forehead like he was trying out as a 90210 extra—although I'd put his age at around forty. *Not that that would have excluded him from being a 90210 extra*, I thought with a snort. I assumed this was one of the guys that kept breaking into the Garcia house, the one with the 'swoopy' hair, as Christopher had called him. He quickly sorted through the junk before tossing the lot of it into the garbage can, all except for… wait, what did he have in his hand? He opened a manilla envelope and removed a dark plastic square which he slid into his coat pocket before turning the lights back off. Whatever he'd picked up hadn't been there before. Someone must have dropped it through the mail slot during the day. What did they call it in James Bond movies? A dead drop? I rubbed my hands together, feeling like a super spy as I walked right behind my guy without him having a clue that I was there. I bet James

Bond would love to have my powers of invisibility, although, in retrospect, they came at a steep price.

His vehicle, a big black Suburban with tinted windows, was parked in the alley behind the shop and I tried to memorize the plate number, repeating it over and over in my head since I didn't have a pen and paper and couldn't hold either one even if I'd had them. He drove to the end of the alley, using his turn signals, and drove the speed limit north through town. Mr. Law Abiding Citizen here, nothing to see, move along, move along. I joined him in the passenger seat, because he certainly wasn't using it, and had a look around the SUV to see if I could find any good clues. He had a docking station for his cell phone in the center console and I could see where the antenna ran under the floor carpeting and up the side of the dash. Interesting. They must travel a lot to need a booster in the car.

The radio station was tuned to country music and as we were heading north on Main Street, Reba McEntire started belting out "Fancy" through the speakers. Mystery Dude was singing right along and apparently knew every single word. He was really getting into it, steering with his left hand and holding his cell in his right as a pretend microphone while he pleaded for Fancy not to let him down. I was glad he couldn't hear me laughing and was so fascinated with his performance that I almost forgot to watch where we were going. I looked up and for a hot minute I didn't recognize which road we were on. My worry was only momentary though, as the headlights soon swept over a rusted metal cowboy and blinking neon sign that said "Vacancy."

I'd heard of the Cowboy's Lodge as it was popular with the local teens and was probably the largest contributor to teen pregnancy around these parts. I'd never been here myself—first of all, I didn't have a boyfriend, actually, now I would never have a boyfriend, which kind of sucked, and second, my parents would have killed both of us if it was ever even whispered that we'd even been in this general geographical area with a boy.

Mystery Dude pulled into the almost empty parking lot in a spot outside of Room 15, the next-to-last room in the row. It was one of those motels where there was only one floor and the room doors lead to the parking lot. One of those places where you know within two seconds of looking at the outside that the bedspread is going to be made out of some slick polyester with that godawful scratchy webbing stuff on the inside that scratches you all night. Sheets that may or may not have been cleaned in the last week and the tub is not going to drain. It was, like, totally gross.

He pulled two sets of keys from the cupholder and walked in, and while I was prepared to launch into a decorating critique of the room, instead, I was completely sidetracked by the sheer amount of trees that had sacrificed their lives in order to create the mess strewn all over the room. There were maps tacked to the walls, stacks, and stacks of three ring binders—the big three inch ones—and they were mostly full, although I couldn't open them to see what was inside. There were more maps and papers and little graphs of things all over the bed, the dresser, the little table by the window and more binders on the floor, stacked along the wall.

What on earth?

Pictures of dirt, pictures of gems, more papers on mineral composition of said dirt. Were they holding a geology convention? Was the mining company going to be moving into the old Spin Time building? And if they were already getting mail there, why was there still a For Lease sign up? One map, half buried under binders on the dresser, had three big red *X*'s on it, all in a cluster. When I looked closer I realized that it was the neighborhood around Mrs. Garcia's house and that the *X* in the middle was right over her house.

Mr. Bad Guy, I'd upgraded him from Mystery Dude because I didn't like the look of those X's, went straight to the bathroom and I continued to snoop. There was no one else in the room but the ashtray on the table was overflowing with—I looked a little closer —yes, two different brands of cigarettes. After reading all of those Encyclopedia Brown books as a kid I was now putting those powers of observation to good use.

However, my fantastic powers of observation were at a complete loss when I tried to read the papers on top of the pile stacked on the desk. Something called "kimberlite" was mentioned a lot, and from the context they weren't talking about a fat-free stripper. It was some sort of rock or mineral judging by the notes about extraction and depths and included more graphs and charts. It mentioned garnets further down the page and at least I knew what those were. So, these were definitely the mining guys. Maybe this was how the Joe Shafer guy who was impersonating a realtor had put Touchstone and Marigold together, obviously the mining company was going to be moving into the space next to Wild Harmony. I'd get Pansy to look up some of the names of these rocks they were mentioning and see what these guys were up to.

There were no tools, no dirty footprints, the sink area was relatively clean so wherever these guys were digging, whatever it was they were looking for, they weren't excavating and then coming immediately here. I wondered if the second set of keys were for another room, and, judging by the pile of binders on the bed, I assumed that was a safe guess. There was no sign of luggage or even a hairbrush in this room. The motel wasn't a busy place, in fact I was pretty sure the rumors about the owner selling drugs as a side business had to be true or he wouldn't be able to keep the place open at all. I figured I'd be safe to snoop into other rooms without invading the privacy of too many other people.

I poked my head into the neighboring room, which was occupied by a middle-aged nearly-naked man lying on the bed propped up with pillows as he watched TV and scratched himself somewhere I never, ever, ever wanted to see again. Suppressing my urge to dry heave,

I took a moment to gather my courage and look into the room on the other side, the last in the row. I was rewarded with an empty room and two twin beds that looked like they'd been slept in, two sets of luggage, and no occupants—naked or otherwise—thank goodness.

So this was the room they were really using to get dressed and sleep in, judging by the quality of the clothes thrown over the back of the chairs. The other room they were using as an office. Which made no sense if they already had a building downtown to use as an office. Which still had a For Lease sign on it. My brain felt like it was working overtime and not getting anywhere. There were ties and leather belts and a pair of leather driving gloves on the table. Highly polished leather shoes were lined up on both sides of the dresser. People who could afford shoes like this didn't stay in flea-bag motels in the middle of nowhere in January. They went to cities closer to civilization or ski towns, not down here in the boonies. It was all very suspicious.

A stack of business cards on the nightstand caught my attention and I floated over to get a better look. Joe Shafer, Touchstone Realty—the same card that Mrs. Garcia had hanging on her fridge. So… if this guy, who I assumed was the guy breaking into Mrs. Garcia's house, was also the same dude who was trying to buy Mrs. Garcia's house, who was also trying to start up a mining business… my brain stopped. None of this made any sense. Why would realtors be starting some sort of mining company? Weren't those two separate skill sets? Unless they were really working for the mining company and posing as realtors. Maybe they were those people who scoped out likely spots for mines and then reported back on their findings. Maybe the business cards were fake and they were dressing like realtors to keep it a secret? I was slowly floating back into Room 15 when I heard the familiar screech and wail of a modem connecting to the internet. A digitized voice announced, "You've got mail."

Oh, mail. And what kind of mail did Mr. Bad Guy have? I briefly imagined a scenario whereby I would watch him signing into his AOL account and then I'd know his Login and password, giving us access to all of his personal emails and we'd totally solve the case. In reality, his hands flew over the keyboard like he typed professionally and I had no idea what keys he'd pressed. I think there was an *r* in it.

His email was equally disappointing. There were no requests for clandestine meetings, no emails from an accomplice laying plans to scare the old woman, just some male enhancement sales emails, a friend had sent a dirty joke—which he didn't even read so I was never going to know the punchline—and an invitation to a real estate seminar in Boulder. Boring, boring, boring. He'd closed his email and reached into the pocket of his coat—which he'd hung from the back of the desk chair – and pulled out the hard plastic square. Under the desk lamp I could see that the dark blue plastic box was a disk protector case and it opened to reveal a 3.5" floppy. Oh, now we were getting somewhere. Someone had dropped this off, so it must be important.

He slid the diskette into the A Drive and brought the computer screen to a DOS prompt to reveal the menu. While I was still half expecting it to be The Oregon Trail or Quest For Glory, the green-on-black screen revealed multiple menus and sub-menus. I was thoroughly disappointed. He brought up the file and it looked like some version of a spreadsheet showing sales figures and lot numbers and a bunch of real estate stuff that I didn't understand. None of the addresses were familiar though, so I wasn't sure which town, or even which state they were in.

Mr. Bad Guy seemed really interested, clicking his tongue over a few and scribbling some numbers on the notepad in front of him for others. I came to the conclusion that I was stalking a real realtor, normal people couldn't pretend to be this interested in house sales. I didn't know what all of this mining stuff had to do with it, but maybe it seemed mysterious because I was a bored seventeen-year-old and I wanted it to be a mystery a little too much. Maybe, Mr. Bad Guy was really just Mr. Hard Up Realtor trying to sell houses in the middle of nowhere where the only people who had good-paying jobs worked for a quarry.

That would be a hard way to make a living. Maybe these guys were trying to scare the old woman because they knew they could make a nice fat commission on the house when it sold. Although, I didn't know who on earth would buy it, but maybe they already had a lead on that. But why would someone drop off a disk in an empty building? Why wouldn't they meet him in public and hand it to him? I was daydreaming about all of my hypotheticals when Mr. Bad Guy Number 2 came in, or Mr. Realtor Number 2, whichever way this was going to end up playing out, and he immediately unwound his Where's Waldo red and white striped scarf and removed his jacket before going to the thermostat on the wall by the bathroom.

"Do you think you have the heat up high enough in here?" With his hands on his hips and his orangish-red hair cut close in a crew cut, he looked like he'd been in the military. He was several inches shorter than Baddie Number One, but leaner and wearing wire-framed glasses. These were definitely the right guys.

"It was cold when I came in, I was warming it up."

"Well, you succeeded. What came in the mail today?" So, old Number Two here had also been expecting the disk.

"The newest numbers for that town over in Escalante. Once word got out, the property prices went through the roof. People can't move there fast enough and are willing to pay top dollar."

"Good, glad to hear it. The faster we can get this place rezoned the better. I'm tired of staying in this shitty town." Well, hey now Buddy, maybe we were tired of you being in our town. And what were they rezoning?

"Any luck tonight, Ernie?" The red-haired guy—Ernie, I presumed—cleared a spot on the nearest bed and sat down with a sigh.

"No, the old lady has that place wired for sound, now. There's a new security sign in the yard and I couldn't get within twenty feet of the house without setting off the floodlights. We're going to have to change tactics on this one."

"She's holding this whole process up, man. I don't know how much longer we can wait."

Ernie's only response to that was to nod, sigh, and then announce his intentions to 'hit the sack' before going next door. Joe must have also decided to call it a night because after a few more minutes of looking at the spreadsheet, he shut the computer down and moved to the room next door. When I got home to Pansy, I woke her up and told her to get a pen—we had a lot of notes to take while it was still fresh in my brain. She wasn't happy about midnight secretarial duties, but I think I remembered most of it.

25

Our two-hour conference in the middle of the night resulted in a plan of action for the following day. Unfortunately, Pansy and Bagel had school so that plan had to wait for the three o'clock bell to ring. Since my attendance wasn't required, and certainly not expected, I headed to the pink house on Sepulveda to get a head start.

"Christopher!" I bellowed as soon as I floated through the front door. "Where are you?"

"Up here," he replied, poking his head through the ceiling and peering down at me. "What's happening? Did you find my mom yet?"

Crap, I hadn't told him that we'd hit a dead end on that front. I'd been too busy trying to figure out Mrs. Garcia's mess. "No, I'm sorry, sweetie. We haven't been able to track her down, yet. But, I have a few more questions for you if you can come down here, please." He floated down and flipped back upright so we could hold a proper conversation. "Did you notice anyone creeping around outside last night?"

"Well, I did notice that the new lights came on. They're really bright."

"Did you go see what was making them come on, by any wild chance?"

"No. It's dark out there."

Geez, kid. "Okay, well, I found out where those guys that have been picking on Mrs. Garcia have been staying. One of them said he was trying to get in last night but the lights kept him away."

"That's good, right?"

"Well, it'll keep her safe for a little longer, but they seem to be getting mad because she won't sell the house to them. If they get really angry they may do something stupid, so be on alert. If they actually hurt her you may have to dial 9-1-1 for her, do you remember how?"

"Yep. But only in an emergency."

"That's right, only in an emergency."

After assuring myself that Mrs. Garcia was secure—she was cozied up in her recliner watching the morning game shows and working on a new crochet project—and that Christopher knew what to do in an emergency, I made my way north to see if the two criminals were still holed up in their lair or if they were out and about.

Ernie was gone, but Bert—as I had renamed Mr. Joe Shafer—was still on the premises, his black Suburban parked out front. He was looking over spreadsheets and typing numbers that meant nothing to me, but I continued to babysit him on the off chance that something exciting happened. It didn't. When the bottom corner of his computer screen showed it was time to meet Pansy and Bagel, I left him to his boring job.

Less than a minute after the bell rang, Pansy walked out the front door talking to Amber, who lit up a cigarette as soon as she stepped into the parking lot.

"Man, I don't know," deep drag and exhale, "I'd say it's been up there a few months."

"So, how long do you normally leave stuff up before you take it down?"

"I'll usually toss stuff when it starts to look ratty, but I know that flier was up there when I hung up the Halloween stuff. I don't think it was up there when we decorated the board for the Back to School theme, though."

"Okay, that helps, thanks."

"Why are you interested in that old flier? You gonna quit school and go work for a mining company?"

"Oh, yeah, my Mom would totally go for that," she rolled her eyes. "It was for Robbie, actually."

They laughed and Amber hitched her book bag up on her shoulder before flicking her cigarette toward the storm drain. "I've got to get to work. Stop in and see me sometime, I get bored."

"Sure will," Pansy replied waving as she sauntered across the parking lot. "I talked to Bagel at lunch and he's in."

"I didn't figure he'd protest." Between school and work he needed some adventure in his life. Dario Ventura, Investigator. Yeah, he'd be all over that.

My boy was leaning against the front bumper of his Bronco and playing with his watch when we walked up. Pansy opened the passenger door and tossed her book bag onto the floorboard before I could warn her that leftover food wrappers were probably going to contaminate it.

"So, are you ready? Do you have your camera with you?" Pansy asked him.

"I told you it was in the truck," he said, jerking his thumb behind me. "I always have my camera with me."

"Well, then, let's go."

"Tell him thank you for being willing to participate and chauffeur your butt around," I said.

"I already told him thank you when he agreed at lunch, thank you very much," she hissed back toward where I was hovering in the backseat.

"She did, that's right," Bagel agreed, nodding in my general direction.

Our first stop wasn't far, just the two blocks to Connekt so that we could do a little research before going on a group stakeout.

We paid for the minimum half hour of internet time and Pansy pulled out a notebook that she'd already written a list of questions from her book bag.

"Dario, why is there a giant ketchup stain on the bottom of my bag?"

Bagel mumbled an apology and started the connection while Pansy went to get a wet paper towel from the bathroom. Once he was connected he reviewed the list and cracked his knuckles before typing.

"Okay, let's see what kimberlite is."

"Kimberlite is an igneous rock that sometimes contains diamonds," Pansy read over his shoulder.

"Are you helping them with a geology report or something?" I heard Lee ask as he came floating in the front windows.

"Not exactly. I finally had some luck while I was watching the building next to Wild Harmony and followed a guy to his motel room last night." Lee's eyebrows raised and I continued. "So, the entire room is covered in papers and charts and maps and to me it looks like they're trying to open a mine, but we needed to look some stuff up."

"Who are you talking to?" Pansy asked, looking around the room before rolling Bagel's chair, with him in it, out of the way and taking his place at the keyboard.

"Lee, I guess he saw us pull in."

"You looked like you were on a mission and you know I can't resist a story," Lee said, running a hand through his overly long hair before squinting at the screen and trying to read over Pansy's shoulder.

"Okay, so kimberlite, lamproite, pyrope… these are all things that indicate where something called a pipe would be, where diamonds are formed when they're pushed out of the earth's mantle toward the crust." Pansy did a few more searches for the other minerals I remembered seeing on the documents, and most were fairly common. However, when you put them all together it seemed to point to diamonds. "But these are things you find in places like South Africa or Australia, not in Colorado."

"Colorado has silver and gold, kid, some coal, lots of gravel, even a little uranium, but not diamonds."

"Well, the charts they have in that room mention this kimberlite stuff a lot, so maybe they're onto a new discovery. Maybe that's why they're acting so squirrelly." I passed along Lee's negative comments and Pansy translated both of our comments to Bagel. The four of us stared at the computer like it was a carnival Fortune Teller spitting out cryptic fortunes.

"Okay, next question, real estate in Escalante." Pansy tried several different versions of the search and we finally pulled up a promising result. It seemed that an intrepid young realtor in Escalante, New Mexico had created an actual website where he could show pictures of the houses he was selling online. However, the pictures took three lifetimes to load.

"Can we skip the pictures, isn't there a way to turn that off so the text loads faster?" Bagel asked.

"I don't know," Pansy replied, smacking his hands away from the mouse. "Just wait for it to load."

"We're going to run out of time, scroll down and see if the text has come up yet."

Grumbling, she complied and then let out a soft, "Oohhh."

"It is a seller's market, folks! Since the Kudney Mine opened for business here in Escalante we've sold every house within ten miles that we had on the market. If you've ever considered moving or selling your house, please call us here at Bershinger Realty where we promise you'll receive top dollar for your home!"

"Huh," Bagel and I said at the same time.

"Where's Escalante?" Lee asked, reading over the half-loaded screen while patting his front robe pocket looking for a notepad that didn't exist.

"Somewhere in New Mexico, apparently. Joe, the guy that stopped at the old Spin Time building yesterday, picked up a three and a half inch floppy that had been sent through the mail. On the disk were a list of properties that had recently sold in Escalante for insane amounts of money. I had assumed that they must be really big houses, but maybe they were more expensive because of the mine."

"Supply and demand," Lee said, more to himself than in conversation.

"Exactly. Okay, so we have time for one more question. What, exactly, are they mining in this Kudney mine?"

Pansy sent the WebCrawler out for another search. "Looks like this one is a gold mine."

"That answers those questions," I said, slapping my hands together. "Are you guys ready to go get some pictures?"

"I guess," Pansy replied. "Dario, are you ready?"

"Sure, why not."

Bagel knew the way to the Cowboy's Lodge because everyone did, so Lee and I floated ahead of the 'had to drive an actual vehicle' division of our strange squad which gave us a good head start. We confirmed that Joe was still there, still doing boring stuff, and I showed Lee the map with the red Xs while we waited. "They've marked the houses on either side of Mrs. Garcia's house. I wonder if they're trying to buy those properties, too?"

"I don't know, kid, but that looks like a project I wouldn't mind checking out for you. If you don't mind me butting into your investigation." As he could actually go through people's mail, lift things that were closed, and turn on lights, I was happy to accept his assistance on the case.

I heard the growl of Bagel's loose muffler and started for the parking lot. "There's Bagel."

"Where?" He glanced around the room and for a second there, I thought he'd lost his mind.

"Uh, he just pulled in." Like, duh.

"The kid's name is Bagel?" He looked confused and disgusted.

"Well, his name is Dario, but we call him Bagel." I started toward the parking lot and could hear him mumbling about stupid kids. Typical adult.

We floated into the backseat of the Bronco and I let Pansy know that Lee was still with us.

"Gerri said that she and Lee are both in the backseat." Since he didn't ask who Lee was I presumed that Pansy had filled him in on the ride up.

"But you can't see or hear Lee, right?" Bagel asked.

"Right. Gerri is the only one that can see and hear everyone."

"No," I corrected her, "Lee can see and hear both of you fine, you just can't see or hear him."

"Never mind, she said Lee can see and hear us too, we just can't see or hear him."

"Well, I can't see or hear anyone but you."

"Jesus, is this what teenagers are like now?" Lee asked, clearly over our stupid argument.

"Mostly, yes," I whispered back. "Pansy, tell Bagel to get out and take a picture of the license plate."

"Ooh, good idea. Dario, Gerri said to get a picture of his license plate. Look, there's a payphone right there at the end of the parking lot, you can pretend to talk on the phone and sneak some pictures." Bagel strolled past the Suburban while pretending to be fiddling with his camera, taking pictures the whole time. He then mimed putting quarters in the payphone and having a conversation before slowly walking back to the Bronco. Step one had been successful, but we needed pictures of the bad guys, too.

An hour later we were all bored and the living and breathing amongst us were getting hungry.

"There are some vending machines over by the office, I'll get us something to eat," Pansy volunteered after her growling stomach had announced its presence.

"Grape Fanta, if they have it," Bagel requested as she slid out of the passenger seat while simultaneously peeling a Payday wrapper off the bottom of her purse. My boy was a slob, but she should know by now not to put anything on the floor.

Bored, we all watched Pansy trotting across the parking lot, laughing when she dropped change and chased a rolling quarter around in circles. But Bagel didn't seem to notice when the white Dodge Ram pulled in next to the Suburban.

"Get your camera, Bagel, get your camera!" I yelled, determined to get his attention. I tried to smack his arm and push the camera toward the driver's side window so that we could get a shot of Ernie, forgetting for a moment that I was dead. He gasped as my hand passed through both him and the camera. It pulled his attention away from Pansy long enough for him to realize what was happening. Pulling the camera up from the strap around his neck, he tried to focus and get the shot before our perp went back inside.

"I don't know if that's going to be good enough. There might be some glare from the window glass," he said, mostly to himself. Great.

Meanwhile, Pansy—having noticed the new arrival— came scampering back to the Bronco hunched over her armload of chips and drinks like she was protecting them from being shot.

"Did he see you?" she asked as she climbed back into the passenger seat.

"No, I don't think he was paying attention, but I don't know if I got the shot or not."

"We can have Lee knock on the door and then take another picture when they open it," I volunteered.

"Wait, Lee can interact with objects, too?"

"Interact with what?" Bagel asked.

"Gerri wants Lee to knock on the door and then you can take their picture when they open it."

"What if they see us?"

"Why don't you start up the Bronco and then we can be pulling out, and look like we're driving away when he knocks. No reason to suspect us because there's no way we can be in two places at once, right?"

"Well, that almost makes sense. But let me set up the right settings on the camera for you, it's starting to get dark so we'll need a wider aperture."

Lee agreed to this plan with a shrug. "Fine," he muttered as he floated out of the truck.

"Okay, he's knocking now," I told Pansy, who in turn told Bagel to start backing the Bronco up.

Bagel drove as slowly as possible while waiting for the door to open. Finally, Ernie stuck his whole head out of the door, looking in both directions to see who was knocking. Pansy took the picture and yelled, "Go, go, go!"

Bagel floored it, the engine roared, the hole in the muffler made all kinds of ungodly noise and the tires chirped as he pulled onto the main road.

"You guys are about as subtle as an earthquake," Lee said as he floated back into the rear seat area of the truck with me.

"But it worked," I replied. Or, at least I hoped it had.

26

With January came the return of Saturday morning trips to the psychiatrist, so Pansy dropped Bagel's film off at the one-hour photo place close to the doctor's office. When Dr. Noonan asked her how her holidays had gone she wasted no time launching into our rehearsed script—about how Mom never left her bed and how Pansy had supposedly overheard Mom's phone conversation accusing Dad of cheating because he was never home, but that she doesn't believe that, and that it was clear that both of our parents were falling apart. Dr. Noonan was so shocked that he spent the hour talking to Pansy about our parents and didn't ask her about drugs or alcohol, even once.

"So, that went well," I said as we made our way down the street to pick up the photos. Pansy pulled the cell phone out of her purse and pretended to answer it.

"Better than I expected. I can't wait to tell Mom and Dad that they both have to attend next week, that should be a lively session, assuming that they tell the truth—that they're both sad and grieving and that neither of them are happy or really living their lives."

"Well, we could always tell them about me. That is an option."

"They'd commit me in a heartbeat and then where would we be?"

She 'hung up' the phone as we entered the drug store where the one-hour photo lab was located.

"Oh, hey, I was just finishing up your prints," the teen behind the counter said, smiling when he saw Pansy. "So, are you some kind of artist or something?"

"An artist?" she asked, confused as to how he could mistake our weirdo stalker shots for art.

"Yeah, the blur and double exposure on some of these caused some really cool effects. It's like, light leaks, but in ways I've never seen before."

"Well, that sounds like art-speak for 'our pictures are crap.' I wonder if I screwed it up when I put my hand through the camera." Pansy glared at me for a moment, unable to yell like she really wanted to.

The kid had already put the negatives in the pocket of the envelope and was pulling the prints out of the dryer. "Look, do you see how the red lights are swirling through this face? It's like a Stanley Kubrick nightmare. Good work."

"Oh, sure, thanks. How much do I owe you?"

"Eight-fifty." More glaring. We were spending the equivalent of half a tank of gas on pictures that were blurred and overexposed and it was probably my fault. I was never going to hear the end of this.

She complained all the way to the police station. We had one half of a usable picture of Joe, nothing of Ernie, but at least the license plate was still legible through all of that artistic light swirling I'd accidentally done. Our plan had been to take the pics to the police station and tell them everything we knew. Lee, who was out doing what he called 'recon' on the rest of Mrs. Garcia's neighborhood, was supposed to have met us there, but since he hadn't shown up and I couldn't exactly send up the bat signal, we went ahead without him.

Pansy introduced herself to the officer behind the front counter.

"How can I help you, Miss Bellafini?" Officer Crane settled in behind his desk while cradling a steaming mug of coffee in both hands. His hands were dry and chapped and looked like he actually used them, so at least I was comforted that he didn't sit and type reports up all day.

"This is going to sound crazy, but I think that someone, at least two men that I know of, are trying to start a diamond mine outside of town. They are trying to make Mrs. Garcia think that her house is haunted so that she'll sell it to them. I have their license plate number if you need it." She pulled the picture out of her purse.

"You're right, that does sound crazy. To be clear, you're talking about the old woman in the pink house south of town?" At Pansy's nod, he continued. "Well, we don't have diamonds here in Colorado so I'm sure that Mrs. Garcia is perfectly safe."

"As there are two men posing as realtors who have repeatedly broken into said house, I feel like she is, in fact, not perfectly safe." Pansy tried to sound polite but

I could hear the edge creeping into her voice. She didn't like being patronized. "Her property seems to be the main point of contention, and I would speculate that the source of the diamonds is actually on her property which is why these men are desperate to get her to sell to them. I'm a member of the Perth Paranormal Society and we recently investigated…"

"Whoa, whoa, whoa. Let's just stop right there, little Missy. Whatever you're up to, I don't have time for it. There ain't no such thing as ghosts and I do not have time to look into your so-called investigation…"

Little Missy? Oh no he didn't. "Whoa there yourself, Mister Man. I'm not claiming that there's anything paranormal at work here. What I'm saying is that these two men are either realtors or posing as realtors, which I feel could be a case for fraud, but they're trying to scare this old woman off of her property so that they can buy it and start a diamond mine."

He had leaned back in his seat at her outburst and was sipping his coffee. "Are you finished? Can I speak now?"

"Yes, sir."

"Why in the hell would anyone want to start a diamond mine?"

"Well, to get diamonds, obviously."

"Do you know anything about diamond mining? No, before you answer, I'm going to guess that you don't. Do you know how much rock you have to blow up before you'd even make enough profit to cover the cost of the equipment you'd need? And then you have to process all of that rock to grind it all down to recover the diamonds. Do you think that someone is trying to mine diamonds on the sly and process them in their garage or something?"

"Well, no, I think they're going to open up a big mining operation. We saw a flier for the company hanging up at the record store with a number to call. They're hiring people."

"Would this flier be for Marigold Mining Company?"

"Yes." Him knowing about it made it seem likely that he already knew more about it than we did, which probably wasn't going to work out in our favor.

"Well, you'll be happy to know that their permit was denied. The survey results they presented showed the mining operation would be too close to residential zoning."

Residential zoning. Ahh, so that's what they were talking about. As long as Mrs. Garcia and her neighbors lived there they couldn't get the permits they needed to open the mine.

"Then why are they still trying to scare her? They're breaking into her house and moving her things around and rattling her windows in the night."

"Has she filed a police report?"

"Yes."

"Then you don't need to investigate anything, do you? It will all be investigated by a real police officer. I'd advise you, Miss Bellafini, to leave Mrs. Garcia alone. There is no point in getting her nose out of joint thinking that she has problems that aren't even real problems."

I think we were being dismissed and for one brief moment I thought Pansy was going to tell him where he could put his problems, but instead she stood, slung her bag over one shoulder and made her way toward the door.

"Miss Bellafini."

She stopped and turned around, although slowly and without her usual smile.

"Just remember that diamond mining is a lot like owning a race car. Do you know how to make a million dollars with a race car?"

"By winning?"

"No, by starting with two million. It's a speculator's game, kid, and there is far too much risk for a no-name start-up to waste that much money on it here in the States when they can go to some third-world country and pay slave wages for labor."

Pansy didn't comment but turned on her heel and made her way down the street to the Firefly. A chocolate shake was in order after that humiliating knockdown. Pansy was halfway through the largest shake the Firefly offered when Bagel came in still wearing his green Foodarama polo. "So, how did it… oooh. That bad, huh?" He slid onto the bench that I was already hovering on. "Holy crap, that was a cold draft… Gerri?" He whispered.

"Yes, and yes. Officer Crane told me that no one in their right mind would start a diamond mine without being able to blow up the entire town to look for a few diamonds which may or may not be there. They aren't going to listen to us."

"What about the pictures? Did you show them to the cops? Maybe they've seen those guys before."

"No, your pictures didn't turn out at all, there's some sort of weird blur over all of them, probably because Gerri put her hand through your camera."

"What? And that ruins film? Point me in the direction of her knee so that I can kick it," Bagel said, looking around him like he was going to pull my ghost out of the air and smack me upside the head. Pansy passed the film envelope over to Bagel.

"Look, I'm sorry," I told Pansy for at least the hundredth time. "It was a panicked instinct and I forgot for a minute. Besides, I wasn't sure that touching film would actually make it blurry, at least I wasn't positive. I did it with the video camera at the McAllisters, remember? Now we know."

"You forgot you were dead." She said it like it was the most unlikely statement she'd ever made.

"Umm, yeah. I was excited and forgot. Sue me."

"I'd love to. Because thanks to you we have even less evidence than we did before."

"Maybe I should go hang out with Bert and Ernie and see if they go to a real office somewhere else or just their makeshift evil lair at the Cowboy Lodge."

Pansy repeated this plan to Bagel who nodded approval. I was getting up to go when Lee came in.

"Don't leave, kiddo. I need you to repeat everything I've learned to the breathers."

Well, alrighty then. Guess I was hanging out for a bit longer.

"Lee has found more information," I announced to Pansy, who passed the news to Bagel who had, by now, obtained his own milkshake.

Lee proceeded to tell us about checking out Mrs. Garcia's neighbors. One had already moved out and the other was in the process of packing.

"The police told Pansy that Marigold Mining had requested a permit but was denied because of residential zoning. But if the other neighbors have already sold to them then…"

"Then Garcia is the last hold out," Pansy interrupted me. "I know that Mrs. Garcia owns a lot of acreage, but what about the neighbors?"

"Mrs. Garcia was small potatoes with her twenty acres," Lee said. "The neighbor to the north owned three times that and the neighbor to the south owned a ranch with over five hundred acres. The ranchers are the ones that are still packing up, I guess selling off cattle and equipment takes a little longer than moving some household furniture."

Pansy filled Bagel in while he continued to sip on his milkshake, thinking it over before he commented. "And the land to the west, the land that actually backs up to the canyon and all the land on the other side is actually Federal, right?" We all nodded. "So, once Mrs. Garcia is out, assuming that the people who bought the neighbor's properties are these same guys, there's no more residential zoning issue. They'll just knock everything down and start a diamond mine."

"In theory, they should be able to get the permit. But getting a permit is not the same as actually finding diamonds," I said.

"And according to the policeman I talked to, there's little chance of making a profit on a diamond mine. So what's the draw? Where are they getting the money to buy these properties?"

"Well, kids, what you need is actual proof," Lee said.

"And where do we get proof?" I asked.

"Good question," both Pansy and Lee replied.

27

Lee Bradley, former Investigative Reporter for the Perth Gazette, was now fully invested in our case. While I found it somewhat comical that after his initial rudeness to me he was now eager to help and be a part of the team, I honestly did appreciate the help. Lee volunteered to stay in the motel room and keep an eye on Joe who rarely left, and I would follow Ernie because he spent the least amount of time sitting in the hotel room. Lee was perfectly content to sit there and watch them scribble things down and send out emails, which, come to think about it, was a lot like what he did at the police station, but I preferred to be on the move. Also, during the times that Joe did leave the room, Lee was free to pilfer through the stacks of paperwork, and being older than I, hopefully, it would make more sense to him.

My Sunday stalking took me to Foodarama, a gas station, and Blockbuster before we picked up pizza on the way back to the motel. Monday stalking took us, much to my surprise, to my own neighborhood.

The first house we visited had once belonged to Mrs. Taylor and her two children, both of whom were still in elementary school. Last I'd heard they'd moved to Fairplay about six months ago and their house was still for sale. Ernie was wandering around with some other guy who also seemed to be a real estate agent. They discussed the pros and cons of the house, built in the late sixties, like almost every other house in the neighborhood, it was one of four plans that had been used in this particular subdivision and was, in fact, a mirror image of my own house. Or, my parent's house. Could I really call it mine if I wasn't technically living in it? I stayed there, resided there, haunted it, if you will, but didn't actually live there. I didn't live anywhere, really. Where was Bagel when I needed to discuss semantics? He was always the best at that kind of thing.

Ernie and his realtor friend were beyond boring as they talked about plumbing upgrades and I tagged along, not wanting to wander too far in case they actually said something interesting. That never happened and I'll never get those two hours back.

After Ernie wrote the other guy a check for a scarecrow or something, we moved on to another house in a different planned neighborhood. It sounded like Ernie was also interested in buying this house, not selling it. I yawned loudly and with exaggerated movements because I could, not because I actually needed to, while a different realtor, a woman this time, was discussing why the family wanted to sell the house as quickly as possible. It wasn't until good Ol' Ernie mentioned his 'clients' that I realized that at no point had I witnessed any clients. Come to think of it, they didn't talk to clients either. They talked to people about sales numbers and mining equipment and people who were interested in selling houses, but I hadn't noticed them taking any walk-ins at the motel room or calling people who were looking for a house to purchase.

Maybe they didn't want to start taking clients until the office space on Main Street was finished. Of course, that would require them to continue working on it and Summer had told us that they'd stopped work weeks ago.

As Ernie and Lady Realtor had entered an in-depth conversation about the heating and air system, I tried to remember if I'd heard them mention the store/future office space at all. I'd definitely heard Ernie say that he couldn't wait to get out of this town, but if they were opening a storefront on Main then he wasn't going to be leaving any time soon. This was all very weird.

Perth is small. There was no local real estate team because no one moved here. People who live here either work for the gravel mine or they work in some sort of service industry that provides goods and services to the people who work in the quarry.

In my opinion, there was absolutely no other reason to live this far from civilization and my goal had always been to move… somewhere. Anywhere else. Ever since I'd been old enough to realize that there were better places in the world, I'd wanted to move. I'd had dreams of living in a big city when I grew up. I wanted to be surrounded by people who actually *did* things and went places that were open after nine pm on weekdays. Anyone moving out of Perth had either found better employment elsewhere, or had committed some infraction so grievous that even the union couldn't save their job at the quarry. Rarely were those job vacancies filled. My father griped about being understaffed at least three times a week.

Ernie was taking the grand tour of this house and kept marking on his clipboard in what looked remarkably like scribbles, unless he was writing in shorthand. I couldn't read shorthand so maybe it actually meant something to him, but judging from his body language and his distracted air it seemed like he was trying to give the impression of being really interested in everything she was babbling about. He wrote this lady a check too. I began to wonder if the checks would bounce because these guys seemed to have a lot of money for client-less realtors.

Our third stop of the day was short and sweet because the person he was supposed to meet canceled at the last minute. Ernie took a quick, unguided look around the outside of the house, mumbling under his breath about there being no damage and that the roof looked good. I breathed a sigh of relief when he got in the Ram and headed back to the flea-bag motel.

"So, what was he out doing all day?" Lee asked as soon as I floated through the door.

"Looking for houses to buy."

"For his clients to buy, you mean."

"Well, maybe. He talked like he was buying them for himself and he didn't have any clients with him."

"Maybe they're out of town and he's looking for them as a proxy."

"I think he's buying them. At least, he signed some paperwork and wrote them checks. He mentioned the checks were for a scarecrow but I didn't see one and it's a little early for Halloween."

"A scarecrow? Do you mean 'escrow?' Wait, you're telling me he bought two houses today?"

"I mean, they didn't go to a lawyer or a bank or anything, but he gave them each a check."

"But why?"

"Why what? Why is he buying houses? I guess he wants to sell them."

"Well, most realtors don't personally purchase a house before selling it, they just take a cut of the profits when it sells." I shrugged. I was seventeen and had only lived in one house. I had no idea how buying and selling houses worked.

"I don't know. They were kind of run down so maybe he's going to put some money into repairs and then try to sell them for more money. I saw Bob Vila do that once on *This Old House*."

"That's possible, I guess. That might even work in a big city but there isn't that kind of demand for housing out here. No one is going to pay more for a house with a fresh coat of paint when they can do it themselves for cheaper."

"Unless there's a diamond mine opening up and bringing people in to work that will need houses."

Lee thought about that one a while. "Demand goes up and so do the prices. I wonder how much Ernie paid out? From the calls that Joe made today it sounds like they're almost out of money."

"I did wonder if the checks were going to bounce. So, what about Bert, or, I mean, Joe. Did he do anything interesting today?" Lee opened his mouth to answer but paused and gave me a look that told me he thought I was immature before continuing.

"No. Joe," he emphasized, "talked on the phone for most of the day. Apparently there was some sort of equipment that they ordered that was delivered broken and he was on hold trying to get a replacement for almost an hour and half. They hung up on him twice. It was actually entertaining." I thought Lee had a warped sense of what constituted entertainment but nodded my head.

"So, where was this equipment delivered?" I asked, looking around the room. It certainly wasn't here. "What kind of equipment was it?"

"A defective motor on a conveyance device. I didn't see what company he called, but he had the Yellow Pages turned to Mining Equipment Sales."

"Well, that's fitting. Did he ever, at any point, actually go look at this piece of equipment?" Wherever it was stashed.

"No, he got a call from someone right after you left, did some yelling, called someone else, yelled some more, and then pulled out the phonebook. He really didn't get a lot accomplished today."

"So… wait. If they're taking delivery of equipment, do you think that they've already started mining? What if this mine isn't just a theoretical-maybe-someday dream, but they've already started without a permit?"

"I think there's a really good chance of that."

I agreed. "Okay, well, I'm going to go tell Pansy what we've learned so far, and then probably stop back in this evening to see if they're doing anything interesting. Thanks for helping out."

"No problem, kiddo. In fact, I don't mind staying here. No need for you to come back tonight, I'm sure they'll get dinner and watch television. I'll keep an eye on them and then poke around the paperwork once they go to bed. I'll see if I can find a delivery address. I didn't have anything planned anyway."

I wasn't sure what kind of plans a person could have when you're all alone and have no one to talk to, which made me incredibly sad to even think about, but I eagerly agreed to not have to sit here and observe these two fine specimens watching TV all evening. There would be no argument from me.

28

I had spent my after-dark hours relaxing and watching videos on MTV and was therefore thoroughly brain-dead by the time I left the house Tuesday morning. I floated north as the sun was rising, glinting off frost-covered trees like a thousand tiny prisms. The Cowboy Lodge was just as depressing in the early morning light as it was at night, but I was happy to see that Bert and Ernie were already up and dressed when I entered. I felt like I should be bringing Lee a Big-Gulp-sized coffee for staying with them all night, but luckily ghosts don't require caffeine.

Lee's face lit up like a Christmas tree when he saw me float in and he immediately started rubbing his hands together like an evil villain plotting the destruction of the world. Most villains would have been able to change out of their wrinkled pajamas and bathrobe but I had to work with what I had.

"Kid, we've had a stroke of luck. Ernie wanted to see the equipment for himself when Joe got back last night so they ate some leftover pizza and then went out to," he made air quotes with his fingers here, "the site."

"The site of what?"

"The site where they're mining for diamonds, Kid. Keep up. They've already got a giant hole in the ground out by the canyon and a tunnel that's running at an angle heading straight for Mrs. Garcia's property."

"So, we were literally within a mile or two of where they're doing this and I simply didn't fly out far enough?"

"Well, yeah, I guess you could look at it that way," he seemed annoyed that I wasn't as excited about his discovery as he was, but honestly I was mad at myself for wasting so much time. I should have thought to look around the property and investigate the neighboring properties. Of course, if you were going to try to scare someone into leaving their home your base of operations would have to be close by. Duh.

"Do you want to hear about it or not?"

"Of course I do."

"Okay, because they've already got this giant auger machine chewing and grinding its way through the rock. They've got a big metal pole barn over the hole so you wouldn't even notice that it's there. From the outside, it just looks like a barn unless you look really close and notice all of the tracks in the dirt where they've been delivering all of this equipment. And there's a lot of equipment."

"A lot? It can't be too much or they wouldn't be able to fit it into the barn." I mean, unless they were some sort of Tetris wizard there was only so much you could put into a barn. Too much stuff outside of the barn would certainly draw attention. And if the barn was too big it might look like an airplane hangar. Do you know what aircraft hangars hidden in the desert or remote mountain areas are used for? Drugs, they're used for running drugs. This was not the kind of attention they'd want to draw.

"Well, there's only so much technically *in* the barn. The rest is under it. They've made pretty good progress digging a tunnel."

"So, I bet that digging this tunnel was what was causing the house to shake every once in a while. Mrs. Garcia will be happy to know that she wasn't imagining earthquakes."

"Okay, so, what do we know?" Lee asked, leaning over Joe's shoulder to examine an email before answering himself. "We know they don't have a permit, but they've started excavation."

"We know that they want Mrs. Garcia's property," I replied. "And they're trying to frighten her into moving and selling them the house. Do you think they'd hurt her if they got desperate enough?"

"Hurt her? Maybe. But they can't kill her because then her estate would be in probate forever and there are three children that would have to agree on what happens to the house and everything in it. That would take way more time than they'll want to spend."

"Are they on a time schedule?" I knew they were getting antsy but hadn't heard anything about when they needed to get her out and the mine started.

"From the calls Joe was making yesterday, it sounded like they're almost out of money and their investors are wanting definite answers on when they're going to be turning a profit." He was still reading over

Joe's shoulder, his bushy gray eyebrows inching closer and closer together.

"So, right now, all they have is a diamond mine."

"No. Right now they have a barn and a hole in the ground. You only have a diamond mine if you actually start pulling diamonds out of it."

"So have they?"

"Not that I saw. They're erecting a second barn now, which has most likely been slowed down due to the weather and the holidays. I'm sure that's where they'll want to process the rock they're pulling up."

"And any of the dirt and rocks that don't have diamonds can just be tossed into the canyon at night— no one will notice."

"Well, I'm sure eventually someone is going to notice, but for right now they're flying under the radar."

"But Officer Crane said you can't make money doing small-scale diamond mining." I was still confused. Why go to all of this trouble if they hadn't even found any diamonds yet? From everything we'd seen on their charts and reports they'd only found the minerals that indicated that there was a possibility of diamonds. It seemed like a pretty big risk.

"They don't seem to be stupid. They're not going to join Mensa anytime soon, but there has to be a payoff somewhere." Lee's face kept getting closer to the screen as Joe typed.

"What is he doing that has you so interested?"

"Well, I could be wrong, but it looks like he's placing an order for a few pounds of kimberlite."

"An order? Like, he's buying it through an email?"

"I think he is."

"But if they have a whole mine of it…" I stopped, realization dawning even as the words were coming out of my mouth.

"Or maybe they just need it to *look* like they have a whole mine of it," Lee finished my thought.

"Do you think we could stop them if we had proof that they were mining without a permit?" I was thinking that we'd have to send in the second string—the ones that could use cameras and drive cars. Which could possibly make them the first string, but whatever.

Lee glanced at me over his shoulder, seeming to already know where my thought process was going. "I don't think that's a good idea. They have the place guarded with real live people carrying real live guns. They don't seem interested in having your sister and your old boyfriend over for a tea party."

I rolled my eyes at him, but couldn't get the idea out of my head that some pictures, pictures that weren't completely ruined by a ghost grabbing the camera, would hold some weight with the local police. I didn't want Mrs. Garcia to have to sell her house because she was afraid. She should be able to keep it and pass it on to her children. And, as unlikely as it was, if there really were a bunch of diamonds under her house then that should go to them too, not these two lunkheads.

"I'm going to go check it out. Where is it?"

"From Mrs. Garcia's house, go out to the edge of the canyon and follow it north. They built a big pole barn about 300 yards from the edge of the canyon on the property that already sold. It's the only other thing out there, you can't miss it."

"Are you going with?"

"No, I'm going to sit right here and watch everything he does until I can figure out why he's doing it."

"Fair enough," I said before turning to leave.

"Geraldine."

"Yeah?" I turned to see if he'd found something else, but he was looking at the ground instead of the computer monitor.

"I wanted to apologize if I came off as rude when we met. I could pretend that being dead for so long has roughened my manners, but honestly, I've always been a little… terse."

"Well, you weren't exactly friendly, but I think we've come to work together really well."

"And that's why I wanted to apologize, and to thank you. I haven't felt this alive, since, well… since I was alive. I've forgotten how much fun an investigation could be and I wouldn't have that without you. So, thank you."

If I could have blushed, I would have. "I should be the one thanking you, you're a pretty useful dude to have around." I disappeared with a wave before it got awkward, but I realized Lee had a point, it felt good to be useful.

Thrilled with my new side quest, I took off for the canyon, feeling all extra special about our case. We were making progress. I had even more questions now than I did last week, but, while our ducks weren't in a row, I felt like we were herding them toward the same pond.

The barn was easy to find if you knew to look for it. The shiny metal roof reflected sunlight like a beacon, but for all intents and purposes it looked just like an innocent barn. The second pole barn had the side beams erected but no walls, giving it the appearance of rib bones sticking up from the earth. Both were in the middle of nowhere, with no livestock or plowed fields around and absolutely no reason for a barn to be there. *Unless you needed to cover up a big old hole in the ground*, I thought as I came swooping down through that shiny metal roof.

Lee was right, they had a heck of a lot of equipment here. And a heck of a lot of guys unpacking and assembling all of the equipment. The decorating scheme leaned toward corrugated sheets of metal held back with steel beams to keep the sand and small rocks from filling back into the tunnel they'd so carefully carved out. The hole was oblong to accommodate the slope needed to drive the equipment underground. I watched a guy in dark blue coveralls start up one of the two bobcats and drive it past two armed guards into the tunnel opening before disappearing around a curve. The sound of several generators running inside the building, their deafening growl bouncing around on all of that steel, made me glad that hearing loss wasn't an option for me, although I still would have liked a set of the ear protectors everyone else was wearing.

I followed the dude on the Bobcat into the tunnel, where our corrugated metal theme continued although the obnoxious sound of the generators lessened as we moved further underground. There were no other employees beyond this point, and I wondered if it was an all-hands-on-deck situation with the unpacking up on the surface. The tunnel continued for quite a ways before widening out to make room for a crap ton of conveyor-belt-type equipment that lined one side. At the end was bare earth, layers of different colored rock and sand. When the guy in the coveralls turned off the Bobcat, I noticed that the generators were just a vibrating hum at this distance.

There was another guy already down at the end, digging a horizontal hole into some of the softer soil on the wall. He had a few bags sitting at his feet so of course, I had to be nosey. The bags looked like they were full of rocks and dirt. A close look at the wall with my untrained eye showed me only sand, more dirt, and the sparkle of sandstone. Wall Guy was using a hand spade to dig and I was trying to figure out why he'd waste his time when I realized that he wasn't removing dirt but placing dirt and rocks from the bag into the hole.

"Hey, Jay, did you bring that bag with you?" Wall Guy asked.

"Yeah, I've got it right here, as well as some more water."

Jay patted a small folded brown paper bag protruding from his front coverall pocket and lifted a five gallon jug of water from the front scoop of the Bobcat. He carried it over to a tub next to Wall Guy that looked like it had been used for cement mixing and started dumping the bags of rocks together in the tub.

"So when are the big wigs supposed to be here?" Wall Guy asked.

"The fax that came through this morning said to be operation ready this weekend because there's a new group of investors coming in to look things over."

"More money guys with deep pockets and no idea what they're supposed to be looking at, huh?"

"That's the idea. Sims is ready to play diamond expert, again. I swear, his fake British accent gets better every time."

They both chuckled and continued to blend and apply their special mixture of rock slurry to the hole in the wall, creating what I assumed was supposed to be a pretend diamond pipe. Operation ready? Money men? I needed to call a meeting.

29

Lee and I met Pansy and Bagel as they left school for the day. I may or may not have screamed her name across the parking lot to get her attention. Either way, it got her attention. She waved to Anne and walked to the end of the student parking lot with Bagel trailing behind. This drew some glances from our peers and I knew the gossip would be all over town by tomorrow, but we had bigger fish to fry.

"Why am I back in this garbage can on wheels?"

Bagel was protesting, but I talked right over him. He couldn't be offended if he couldn't hear me, right? Pansy put her hand in front of Bagel's face to silence him and turned to the back seat to face me.

"Lee is here with me and we need to let you guys know that we've found the site where they're mining. Well, Lee actually followed them out last night, but I went out today to look at it, and it's, like, a whole thing."

"What do you mean, 'where they're mining?' I thought they didn't have a permit?"

"They do not, but that hasn't stopped them. They had a bunch of equipment and probably twenty guys running around the property."

"Tell her about the armed guards," Lee reminded me.

"Yeah, they also have armed guards in a truck by the main road, and at the gate around this giant pole barn that they've got covering up an even giant-er hole, and there are more guards inside."

"So, wait, where are all of these people staying? I mean, this is a small town, you can't just bring in twenty or thirty new people and hope that no one notices."

"What people? Where? You've gotta give me the 411 or I'm not going to be any help, here." Bagel was done sitting passively.

"Gerri has Lee with her and they've found the site, where is it?"

"North of Mrs. Garcia's house on the canyon rim," I supplied.

"North of the Garcia house. Anyway, these realtor guys already have a full mining operation going out there, permit or not, with like twenty workers and a handful of armed guards. There, now you're caught up." She turned back to me. "So where are they all staying?"

"The people that had lived on that property have already sold it to the realtors and moved out. I went through the house and it looked like there were several living in the house, some bunking in the garage, and several RVs parked around it. There's that windbreak of trees planted in front of the house so you can't see any of that from Sepulveda."

"Gerri says all of these people are living and basically hiding down there on the property."

"Okay," Bagel said, one elbow propped on the wheel as he faced the backseat too, even though he couldn't see us. "So, what we need to do is get onto the property and get some pictures of all of that, right? Even if all we can prove is that they're mining without a permit then once the police start going through all of their stuff they'll see that they've got some kind of real estate scheme going on, right?"

"Have any of you kids ever heard of a Ponzi scheme?" Lee asked. I passed the question on to Pansy.

"Lee wants to know if anyone has ever heard of a Ponzi scheme." Pansy repeated the question to Bagel but none of us had ever heard of it.

"The gist of the con is, you promise rich people some pie in the sky idea that's going to make them richer. People with money always want more of it. The conman needs to be a good salesman and since these guys are real estate agents, they already have the fundamentals down cold. Now, you promise this thing, which is never going to happen, like a diamond mine in Colorado, but the more real you can make it look and sound, the more money you can get out of your investors. In order for a Ponzi scheme to be successful, you absolutely have to keep luring in more and more investors. When it comes time to pay the first investors their dividends, which don't actually exist because you're not earning anything, you pay them with money brought in from the second and third rounds of investors. Then when you're handing over the check, you might casually mention that if they'd like to reinvest, they're practically guaranteed to make an even larger return. Odds are good that the victim will agree. The ones that agree to reinvest might even give you more money on top." I interpreted sentence by sentence and then Pansy repeated it back to Bagel. By the time we were all on the same page, Bagel's was the only vehicle still sitting in the student lot.

"So they're desperate to get rid of Mrs. Garcia because she's holding up their mining permit. If some investor took time to actually investigate their fake mine, they'd find out really quickly that it's illegal," Pansy said.

"Not just that, they're double dipping," I added. "They know that when that mine opened in Escalante it drove the price of homes through the roof as people tried to move closer to where they worked. That's why they're buying up empty houses here. As soon as they get a permit they're going to advertise for jobs that don't exist and drive up the property prices here, too. That's like, a whole extra layer of fraud."

Pansy relayed that bit to Bagel. "It makes me wonder if the mine in Escalante is even real," he contributed.

"Tell them that I wondered the same thing, so I took a look through their checkbooks while I was hanging out last night," Lee said. "Guess who is also managing the development of the Kudney Mine in Escalante? Marigold Mining has a whole separate account for that mine, and it has multiple hundred-thousand-dollar deposits in it exactly like the checkbook for the Perth mine does. It doesn't prove that it isn't real, but it certainly looks suspicious."

"We need to get in there," Pansy said after Lee's message had been relayed. "We need proof to stop them before they rip off more people. Especially if they entice working people here and then overcharge them for a house. What a bunch of creeps."

"My camera is in the back seat, but I'll need to pick up some fresh film. We can stop at Foodarama on the way out there."

"You can't go out there," I told Pansy.

"Well, I don't know how you think you can stop us," Pansy replied.

"I don't need to, the guys with the guns will, remember?"

"I can be really sneaky when I want to be." Bagel, Lee and I all stared at her. She was wearing her silver coat that was so reflective she may as well have been wearing aluminum foil. So stealthy.

"Maybe we should try the police again," I said.

"Just because we know more doesn't mean that I can explain how I know it. We're going to need real tangible proof to get rid of these guys."

"I wonder if I shouldn't go on down to Escalante and check out the other mine. I might find something there that would give us the proof we need."

"I mean, it can't hurt. Pansy, Lee is going to go check out the mine in Escalante and see if there's anything really there or not." I turned back to Lee. "Do you need Pansy to get a map for you to look at before you go?"

"No, they had one laying on the bed so I've got the general idea of where I'm going. I should only be gone for a day or two."

He was gone before I could tell him to be careful.

30

After securing a promise from Pansy that she would remain at home with her fresh stack of homework, I began heading toward the motel to keep an eye on Tweedle Dee and Tweedle Dumb, but decided that I'd rather go check on Mrs. Garcia and get Christopher up to date. I floated south, following Sepulveda to the pink house. Christopher was thoroughly interested in what we'd learned so far and had a whole bunch of questions. While none of it directly helped him and his search for his parents, he was fascinated to learn that there was a real mine so close by.

"Are there really diamonds in it, Gerri?"

"I feel like there probably are some now, but I think they carried them in in a brown paper bag to make it look like they were found there naturally."

"So they're a bunch of liars and meanies."

"That sums it up. I'm going to go back over to the mine and see what goes on at night over there. Do you want to come?"

He declined, and as interesting as watching *Nick at Nite* with Mrs. Garcia was, I floated out the door and across the yard. It was fully dark out, now. The moon was no longer full but there was still a big chunk of it up there throwing light all over the place, especially out here in the middle of nowhere where the artificial light was few and far between. The days had been warmer and it hadn't snowed since the new year had begun, so the landscape was multiple variations on the theme of brown. Or, at least in the daylight, right now it was just gray on darker gray.

The mine itself was empty of all but two guards who were guarding the doors. The large overhead lights were turned off, but there were smaller lights spaced evenly around the barn so that a living person could walk around easily without tripping on everything and to give the security cameras enough light to film I thought when I noticed them high up in the rafters. After poking around the equipment for a bit I noticed a desk with a few filing cabinets and a phone/fax/copier/scanner set up in the very far corner. This must be what passed for an office when you didn't have walls. I hadn't noticed it earlier when people were here and there was chaos, and it was far enough out of the way of the lights that most of the desk and the scattering of paperwork on it was so dark that I couldn't make out any of the writing. I tried to turn the desk lamp on but that was a no-go.

There was a manilla envelope on top of the pile and I could only make out the words Confidential stamped across it because the writing was so large. What I needed was someone that could open this for me. I tried, and failed, multiple times to open the envelope and would have thrown something in frustration if I'd been able. Although, if I'd been able, I wouldn't have been so frustrated in the first place.

Lee was gone, I was afraid Pansy would only be able to control her curiosity for a few days at the most, and I needed proof for the police. Finally, I decided that

Christopher was being drafted into this investigation whether he wanted to be or not. I was back at the Garcia house in a matter of minutes and found Christopher exactly where I'd left him, floating near the sofa reading the closed captioning of Green Acres.

"Christopher. I need your help. I need you to come with me."

"Out there?"

"Yes, I know it's dark and you're, well, maybe feeling a little vulnerable, what with the lack of clothes and all, but you could break this case wide open."

"Like on Law and Order?"

"You know about Law and Order?"

"Mrs. Garcia never misses an episode. She thinks that lawyer, Mr. McCoy, is cute."

I took a moment to process that. "Okay, then yes, exactly like Law and Order. You can be like the detectives, finding evidence to make these bad guys go away to jail for a very long time. Please, Christopher, I really, really need your help with this."

"Okay, but you have to pinky promise that no one is going to get mad at me because I'm outside without shoes."

I felt this kid had some trauma we would need to unpack at a later date, but for right now, this was an easy promise to make. "Trust me, if you can help me with these papers, everyone will have only good things to say about what an awesome little dude you are. No one will be mad, I promise."

I could see that he was waffling, I almost had him.

"Alright, but don't float off and leave me, okay? I'm really afraid that I'll get lost and not know how to get back home."

"I'll be right there with you. I will not leave you, I promise."

And so, for the first time in forty-three years, Christopher Fairchild left his house. Our return trip to the mine was moving at a negative speed. I'd babysat a little kid once and when we'd gone out for a walk we had to stop and look at every single thing we'd passed. Christopher was a lot like that. Trees had grown bigger, shrubs had grown up, and all of the things he remembered had changed. He saw headlights on Sepulveda and sped off in that direction.

"If you want me not to leave you, you have to quit running off. Thankfully you're so white you practically glow out here in the moonlight."

"Like Casper!" He giggled.

"Exactly."

"This road was just dirt when I was alive. Look how big and wide it is now! I bet you could go really fast on it."

"Well, it's wide and flat but it's also full of potholes, so I wouldn't suggest going too fast." We floated north along the road and I planned to eventually cut back across the scrub when he spotted something up ahead.

"Look, someone pulled off the road up here. I wonder if they hit one of the potholes."

I started to respond when I noticed that the vehicle he was pointing to looked familiar. Like, very familiar. In fact, it looked exactly like Mom's Explorer had been driven off the road and somewhat hidden behind some weeds. If we hadn't been floating a good fifteen feet above the ground we wouldn't have noticed it. I floated closer to confirm how mad I should be.

Sure enough, it was definitely my mother's SUV and I was one hundred percent certain that she had not been the person to drive it out here.

"Christopher, we may have a problem. I think my sister is out here somewhere. If she is, there's a good chance she's going to get into trouble. These guys not only have guns, but security cameras all over the place. We have to find her."

"Trouble like they'll make her go to jail?"

"That would be a best-case scenario, honestly." I was thinking shoot-her-and-throw-her-in-the-canyon trouble, but I certainly wasn't going to tell him that.

We sped across the open landscape, trying to keep an eye out for anything out of place. I wondered how long Pansy had been out here. Had she left right after I had? Had she waited until dark? She wasn't wearing that reflective coat was she?

As we came over a stand of pines I saw the beam of a flashlight bobbing in the darkness, heading straight for the barbed wire fencing surrounding the completed pole barn. She must have walked for a mile in the dark to get this far, but she was steps away from being picked up on camera.

"There she is!" Christopher pointed. His nervousness about being outside had been completely replaced by excitement. It occurred to me that while I'd been playing Supergirl out here, flying around in the dark, Christopher had not experienced this pleasure before.

"Yep, chances are good. Let's go get her."

We flew through the night as fast as we could and Pansy screamed out loud when I stopped in front of her. I was glad to see that she'd at least worn a black hoodie.

"Turn the light off, there are security cameras and they're going to see you."

"I thought you were going to go hang out in the hotel room tonight."

"I changed my mind. I thought you were doing homework."

"Well, I changed my mind, too."

"These guys are not playing around, Pans. They have guns and cameras and a barbed wire fence surrounding the whole thing. What were you thinking?"

"I was thinking that I wanted to help," she hissed, turning the flashlight off. "You and Lee can sneak in anywhere and eavesdrop and spy and are like, super ninjas or something, but what have I contributed to this? It was time I stepped up."

"Lee and I are invisible and can't be shot. You can. You didn't drag Bagel out here, did you?" I asked, looking around for another shadow skulking in the weeds.

"No," she hissed back.

"You've got to leave. I've got Christopher with me, he's going to help me go through some paperwork on the desk in there. Go home."

"I've got a disposable camera with me. We can take pictures of anything you find as proof for the police." I heard a zipper open and she turned the flashlight back on to dig through the fanny pack she had strapped to her waist.

"Look, I'm not great at this stealth thing because I have any kind of skill. I'm just dead, Pansy. I'd prefer you not to join me."

She pulled out the cardboard camera and paused, torn between fear and a desire to help.

"Go home, Pansy. It's not worth getting caught. We'll find a way, but not this."

"I saw a light over there!" a man shouted from the direction of the pole barn. Crap, crap, crap.

I was sure that Pansy's look of fear mirrored my own. "Turn the light off, now!" I yelled. She turned it off and Christopher floated up to get a better view of the man running toward the front gate of the fencing. The screeching of metal on metal as the gate slid open resonated through the night and Pansy took off running through the waist-high grass and brush. The wrong direction.

"Wow, that guy is really big," Christopher said and I nodded. Yes, all of the security guards looked like they spent three hours a day in the gym. They weren't mall cops.

"Not helping, Christopher. Come on, we have to go."

I floated up to get a better view, or at least as good a view as I could have in the dark.

Pansy tripped over something, I couldn't tell what, and the flashlight went flying ahead of her, bouncing off a rock, which made it turn back on.

"There! I see it again!" the man yelled.

"Who's he talking to? Are there two of them?" I asked Christopher.

Before he could answer I heard the crackle and beep of a reply coming through on a walkie-talkie to tell him that it was confirmed on video and for him to go find out what it was.

Great.

Pansy scrambled back to her feet and snatched the offending light off the ground, turning it back off and setting off in a blind run toward the canyon.

"Hey, I know where we are," Christopher offered. "I used to play in a cave over here. It was a great place to hide."

"Lead the way, kiddo. We're right behind you. Pansy, follow me, Christopher knows where there's a cave up ahead."

"A cave?" she grunted, trying to maintain her footing in the dark. "How can there be a cave? It's flat as crap out here."

"Oh, it's down the canyon wall a little bit," Christopher offered. As if scaling canyon walls in the dark was no biggie. The kid was overcoming a lot of fears really quickly here.

"Look, don't ask questions and just follow me, okay?" There was no chance I was telling Pansy that she was going to need to climb off the edge of the canyon until the last possible second.

Christopher led the way and I followed, trying to point Pansy around the larger rocks and brush that I could see when she suddenly stopped and squatted down in the weeds.

"What are you doing?"

"I'm trying to find the cell phone," she whispered, wrestling with the fanny pack in the dark.

"Who are you going to call?" I mean, technically she was the one trespassing.

She finally got the phone turned on, only to see a message about roaming light up on the screen. There was zero service out here and no way to call anyone if she got hurt. Cursing softly under her breath, she put the phone back. The guard had stopped moving so he could listen for her and he must have heard the zipper because we were instantly lit up like deer in headlights.

"You there, stop! You're trespassing on private property!" The man yelled. There was a beep and a crackle. "I've spotted them, looks like a kid."

"Kid or not, they can't get away. Stop them."

We heard the gunshot as dirt and rock exploded a few feet in front and barely to the left of us. "That means go faster, Pans!" I yelled. Yelling probably didn't help her any, but it was my natural response to the stress I was under. Pansy, still hunched over, took off in a scrambling kind of run. We lost him around a scrubby pine and evaded being caught in the beam of light again for the next few yards. We were starting to make progress *away* from the man when all of a sudden, Christopher dropped out of sight.

"Stop, stop, stop," I yelled again, a greater swath of darkness coming up in front of us. We were at the canyon edge. Pansy, still bent over, came to a stop. We could hear the guard coming closer.

Christopher finally popped up a few yards away, waving at me.

"It's over here. The path down is right here."

"Okay," I told Pansy. "Keep low so he can't see you and follow me."

"Is that the freaking canyon?" she whispered, ducked so low she was all but crawling on her hands and knees. I didn't reply because the answer was obvious.

"I've lost him," the security guard said behind us into his walkie-talkie. Moving crouched over had slowed Pansy by a lot, and the dude was definitely catching up to us. Pansy stepped on a branch, the snap making his flashlight beam swing directly to us once again.

"Run, just stand up and run," I yelled. "We're almost there."

"There, where?" she whispered, standing and sprinting toward the edge of the canyon lip. The man behind us picked up his pace and wasn't going to let her escape again.

"Okay, be careful, there's a path here," I said as she approached me. It was wide enough to walk on without clinging to the wall in most areas, but it was a steep descent to a ledge about two stories down the wall.

Christopher was hovering down at the ledge, pointing to what turned out to indeed be a cave-like hole in the canyon wall. Pansy was almost to the entrance when she slipped on some loose rocks and one foot slipped off into the void, bringing her to her knees with a thud and a scream. The flashlight beam flashing overhead came closer to the edge of the canyon rim.

"Where did you go?" I heard him mumble. Pansy scrambled to her feet again.

"It's right here, you're almost there," I stood in front of her, mad because I couldn't physically help her.

Pansy had just made it into the cave when the security guard found the path down, no doubt able to follow her trail of flattened grass and broken twigs.

"Hide, go to the back, as far as you can."

"It's not a very big cave," Christopher said. "I don't think she's going to be very hidden."

I did not pass that information along.

I couldn't see her, the moonlight was still too far to the east to be of use on this side of the canyon wall. Pansy was in complete darkness, but I heard her scrambling to the back. Unfortunately, the security guard heard her too. He continued down the path, his wider body slowing him down, but he had the aid of a flashlight. In what felt like two breaths time, he was at the entrance of the cave flashing the beam all around.

"There you are," he said, aiming the beam directly at Pansy. His other hand held a pistol, which was also pointed directly at Pansy. If my heart could have exploded, I'd have worried about it.

I floated in front of Pansy, knowing I couldn't block her but not knowing what else to do to protect her.

"Come out of there, kid. We need to have a word with you."

His flashlight beam highlighted her and everything around her, which made me gasp when I saw something that shouldn't have been there. Pansy saw ammunition. She picked up an old metal lunchbox, and flung it at the man.

"Leave me alone!" she screamed.

The lunchbox surprised him, but bounced off his chest with no harm done. He'd managed to make a, "What?" sound when the lunchbox was followed by a baseball to the forehead. That surprised him enough to make him take a few steps back. *But was it far enough?*

With a scream of my own, I rushed at him, channeling all of my fear and anger in an attempt to push him off the narrow ledge. I concentrated harder than I'd ever concentrated on anything in my life. In the split-second before I made contact, I prayed to who or whatever was out there that I'd be able to save my sister. Instead, I went right through him with zero resistance.

Christopher, however, was right behind me, his body practically glowing with the effort he was making to "touch something" and he "touched" the security guard so hard he sent him stumbling backward and over the edge. The dude landed on a larger ledge about fifteen feet down the canyon wall with a thud that didn't sound healthy. His groans were interspersed with curses, confirming that he was alive, but not going to be a concern for the foreseeable future.

"Oh my God, did you do that?" Pansy asked. She had managed to turn her flashlight on, and I was thankful that she'd had the foresight to hang onto it and not use it as a weapon.

"No. That was all Christopher."

"Is the guy dead?"

"No, he'll live, but he's stuck on a ledge so you're safe for now. Are you okay?"

She shined the light over her knee, her jeans torn and bloody where she'd lost her footing, but she was nodding her head. "Yeah, I'll be okay."

"Great. Now, promise me that you aren't going to freak out."

"No, I think I'm okay."

"That's not what I mean. I want you to turn the flashlight to your left, but don't freak out."

"Oh my God, is there a spider?"

"It's freaking January, Pans. No, just do it, okay? But don't yell in case reinforcements are out there somewhere."

She turned the beam of the Maglite to the left and let out a gasp of her own. There, amongst a random collection of toy cars and building blocks, was a bundle wrapped in a blanket. It was suspiciously the same length and size as Christopher, and I suspected that we'd solved at least one mystery tonight.

"Is that…?"

"I think so."

She leaned closer.

Christopher floated closer, too. "Hey, that's my blanket."

"Yeah, buddy, I think it is"

"I'm not unwrapping that," Pansy said firmly. I would have, but she always had been the squeamish one. "But, it looks like there's a note."

Standing, she walked the few steps over to the body. The paper was brittle, tucked into the folds of the blanket, and she pulled it out carefully. "It just says 'I'm sorry.'"

"He must have spent a lot of time out here and she knew this is where he'd be happiest," I said. Pansy swept the flashlight around the small cleft in the canyon that Christopher had called a cave and Christopher, who'd been staring in puzzlement at his own body, suddenly yelled.

"Stop! Go back! There it is!"

"Pansy, he wants you to swing the light back over there," I pointed and Pansy complied, highlighting the area where the lunchbox had landed after bouncing off the security guard. It had opened when it landed, spilling its contents onto the rocky floor. There were some jacks, a yo-yo, and a few baseball cards.

"My Willie Mays card!" Christopher flew directly to it and held it up with both hands. "Now Daddy won't be mad at me."

"I think you're kind of beyond that now, kiddo…" I trailed off as Christopher's little white body, blinding in the glare of the flashlight, took on an extra strength glow. With an intense flash of light, he was gone.

"Christopher?" A howl of wind through the canyon was the only response.

"Gerri, that card was floating in the air." I wasn't a hundred percent sure what the signs of shock were, but I felt like Pans had to be getting close. I knew that I certainly was.

"Pansy, we've got to get out of here. Hopefully, Mr. Security Dude dropped his walkie-talkie when he fell, but either way, when he doesn't come back they're going to be looking for him. We've got to go."

After a slow and careful crawl back up to the top of the canyon, we hurried to Mrs. Garcia's house to call the police.

31

"Well, you see, I'd lost my kite." Pansy laid both hands on the table like she was offering this statement up for sacrifice to the police officer across from her.

"Your kite." Officer Crane did not look convinced.

"Yeah, so, like I told you before, I'm a member of the Perth Paranormal Society, and we recently completed an investigation at the Garcia house. While we were there I'd noticed that giant field next to the house and the wind was always pretty steady through there, so, after school I'd gone out to fly my kite. It seemed like the perfect place." We'd rehearsed this bit of nonsense a few times at home but she was killing this performance.

"So, you were flying a kite at night?"

"Oh, no, no, no. You see, my string broke, and my kite went flying off, and I tried to find it, but I had to go home for dinner or my Mom would have been really mad." She all but batted her eyelashes. "But then I got to thinking, what if the kite is stuck on some scrub brush? But if I don't hurry up and find it then the wind could blow it into the canyon. I'd never find it again. So, after dinner, I told my Mom that I was heading to a friend's house, but really I went back to look for my kite. I mean, I couldn't tell her the truth, it's all kind of dumb, don't you think?"

The man could not disagree. "And while you were out with a flashlight looking for your lost kite, what? Explain to me what, exactly, happened next."

"Well, Mrs. Garcia had told me that the people that used to live there had moved out and she didn't think anyone had moved in, so when I saw this big barn and fence and all of these lights on, I was curious. I thought I should ask if they'd seen my kite."

"Go on." I started to cackle at the officer's expression, but Pansy shot me a warning look.

"Well, I guess they saw my flashlight and this dude that looked like a professional wrestler came running out of the gate and started shooting at me, so I took off running. But, I was like, lost or something? I guess I went the wrong direction and instead of running to the road I literally slipped off the edge of the canyon. Like, I could have died." She clutched her chest here and I snorted. This man was going to think that she was the dumbest human being on earth by the time we were done.

"But you didn't."

"No. But only because when I fell I landed on this little path, and I followed it down on my hands and knees until it came to a cave."

"And then…"

"Well, this giant dude followed me and pointed a gun at me so I threw a baseball at him. I guess it startled him enough that he lost his footing and fell."

"So, you were completely unaware that this, 'giant dude,' as you refer to the suspect, was actually employed by the very same mining company that you came here to complain about just last Saturday?"

"Oh, was he?" Her tone slipped a little there from innocent *almost* into sarcasm.

"He was. And you were also unaware that Marigold Mining had moved onto the property and was already mining without a permit."

"I was completely unaware of that." As of last Saturday, yes, she'd been completely unaware of that.

"Sure. Okay. And now, we come to item number two. The dead child you found in the cave. We've recovered the remains and will be working to identify the child. You wouldn't happen to have any insights into how it came to be there, would you?"

"Well, actually… yes. When we investigated the Garcia house, with the PPS you remember, Blake, our historian, had pulled up information on the original owner of the house. Chester and Margaret 'Maggie' Fairchild. Apparently, sometime in 1953, they were getting a divorce and he was demanding custody of their seven-year-old son, Christopher. Well, the kid went missing, and then two months later the mother left town."

Officer Crane was writing all of this down as fast as he could, stopping her to confirm the names as he went. "Well, the bones were certainly the right size for a small child. The state will want to do a DNA comparison, but this will certainly help us begin the search for the parents or any living family so that we can compare it." He closed his notebook and leaned back in the metal chair. "Well, I think we're done here, for now, Ms. Bellafini. Once we finish collecting evidence from the site on Sepulveda, I'm sure we'll have more questions for you."

"Don't forget the hotel rooms."

"What?"

"My original complaint, if you will recall, was that the two 'real estate' agents," she used air quotes here, "involved in this mine were staying at the Cowboy Lodge. I'm sure you'll find plenty of evidence there, too."

He gave her the hairy eyeball for a moment before nodding. "I'm sure that *you're* sure and for now, I'm not going to question *why* you're sure. You can go now, Ms. Bellafini, but don't leave town."

Pansy gave a real laugh at that, about an octave lower than the fake giggle she'd been using during the interview. "Of course not, Officer. I've still got to find my kite, after all."

"Well kiddos, you've got the police station hopping. I've never seen it that busy. We've got Staties, Feebs and every badge in between boxing up documents and taking all of the eight-by-ten color glossies that they can. It's been a hell of a show."

While Lee had been upset that he'd missed the most exciting part, he'd kept himself busy reading every report as it was typed and reporting back to us, his only audience. I repeated his comments back to Pansy who then relayed them to Bagel.

Bagel flopped backward across my bed, hands firmly grasping his head as he made what I referred to as his 'thinking face.'

"You know, you and Gerri did some incredible good here in the last few months. I mean, you were both always awesome, but you've taken it to a whole new level. And you too, Lee," he looked around the room, unsure where Lee was at the moment and finally waved an arm around the room, in general. "You were super helpful. You guys solved a murder, stopped some con artists, oh, and don't forget, solved the 'haunting' of the McAllister's house. What's next?"

How about me? I thought. *Can we get back to solving the Case of Why is Gerri a ghost and how do I poof like Christopher?* Although, maybe I should change that to how do we *avoid* me poofing like Christopher? Pansy still needed me, after all.

"Well, I've been thinking," Lee started, pace floating back and forth across the bedroom. "I have a few cases that I would really appreciate some help on. You being able to speak to a living person, well… I never imagined it could be done. This will open so many doors in my investigations."

"Lee has a few more cases for us," I told Pansy.

"Can I just graduate high school like a normal person, please? They wrote up this article in the paper about the PPS investigation into the Garcia house and then literally gave me credit for bringing the 'potential illegal activity' to the attention of the police *and* for locating a dead body. All in one night."

"Actually, they said an unnamed underage member of the PPS," I offered.

"Oh, and how many underaged members are there? Huh? One. Me. That's it." She turned in her seat at her desk. "So now, everyone that didn't already know that I'd joined the freaking Ghostbusters, knows now. Oh, and they think I'm dating Dario because we've been seen all over town together."

"Well, excuse me for ruining your life," Bagel said, getting up from the bed.

I felt guilty as I watched Pansy's shoulders droop. She'd never been comfortable with attention and this was obviously pushing her into the spotlight in ways she absolutely did not want.

"No, don't go. I'm sorry, that's not how I meant that to sound. It's just," she gestured to the newspaper on the desk in front of her. "This is not how I'd planned for my senior year of high school to go. I had a plan and it, well, it wasn't this."

"Tell her to put on her big girl panties. We've got a lot of work to do." Lee said, not at all sympathetic to teenage angst.

"I will absolutely not tell her that, thank you very much, but we do have something to do right now. Something that desperately needs to be done before Mom and Dad go to the therapist tomorrow." I turned to Pansy. "Are you ready?"

"As I'll ever be." She grabbed the deck of playing cards and motioned for Bagel to follow. "Dario, I'm sorry I keep hurting your feelings. Please don't leave yet. I'd really appreciate it if you'd come down and help me with this."

My boy didn't look happy, but nodded and followed her down the stairs to the living room where Mom and Dad were watching TV together. Since Pansy's near-death experience they'd been home and hovering. Lee followed because he didn't want to miss the show.

"Mom. Dad. We have something to tell you."

Get a sneak peak

A Ghost of Spring
Book Two of the Perth Paranormal Series

"Did you look in the hall closet?" Mom yelled up the stairs.

"Twice! I still can't find them," came Pansy's muffled reply from the depths of our closet where she was currently on her hands and knees. A red leather mule came flying out to land in the small pile of shoes and sweaters behind her.

"Well, they didn't just disappear," I heard Mom say from below.

"You wore the blue-and-white striped scarf to school on Friday, but I don't remember you having it on when you came back out," I offered. As amusing as it was to watch her tear through every closet in the house, we were going to be late.

Pansy paused in her digging and sat upright. "You're right. It was almost sixty degrees out by the time school let out. Crap."

"Did you wear gloves that day? I don't remember."

"Umm… yes, I remember having to take them off to work the combination on my locker."

"Where they probably still are." Not having to keep track of gloves and hats and scarves and all of the things you needed in a Colorado winter was firmly in the plus column for being dead. "Well, if you hadn't ruined my scarf and gloves at the Henshaw investigation you'd have those to wear, wouldn't you?"

"How was I supposed to know they'd be so flammable?" Pansy asked, standing and brushing the carpet lint from her black jeans. Rather, my black jeans. Investigations were hard on the wardrobe and heaven forbid we endanger her prissy sweater sets and poet blouses. I followed her back down the stairs, my boots that she was also wearing thumping on every tread.

Mom heard her coming and poked her head back out of the doorway to the kitchen. "What about the set with the sunflowers that I bought you for Christmas?"

"I haven't seen them since February. I think I left them at Bagel's."

"Well, can Gerri float over and check with him? Have him bring them with him?"

"I can't deliver messages, Mom." Once the initial disbelief had passed, the parents had adapted surprisingly well to my ghost self.

Pansy didn't translate and just waved me away. "No, he's meeting us at Sycamore Plaza directly from work, he's not going home first."

"Well, I've got a thermos full of hot cocoa for you. Did you maybe find something of Gerri's to wear?"

"You mean besides my jeans and combat boots? And is that my Nirvana shirt you've got on under that?"

"Yes. Why, were you using them?"

Hardy har har.

Mom made an 'aha' face and hurried off while Pansy packed the thermos into her book bag. She was zipping it back up when Dad walked into the kitchen to rinse his now-empty ice cream bowl. He pointed at the clock on the stove.

"Aren't you going to be late? I thought you were leaving at seven-thirty?"

"I was supposed to, but I can't find any of my cold-weather gear."

"How is that even possible?" Dad had never been a teenage girl and sometimes it really showed.

"Look, it warmed up and I didn't need it, but I haven't found enough matching pieces." I mean, if we were just walking from a heated building to a heated car or vice versa, we usually wouldn't even wear a coat. Still, tonight we were investigating the Chivington Sanitarium, or The Castle, as the locals called it, and the five-story monstrosity was under construction and had no heat.

"Is that my Maglite in your pocket?"

The giant flashlight didn't completely fit into the front pocket of her puffy silver coat, so it wasn't like she was trying to sneak it out or anything.

"Umm, yes. Can I borrow it?"

"If you wear the batteries out, you know who's buying the next set, right?

"Yes, Dad. I know."

Mom returned, carrying a hot pink toboggan with a giant white pom-pom on top and the matching scarf and gloves. Both the scarf and the gloves were also adorned with cute little white pom-poms. They'd been

Pansy's when we were in the sixth grade. I didn't even want to know where she'd had these stashed.

"Absolutely not. No." Pansy shook her head and held both hands up in front of her to ward off the evil.

"They match, and they're warm."

"I don't even care if they match, they're *childish* and that toboggan has a pom-pom the size of a grapefruit on top."

"Then I guess you'll be cold."

"Can't I just wear yours?"

"Have we not established that you've lost three sets of gloves and two scarves in the last month and a half?"

"I mean, they're probably not lost-lost, I just don't have access to them right at this very moment."

"You can wear these or you can be cold," Mom shrugged. "It's up to you."

"Fine." She pulled the gloves on, wrapped the hot pink scarf around her throat, and pulled the toboggan over her ears. "Fine," she mumbled again.

"You two have fun," Dad yelled from the kitchen before Pansy stormed out the front door and headed towards her new wheels. Mom and Dad had bought her a bright yellow Geo Tracker a month ago because Mom was tired of sharing her SUV. It had immediately been decorated with Looney Tunes stickers across the bumper and Bagel had hand-painted Tweety Bird onto the vinyl cover for the spare wheel.

"You're late," I commented from the back seat.

"I know," she growled, putting her seat belt on.

"Well hurry up, I can't wait to see this one."

"You haven't cheated, have you? You haven't already gone over there without me?" She somehow managed to back out of the driveway and head towards Sycamore Plaza all while shooting me dirty looks in the rearview.

"Did I think about it, or did I do it?" I mean, yes, I'd thought about checking out The Castle before the PPS got there, but that was like searching your parents' closet for your Christmas presents before Christmas. The suspense was part of the fun. "I promise, I haven't been there yet. Besides, watching you and Bagel explore is part of my entertainment. If I'm going to go somewhere new, I don't want to do it without you."

"Do you think we'll find anything?"

The publicity from the Garcia investigation had caused considerable interest in the PPS and we'd been getting steady requests for investigations since January. Unfortunately, the last few cases had all been kooks, weirdos, or even worse, easily explained by a reasonable, common-sense approach. The Castle though… if any place was haunted, surely it would be.

"I mean, it was a tuberculosis ward at the turn of the century and then a nursing home for decades after that. Blake couldn't even begin to *guess* how many people died in the place. So, yeah, Pans, I think we will. I have a really good feeling about this one."

A Ghost of Spring

A.B. Hooser & The Henlo Press 2024

I want to start by thanking my friends who volunteered to be characters in this book. J'Shawn and Chandra, Autumn, Paul Brandon, Amber, and Annie, may your characters live on forever.

I also want to thank Carrie for asking for a YA novel for her girls way back in 2016. They wanted ghosts and no romance and while they're both in college now, they'll probably still enjoy it.

And most importantly, I want to thank my publisher, The Henlo Press. Thank you for believing in me and my little ghost story, I appreciate all of your hard work more than words can convey.

Sincerely,
A.B.Hooser

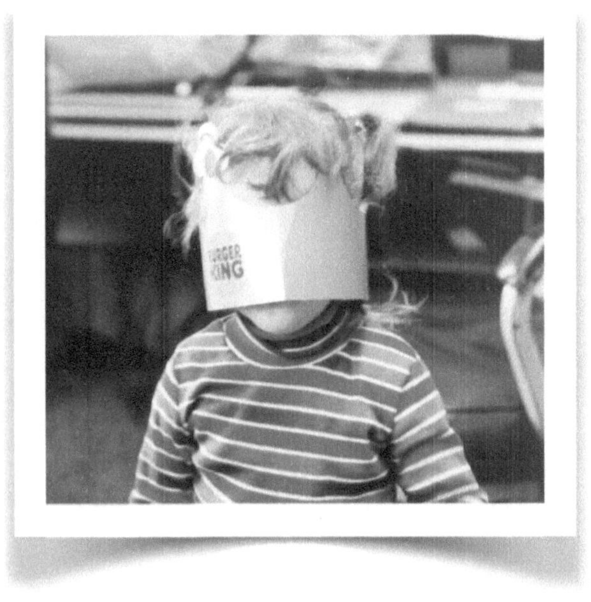

About the Author

Author A. B. Hooser lives in Huntington, WV with her family and two dogs. Artist, gamer, writer, she lets the ADHD lead her into every new adventure. She tells people that she has mastered the art of procrastinating by creating an entire sticker business to avoid finishing the multiple books she has half-written.